WEALTHY PLAYBOY

SLOANE HOWELL

ALEX WOLF

ALEX WOLF

Publisher © Alex Wolf & Sloane Howell October 2nd, 2020
Cover Design: Chelle Bliss
Editor: Spellbound
Formatting: Alex Wolf

WELLS COVINGTON

Wells Covington

I FUCK women in pairs because odd numbers bother me.

One of the lucky ladies from last night stretches her arms up toward the headboard like a cat, then rolls over onto her friend and goes back to sleep.

This is my life. Nothing to complain about, at all.

Orson, my personal, well, everything, meets me in the living area of the suite I always rent during the week. At least, when I have early meetings in downtown Chicago. I couldn't live without this guy keeping the mundane tasks of my life in order, and his British accent makes it perfect. I feel a little like Batman.

"Sir, do you prefer the Tom Ford or Brioni?" He spreads two suit bags over the sofa.

My eyes flit back and forth between the two of them. "Which one is best for crushing a piece-of-shit CEO's hopes and dreams before breakfast?"

"The Brioni, sir." He picks it up and hands it to me.

I laugh and take it from him. "Thanks."

Ten minutes later, we're power walking to the elevator. I like to get ready as fast as possible. Efficiency is key in life. If I can knock ten minutes off my morning routine every day for the next fifty years, that's one hundred and eighty-two thousand, five hundred minutes, or roughly one hundred and twenty-seven extra days of doing more productive things than making sure my hair is perfectly slicked back for a meeting in which I'm the only one capable of firing myself.

Orson and I ride down the elevator to the lobby, then walk toward the front of the hotel.

"Can you take care of the women?"

"What do you require, sir?"

"Feed them breakfast, then they can be on their way."

"As you wish." He stops at the front door.

I turn to face him. I'm not really sure he realizes how much he means to me, but I'm terrible at communicating things like that. I've never had what the world would call great social skills. Enough to get by, but showing affection is difficult and awkward and usually a waste of time. I don't understand why people crave it so much. Well, I understand it, the logic just doesn't compute.

"See you at the house later?"

"I'll be there after *feeding the women*."

I laugh. "Thank you."

He nods, turns on a heel, and heads back to the elevator.

I walk out into the Chicago morning air, over to my car and driver. I've perfected this routine a million times, so there's nothing interesting about it. What will happen when I show up at Dresden Retail's headquarters, will be the interesting portion of the morning.

I step into the back of the car and have a seat as the driver maneuvers us through the city. Swiping through my phone, I hit up my usual morning routine, checking Bloomberg, Twitter, CNBC, and several other applications. Next, I begin to whittle my emails down and put out any fires before they become something that could consume an afternoon. Investors are needy pricks, and I like to anticipate those needs.

As we turn down the street toward Dresden, my heartrate spikes, in a good way. Dopamine fires through my nervous system, a rewarding chemical that my body welcomes. These types of situations drive what I do. Finance is scientific, but there's also an art to it, much like chess. Performance is often necessary—drama, manipulation, seeing three steps ahead of an opponent. It's the key to a large return and a reward of excess resources. It's never about the wealth, though. That's the trophy. Playing the game is the exhilarating part. Winning is everything.

The driver pulls up to the front of the building and lets me out. I stare up at the skyscraper in front of me and grin.

Time to go to work.

I walk through security, all business, expressionless face, and take the elevator to the executive floor. Personally, I think it's a bit chivalrous for me to make this move before a board of director's meeting. I'm doing this CEO a favor and helping him avoid embarrassment.

When I walk through the front door, he's leaned up over his secretary's desk—smiling, not a care in the world. She looks as one would expect an employee to look when the CEO is hovering over you—nervous, uncomfortable, trying to be nice.

His eyes dart over to mine, then he smiles. Fuck, this guy is creepy as hell. It helps ease what little of a conscience remains in my soul. He's a pompous dickhead too, and that's saying something, coming from someone like me. He's coasted through life on his father's name and nepotism. My achievements are through hard work.

It's okay. I'm about to destroy his future. Well, that's untrue. It's going to hurt for a while. I'm sure he'll land on his feet somewhere down the line, though. His type always does.

He walks up and holds out a hand. "Covington." He does nothing to hide the contempt in his voice. "Didn't realize we had something on the books."

I take his hand. "We didn't."

He just stares back at me.

Let him do it. Patience.

Here he goes. His lips curl up into a smile.

"If you think you're getting control of the board, you're mistaken. Might as well just turn around and march your ass right back out the door, if that's why you're here. Otherwise, if you want a tour, I can have Maggie set you..."

"No tour necessary." I draw this out not because it's needed, but because it will send a message. He'll tell this story for years, and I want CEOs of companies with which I'm invested, to have a healthy dose of fear. Complacency is an enemy of profits, and I live for profits, nothing else. This asshole runs around with other people I do business with. If they want my capital, the fear comes with it. It's a package deal.

"Then, I guess we have nothing else to talk about. Enjoy the, uhh, floor." His eyes dart around, then he turns to walk away.

Now, it's time.

"Oh, but we do."

He whips around, this time his face is red. Anger and frustration as anticipated. "Get to the point then. I'm busy."

I shake my head at him. "Do you lose your cool so easily when managing operations? No wonder I'm here."

"The hell you talking about? This some kind of test?"

"Oh no." I shake my head. "The time for tests is done, as is your tenure at Dresden."

He laughs, but I can see the insecurity written all over his face. "Did you not hear me? I have the votes."

"Oh, I have no doubt you *did* have the votes, yesterday morning. I'm sure you kissed all kinds of ass, and made all kinds of promises for the quarter, threw your family name around." I pause. "Begged, even."

His face goes pale, then comes denial, as it usually does. "You're bluffing."

"Why would I walk into your office and bluff? That's beneath me." I step up closer to his face. "I don't play a hand unless I'm sure I will destroy."

He shakes his head, as many men do when they feel power and wealth slipping through their fingers. "Don't believe you. I talked to..."

I cut him off. "You talked to Shirley and Dan yesterday, convinced them with cherry-picked data and threats to vote your way. Yes, I know. But what you don't realize is I've watched

4

you for months, and your managerial talent is fucking lacking. Look around this place." I make a show of craning my head around. "This is the twenty-first century and it looks like the company is a hundred years behind the times on management diversity. Not that I give a fuck. I'm driven by numbers and performance, but optics affect numbers and performance. You've had three run-ins with sexual harassment claims I'm sure you paid to go away, nearly every senior position is an old Caucasian man, and that's nothing compared to the fact your entire strategy with a retail company is to build more stores and ignore all things digital. You're a fucking dinosaur in this industry."

He shakes his head. "You're wrong. On all that. Just like you little hedge fund babies, trying to come into a place that actually makes products, for Americans, a company that builds things, contributes to society... And you want to swing your dicks around like you actually know anything about business."

"I know you lost another ten percent of market share last quarter. How you lost double digits in one quarter is astonishing in itself, but I'm tiring of this conversation. It's boring." I glare right at him. "*You* are boring. A fucking cliché. So, let's get to how I made it possible to eradicate you from the company your family built, that you've destroyed. Yes, you had the votes to secure your position for another quarter. But what you fail to realize, is you have a narrow manufacturing line that accounts for eighty percent of everything you sell. Not only did I buy your suppliers, yes, I control the *American* companies that make all those *American* products you do nothing but *sell.*"

His face goes white as ash, because now he knows it's over.

I continue. "To make sure you didn't weasel your way out, I found your three biggest debt holders, and convinced them to convert their debt to shares so I would have the votes. I promised them with their support, I would take inventory of the firm's assets and begin selling off holdings, and take this company apart piece by piece, so shareholders can still get a return on their investments, since they're not getting shit from your leadership."

5

He looks like he might cry. It's beautiful, and he deserves every fucking ounce of it.

I have no sympathy for him. He was responsible for every employee in this company and he failed them, with poor decision after poor decision. He's like an asshole cheating partner, stringing someone along instead of cutting them loose so they can move on. Institutions like this need to die off. They're a drain on the economy and hold us back, all so this prick can have a personal piggy bank. In my scenario he'll still make out with millions and millions of dollars, he just won't get to make bad decisions that affect his workers and shareholders.

"You can't do this."

"I *am* doing this."

"This is my legacy. My family's company. I'll be a pariah. It'll ruin our name."

"You should've thought about that a long time ago, not now. It should've been on your mind with every single decision you made for the past five years. You were complacent, lazy, privileged."

He looks up at me.

"And now, you're fired. So go get your things. Security will see you out, and I'll have your checks sent to you. You're welcome."

He balls up his fists, and just maybe I underestimated him. This did just get interesting.

I take a step toward him. I'm six four and he's five nine. It wouldn't be a contest. I glare down at him and lower my voice where no one can hear. "Don't embarrass yourself twice in one day. Have some fucking dignity."

He finally stomps off. "This isn't over. I'll see you in court."

"Yeah, good luck with that." I walk over to his secretary's desk.

She clearly heard everything, and judging by the smile on her face, all the bullshit people reported about that guy was true.

"Tell Cory Roberts he's in charge until he hears from the board this afternoon."

"Okay then." She flashes me a smile.

I walk back to the elevator.

My phone rings as I step off. It's Lipsy; aka Brian Lipscomb, my second in command at the firm.

I hold the phone to my ear. "What is it?"

"Parker Project. We're exposed."

"How exposed?"

"Sharon Stone is giving Michael Douglas an interrogation delight."

"Fuck, that play is becoming a pain in the dick. I'll stop by. It's on the way."

"See you in a few, boss."

I hang up the phone. Goddamn it, this might ruin my morning. The Parker Project. Should be easy money. We're converting an old hotel into a high rise on Michigan Avenue. Complete renovation, head to toe, with lake-view condos. It'll turn a piece-of-shit old building into a revenue-churning machine for the city of Chicago. I already have interest from all over the world, businessmen with offices in the city who want a luxury apartment while they're in town, foreign oligarchs who like to flex their oil money in the windy city.

Seventy-five percent of the units were contracted before I put a dime into the place. Yet, it's been one goddamn legal snag after another and there's a pattern to it. Depending upon the severity of this little problem, it might actually push this guaranteed profit haven's projections into the red.

I don't like people fucking with my business, and someone is. My money is on Bennett Cooper, but I don't rely on guesswork. I worship at the altar of facts, science, and logic.

Lipsy greets me at the curb when we pull up.

I say, "What is it?" as I step out of the car.

"Oh, you'll enjoy this in a morbid way."

I raise an eyebrow and start toward the building.

Lipsy hurries to match my pace. "Part of me wants to hold out, let the tension build, then watch you react when you see it."

I shake my head at him and grin.

We pass some local media vans and reporters as I head toward the building. What the fuck are they doing here?

Their smug faces turn to smiles when they see me. One of them steps in my path. "Any comment, Mr. Covington?"

"Fist yourself with your mother's hand," says Lipsy. "We'll find you when we have a comment."

I snicker, but it's short-lived. My mind is on the project, but somehow Lipsy always lightens the mood just enough.

The reporter's face turns pink and he keeps walking with his camera man trailing behind. *The Chicago Tribune* hates me. We go back a long way. I'm nothing but a Manhattan, one percent, corporate raider who pillages their city siphoning resources and destroying the middle class. Their words, not mine. They always conveniently forget I grew up here with nothing.

"Lipsy, what the fuck happened?" I ask as we walk through the front, but before he can say anything, I freeze right in my tracks.

Lipsy turns and stares at my face, partially smiling, taking in my reaction with a morbid fascination like he's been waiting for this moment all morning. It's just who he is.

My jaw clenches. More of the media run up and snap photos before being shoved away by a few police officers who approach me.

Finally, I cock my head slightly to the side, taking it in, trying to find the meaning in it. Not the actual meaning of the literal words, but the motive behind what is spray painted across the brand-new, twenty-five-square-meter marble wall we just had installed. It's not just any marble either. It's Lux Touch from Pietra Firma and John Hardwood designs. It's a work of art, symbolizing the luxury you get when you pay the price for one of our units.

Every inch of it consists of black marble, finely cut diamonds, mother of pearl, abalone shell, and black onyx. It retails for one million dollars per square meter. I don't even need to do the math to know it's a twenty-five-million-dollar wall, because I wrote the fucking check.

I stand there, basking in the fact it now has red spray paint across it that reads, "ONE PERCENT NOT WELCOME!"

The press continues to snap pictures of me and the wall.

Lipsy turns to me. "Already spoken to several experts, it can be restored and, of course, it's insured."

I shake my head. "Not worried about the money or the wall." I glance at the reporters and back to Lipsy.

He nods. "I know."

Two officers approach me. "Need you two to come with us, please."

I nod, happy to get away from the reporters. The officers lead us around a corner, and there's a young woman in a room. I can't get a very good look at her, but so many things are obvious about her. She's dressed like one of those hippie Occupy Wall Street protesters, and she's confined to the small room.

"She did that?" I ask, gesturing back to where my defiled wall stands.

One of them shakes their head.

Lipsy starts toward him. He's used to more concise information being offered up to him from junior analysts and not city bureaucrats dragging things out. "Well what the fuck is she doing here then? Get to the point, Mahoney."

The guy looks at his partner and shrugs, obviously missing the *Police Academy* reference. "We think she was an accomplice. The artist, so to speak, ran away, but we caught up with her. The silent alarm tripped when they broke in."

I can't stop staring at the woman in the room. She looks calm as can be, almost like she's enjoying this experience. I want a better look at her, to see her reactions, read her mannerisms.

Lipsy looks like he might have an aneurysm dealing with the two officers. "Okay, let's slow this down then. You got here. Artist ran. She stayed behind? She tried to run, but you caught her? So, what the fuck? She's been Keyser Sözeing you in there with a goddamn barbershop quartet in Skokie?"

I interrupt him. "Can I go in there?"

The two men look at each other. One of them shrugs. "Sure, I suppose."

I walk off, leaving the three of them there while Lipsy chews their asses out trying to get facts. I'll get more out of five seconds just watching her up close.

As I walk through the door, I realize she's way hotter than I thought.

When her light golden-brown eyes meet mine and I finally get a look at her face, it stuns me for a second. Just a second, though. There's something familiar about her. Something I can't place. I quickly recover. She's the most non-threatening person I've ever seen in my life. Looks like a grad student working on a Ph.D. in something like intersectionality.

Surprisingly, her breathing stays completely steady. No elevated heart rate. She's one hundred percent relaxed, considering I hold her future in the palm of my hand. Even though she's sitting down, I can tell she's short, maybe five three at best. Light brown hair that would usually fall to her shoulders, but she has it up slightly with a rainbow bandana. There's a hemp necklace around her neck.

I take a seat across from her, a desk separating us. The top of her t-shirt tells me it's from Yellowstone National Park.

She doesn't say a word, but I see her eyes searching me for the same types of clues. Certain people, you can look at them and you recognize something kindred, you can tell when they're calculating, the same as you. There's some kind of unquantifiable force at play, a sixth sense of sorts.

She doesn't say a word, though. Remains completely silent.

Fuck, she really is beautiful, in this natural, down-to-earth kind of way. She looks like a genuinely nice person, who means well, but has never had to scrap in the real world, fight for anything. So, she picked wealth inequality as her cause. Everyone needs a cause, something that drives them, something to fill their calendar with as the earth spins and revolves around the sun over and over.

Finally, I break the silence. "You ruined a very expensive wall, Ms…" I intentionally leave the sentence hanging, waiting for a response.

Silence fills the room, and I find my anxiety about the situation rises, much more than hers seems to. What the fuck is happening here?

I wait a bit longer.

Finally, I say, "The police will give me your name. For someone whose life is in my hands at the moment, it's no time to be shy."

It's like my words don't even register, even though I'm certain they do. Why is she so disarming? Why am I on the defensive here? I already know I'll spend my entire night trying to analyze this encounter, something that should take me no longer than three seconds to sum up.

"Meadow."

Her voice is soft, feminine, almost like a purr, but with a side of innocence along with it. It's clear and concise, but there's no malice. Her actions are so unlike the person she's trying to sell me right now. It might not be obvious to a couple rookie cops out there, but the nuance sets off all kinds of warning signs with me. She's no hippie tree hugger. There's more under there, somewhere. She has leadership written all over her.

"Ms. Meadow? That's your last name?"

"Meadow Carlson."

Has to be a fake name. It's the most hippie-sounding shit I've ever heard.

"Okay, Meadow. Why did you *attempt* to destroy my wall?"

She smiles, and it should make my blood boil, how smug she is, but I'll be damned if it isn't hot. Her confidence is off-the-charts doing something for me. I crush grown men like the CEO earlier, day in and day out, but Meadow Carlson might just be a worthy opponent. Only time will tell.

"I didn't." She shrugs.

"Then who did?"

She laughs.

I grin back at her. "Something funny?"

"I mean… yeah." She stares at me like the question was the dumbest thing she's ever heard.

"Enlighten me. I'm bad at social cues. Don't always catch the joke."

"I have no doubt you're always a step behind." She raises an eyebrow, sarcasm oozing from her words.

Two things happen simultaneously inside me. One part of me

rages, wanting to lash out about this project losing money every day, the fact I can't get a full read on her, and it's taking me far longer than normal to figure out what's happening here. The other half of me is strangely aroused, and not just sexually, though I would love to bend Meadow Carlson over my bed and spank her faux-hippie ass until she begged for it over and over. It's more than that, though. Yes, she has a nice body, young and firm. But there is something a million times more attractive about an intelligent woman who can hold her own in a room with me, giving off minimal clues as to her motivations. Who calls me on my bullshit, because yes, I see exactly what she's doing.

"Never mind. And there's no need."

For the first time, I get a reaction out of her. She's on her heels.

"For?"

This time, it's me who grins. "Oh, I think you know. What you were about to ask for." I stand up and walk out. I have all the information I will receive, and it's time to make sense of some of it. She was two seconds away from telling me she wasn't saying anything else without a lawyer present. She knew I'd counter with an intimidation tactic about the size of my legal team. I could see it playing out in my mind, started to get a read on the flow of the conversation.

Now, she's wondering what I'll do.

I already know.

I walk up as Lipsy continues berating the officers and their bosses who have just shown up, telling them all the things he'll do to their family, like it's some kind of scene from a mafia movie.

He's very protective of me and the business, and I sometimes wonder if he's actually serious about the things he says.

"Cut them some slack, Lipsy. It's all good."

He immediately morphs into a cheerful mood. "Okay, fellas. Well, good chat."

They stare at him like he's nuts.

One of the bosses, I'm assuming because he's in a suit and

not a police uniform, approaches me. "We can book her on B&E, vandalism—"

I hold up a hand. "Let her go."

Lipsy's eyes widen. "Go?"

The cop looks at me the same way.

I shrug at both of them. "It'll clean off and it's insured."

The officer stares back and forth at us, then finally says, "Okay then." He drags out the words like he can't believe his ears, then turns to his coworkers. "Let her go."

I don't stick around for any more of the conversation. Lipsy and I march past the media who continue to snap pictures, and there are actual video crews here now, complete with reporters standing with microphones talking into bright lights.

I shake my head at the situation and walk past, ignoring the questions, Lipsy matching my pace.

When we're out of earshot from everyone, marching toward the car, Lipsy continues looking straight ahead, but says, "Minimize press coverage?"

The driver opens the door for me and as I step in, I say, "Yep."

Lipsy glances around. "Office?"

I nod. "Office."

Meaning we're not saying shit else about any of this until we get there. I roll down my window as he starts to walk away. "Lipsy!"

He spins around. "Yeah?"

"Let's get Decker Collins in on the meeting with Dexter and Paisley. He's the PR wizard there."

Lipsy cocks an eyebrow up. He doesn't even need to say the words for me to know what his concerns are. Decker likes to stick his nose in our business sometimes.

"It'll be fine. I think he may be able to help. And I need to drive home a message."

Lipsy shrugs. "Done."

"Good."

The driver starts to pull away, but I hold up a hand and tell him to pull around to the side of the building. About five minutes later, the police open a door and Meadow Carlson is released into the alley.

I roll my window down, making sure she takes notice. There's still something about this woman. Even the way she walks; there's authority in it. She doesn't carry herself like some kind of activist.

She glances over and catches me staring right at her.

It doesn't rattle her at all, not that I expected it to at this point.

I'm pretty sure her lips curl up into the tiniest smile, then she turns and heads the other way.

I know that smile. I know that look.

I've seen that look of confidence on plenty of people, in boardrooms across the world. It's a welcome-to-the-battle smile.

There's way more to this woman than what she's letting on, and I'll know everything before the sun goes down.

I haven't had a good challenge in a while. My blood pumps through my veins, adrenaline flooding my limbs.

Shots fired. This feels like the beginning of a war.

And I'm going to enjoy it.

MEADOW CARLSON

I FINISH TYPING a blog article under one of my several pseudonyms, covering the vandalism at the Parker building and lambasting Covington for another monstrous, benefit-the-wealthy endeavor of his. I'll spread this through all the small grassroots outlets I own, and it'll catch fire with big media by the end of the day. I'll give it a little extra shove to take it national. My small network has that ability.

I look around the office of my impact fund. It has no real mission per se, other than each investment must provide positive social change. Yes, I run a fund. Yes, I make profits for my clients. That's how I retain a large supply of capital to create change. Some people go the nonprofit route. This is how I make a mark on the world. All of us have a skillset. This is what I'm good at. It's how I protest for change, and I prefer to do it under the radar, drawing minimal attention to myself.

The only person who needs to know I helped change the world is me.

My assistant and three junior analysts are aware too, of course, but I couldn't run this place by myself. They were carefully chosen and know how to keep their mouths shut and not brag about our achievements.

I hit publish on the article, share it across my small media outlets, and it should trend on Twitter within two hours. Not a bad morning's work.

I stand up, stretch my arms over my head to work out the knot in my shoulders from sitting in that interrogation chair for two hours, and head over to the coffee maker. When I'm halfway there, I hear raised voices from the other side of my door.

"You don't have an appointment."

"No worries, she'll be happy to see me."

Shit. What in the hell?

I know that condescending, sarcastic voice. It's been imprinted on the hard drive that is my brain for the past twenty-four hours.

I can't even register his name before the door opens and his six-four figure fills up the frame. It's so weird. Most men his height are proportioned differently. They're either very lanky, or very wide. They always look out of place in a room.

Wells Covington is just hot and built perfectly, like a larger version of a GQ model.

That's beside the point.

A million questions fill my brain at once. What does he know about me? What is he doing here? Why'd he not press charges? That was the plan. It was the only reason I went to his building and allowed the police to find me there.

I was in complete control of our little confrontation until the very end. The winds shifted, his demeanor changed, then he just let me go. I'm not used to things not going to plan, though I'll recover easily. He's a perplexing man, but I'll still win. I always win, and for the better of the world, not to enrich myself.

"How'd you find me?" It's a stupid question, and I regret it the second I ask it. What the hell is wrong with me? Why am I suddenly rattled when he's in the room?

It's his eyes. They're calculating. He's intelligent, but there's a hint of danger every time I see his irises too. Perhaps I under-estimated him? Not likely, but I don't like a single shred of uncertainty.

He doesn't reply. Just cranes his head around, taking in the room, then starts toward me. "Don't worry. It took no real sleuthing efforts."

He's such a smug asshole. Who the hell talks like that?

"I have a feeling everything takes real sleuthing efforts with you."

He walks right past me, stands in front of a chair in front of my desk, then holds his arm out as if asking me to have a seat. "A discussion is warranted, Ms. Carlson."

Amused, I grab my coffee and head around to my desk. I shouldn't entertain this. I should tell him to leave, but there's something about him. He's like a good book you can't put down, even if you want to. Despite his arrogance and the way he wields his wallet for power over the world, he's interesting, magnetic. He could probably be a damn cult leader.

Surprisingly, he waits for me to sit at my desk before he takes a seat. The devil apparently enjoys playing the role of a gentleman. It's somewhat comical. He'd crush me under his Berluti heel at the first opportunity if one presented itself. I'm highly aware of this fact.

The second my butt hits the chair, he speaks.

"March of last year, I acquire the former Parker Hotel with my one-billion-dollar investment projecting a return of five hundred and thirty-two percent over the first five years. Three months post-acquisition, a licensing issue occurs through political back channels that receives local media attention, lowering projected ROI to four hundred and sixty-five percent."

Do not smile. Do not give him the satisfaction of you boasting through facial cues.

"Still an acceptable return, and unforeseen circumstances and market forces can affect projections. That's why they're called projections in the first place. Yet, four months after that, contractor rates for construction in downtown Chicago enterprises rise ten percent out of nowhere, due to causes no one has yet deciphered, lowering my projected return to two hundred and twenty-four percent. Are you noticing a pattern here?"

I offer a shrug, like *sorry you'd only make two point four billion dollars in your first five years.*

"Magically, the *Wall Street Journal* caught wind of this and asked for comment on my decision to still go forward, and I spent an entire day fielding calls from investors who still read the paper."

"It's tough doing business, Mr. Covington. So I've heard anyway. I don't know much about the economy."

He continues like I didn't even speak. "I think we both see where this is going. Additional financial audits, government interventions—" His face hardens and his teeth grind. "Additional bullshit, nagging details I don't appreciate, to the point where miraculously my high rise might end up in the red now, especially after a picture of your little wannabe Banksy artwork ends up plastered across the web." He relaxes a little and fakes a smile at me. "Let's get to the point. What is it that you want?"

"What do you mean?"

He smirks. "You may think you're operating under some guise of stealth, but I sniffed out the pattern in one night. So I repeat. What do you want?"

Damn, he's pretty good. A little smart, I'll give him that. I allow myself one small, smug grin as I lean back a little in my chair. "I didn't think I was stealthy at all. My friend wrote what we meant on the wall. I think the meaning of it is obvious. It's more about what we don't want."

He leans in a little. "And what is that?"

I narrow my eyes on him. "A monument to corporate billionaires in the middle of our city. A giant monolith to capitalism, where the wealthy rest at night, looking down on all the hardworking people from above, lording over Chicago. Men who calculate the bare minimum they can pay employees using an algorithm, and hire the best lawyers in the country to get them out of paying any tax possible, while ravaging the environment so shareholders can have an extra vacation home."

Covington smiles. "Ahh yes, an idealist. It's cute, really. You turn rich people into a cartoon so you have someone to blame for the world's problems, ignoring the amount of jobs created, the generation of wealth, the business it brings to your beloved city, providing the very economic engine that fuels the working class.

My fund is privately held, as are the companies responsible for this high rise. You have no idea what wages will be paid because employees have not been hired yet."

I start to speak, and he holds up a hand.

"You have no idea what taxes I pay and those that I don't. Nor is that information available for any potential tenants of my building, because it's not public information, not to mention they each have nuanced circumstances."

I shrug. "I guess you got me. I'm just an idealist. No idea how that kind of thing works."

"Bullshit."

He catches me off guard with that. "Excuse me?"

"The entire timeline I just gave was extremely calculated. Someone knew my processes and went through a great deal of trouble to sabotage the high rise in a very particular manner, and they knew exactly how to maximize my exposure."

I laugh. "What are you insinuating?"

He stares back at me, but not in anger. It's a hint of amusement, and maybe even slight adoration. This little sit down might be more dangerous than I suspected. He doesn't respond.

"You think I'm responsible for all those things that happened to your project?"

Still no response.

"I'm flattered, Mr. Covington, but I don't know what half of that stuff you even said means. I think you're giving me far more credit than I deserve, and trust me, I'd love to be responsible for all that."

He glances around the room once more, like he's taking a mental picture of every detail, then stands up and leans over my small desk. He's so tall he's damn near right in my ear, totally invading my personal space.

I want to punch him in the face or scream, but I don't, because at the same time my heart redlines in my chest and my face flushes with heat. I smell his expensive cologne and aftershave. Part of me, I think, enjoys it.

What the hell is wrong with you?

He exhales warm breath in my ear as he speaks and says, "I guess we have no more to discuss then."

At that, he leans back and starts for the door. My face is so hot I want to fan it, but I don't. I won't let him intimidate me or turn me on. Not going to happen.

When he gets halfway to the door, he freezes in his tracks but doesn't turn around to look at me. He just says, "The bullshit stops today, or I'll be back."

He's so mysterious and arrogant and rude and—hot.

Wait what?

I have to be honest with myself. I'm turned on right now and it's not just the physical, even though it's overwhelming, and I hate myself for it. It's the mental part of it. I've never met anyone who seems to see the world like I do, the calculations, ten moves ahead like a chess game.

He worked all that out in his head, and he knows I'm responsible for it. It doesn't matter. He could never prove any of it.

How the hell did he figure it out, though? Now, I have to know.

WELLS COVINGTON

"Did you really say all that to him?" Dexter Collins, one of my best friends and my financial attorney, snickers as he pours himself a drink. Paisley Williams, the other financial partner and fiancée of Donavan Collins, shakes her head.

I shrug. "Of course, what else would I say?"

Dexter laughs. "I don't know, maybe just 'you're fired.' Or wait for an actual vote to take place on the board of directors?"

He hands me a drink. Paisley remains silent, probably judging both of us.

"Where's the fun in that? Revealing how you beat someone is almost as good as beating them. Almost." I sigh. "Anyway, I need you two on top of the paperwork and procedures…"

Decker Collins, managing partner of the firm and big brother to Dexter, walks in and interrupts. He glares right at me. "Sorry I'm late."

We don't like each other. Everyone is aware of this.

"Not to worry. I'm sure there were important things you were doing."

Dexter mumbles, "Fuck."

Decker's eyes narrow farther. "I apologized."

I shake my head. "A sincere apology, I have no doubt. I'm sure you were combing through every last record of mine to make sure my business remains pure as snow, one hundred percent ethical. It's why I pay you." The Collins brothers run the Chicago offices of The Hunter Group, a now national firm. I have to dig in with these assholes, because they are stubborn as shit, even if they are good friends.

Dexter cringes.

Decker's face reddens. "How was I supposed to know you were an FBI informant, taking down a trafficking ring?"

Decker kept pushing and sending his PI to investigate several of my holdings earlier in the year, even though I told him to back off. That's the problem with nosy people. They can fuck things up, and Decker did exactly that.

"You weren't. That's the whole point of being an informant; anonymity and secrecy." I turn to Dexter and Paisley, completely ignoring Decker's brooding looks of contempt. "As I was saying, I need all the legal paperwork in order to begin dismantling the corporation, restructuring the equity, valuating the assets."

"Raided another company?" Decker snorts.

"Turning a piece of shit into something profitable, so it can be replaced by something better. I'm sure you earned all this—" I crane my head around the room. "With altruistic standards and practices, but losses are unacceptable to me, or my clients go elsewhere."

He's emotional because he fucked up. I get it, but I can't tolerate it. It's saying something, coming from me, but he's maybe the most egotistical man I've ever met. He'll never admit he made a poor decision.

"I, at least, try to have some ethics."

I take a step toward him and look down my nose, considering I'm about two inches taller. "Let me make one thing clear. I stick around as a client of yours because of Dexter and Paisley. They're my best option, mathematically. Donavan is the best criminal attorney in the world. This place is like family to me." I point a finger at him. "But don't push me. I'm a bad enemy to have. This relationship between our companies is malleable. Bennett Cooper is willing to accept me back with one phone call, or I could move a lot of this legal work in-house and take half your employees with me. I have far deeper pockets than you ever will. All these *little* clients you have from Wall Street came here because of me. That can change. I'll hire your cousin Harlow and keep her busy for a decade and end your new stream of clients from her advertising strategies. I dismantle companies when they fuck with me and my business, so get on board or get fucked up."

You could hear a pin drop in the room. This conversation needed to happen. He needs to understand his place if he wants his law firm to survive. His vanity is a weakness.

Decker glares across at his brother, then turns back to me. It takes a moment, and he stares into my eyes, but all he'll see is the truth; that I mean every single word. Dexter and Paisley look on as if the fate of their firm depends on what comes out of Decker's mouth next.

"We will no longer research anything about your companies that is not laid out in our engagement letter."

I nod. "Apology accepted."

Decker's eyes widen a little. "I didn't apologize."

"We both know that's what you just did. Now, I need some PR work. Your brother can fill you in."

Decker remains silent.

I turn to Dexter. "We all set then?"

"We're all over it," says Paisley when Dexter doesn't respond and keeps his eyes trained on Decker.

I wouldn't want to be in the room when I leave. They'll have it out. Decker will need to lash out at someone who doesn't have authority over him. It's what men with his temperament do.

"Thank you, Ms. Williams. Look forward to attending your wedding."

Finally, she smiles, glad for the change of subject no doubt. "Do we need to reserve a plus two for you?"

I smile. She knows me so well. "More than likely. Have a good day, everyone."

I walk out of the conference room.

On my way to the exit, I spot Dominic Romano and his fiancée Mary Patrick. Fuck me if these two didn't cause me a ton of stress over the past six months, but this is fortunate. Dominic pauses when he sees me, but Mary continues on to her cubicle.

"Covington." He holds out a hand.

I shake it, then pull him to the side. "I need you to take on a side gig. You free over the next few weeks?"

"Not at all."

He's lying. This man has a genius IQ and is even more of a genius at hiding that fact, but I know what he's capable of. He's by far the best investigator I've ever met in my life.

"Enough bullshit, Romano. Let's get to the heart of this transaction. What do you want in return?"

Dominic grins. "I love how you don't fuck around. It's refreshing. Let's see." His eyes roll up to the ceiling, then he turns in the direction Mary just walked in, then back to me. "I want one of your yachts for a weekend."

"Done."

Dominic continues. "Want to take Mary out on Lake Michigan, five star—" His eyes dart to mine. "Done?"

I nod.

"Must want this pretty bad. I think I undersold myself."

"Don't fucking push it. You still owe me. You're lucky I'm entertaining this yacht idea at all."

"What do you need?"

"Meadow Carlson."

He snickers. "That a person? Fucking Meadow."

I nod. "Want to know everything about her. She's trying to sabotage one of my developments, forcing a loss on it. I need everything there is, no detail left out."

"Seems easy enough."

I shake my head. "Don't let the name fool you. Won't be easy at all, trust me. Why do you think I gave up the yacht so easy?"

Dominic's brows narrow on me, and he nods. "Give me a week or two."

"Thanks."

He starts to walk off when I spot a guy named Penn, one of Donavan's good buddies who came from Cooper and Associates.

I used to see him around at the Cooper offices in Manhattan. I hold a hand out and stop Dominic from passing by. "Penn Hargrove. He handles all the non-profit entities now?"

"Yeah. He's all about the charity shit. Slays a lot of ass but seems to actually care about the work he does around here. It's how Donavan got him on board. I don't work with him much."

"I want a meeting with him."

I walk off before Dominic can respond. Things to do, chess pieces to position.

MEADOW CARLSON

My phone rings, an unknown number, as I push a cart down the aisle at Home Depot. When I answer, it's an automated message.

"This is a collect call from Butner Federal Correctional…"

I end the call. I have no desire to talk to the person on the other end, sitting in the nicest, white-collar prison in the country, probably playing cards with Bernie Madoff.

I have more important things to do, like gather some supplies for the next stage of shutting down Wells Covington's project. I really shouldn't expose myself as much as I have, but there is something about that man and his arrogance. I shiver a little, just at the sound of his name in my head.

I glance at my list on the Notes app on my phone, then take inventory of my basket again. As I approach the end of the aisle, an extremely tall man steps around the corner and stares right at me.

I nearly shriek and have to clutch my chest. The complete shock of the moment slowly turns to rage as I take a few deep breaths. My face heats up, skin prickles, adrenaline spikes.

Play it cool. He wants this reaction. What the fuck is he doing here?

"Ahh, Ms. Carlson." He cocks his head a little. "What a coincidence. Small world."

I start to push past him, and his hand comes out and slams

into the end of the cart, stopping me in place. It's forceful and deliberate, but a smile remains on his face. His eyes dart down to the contents of my basket, as if he already knew what he'd find.

Does he know what I'm doing?

Don't be ridiculous. He's smart but he can't know everything. He knows.

I wish my brain would shut up for two seconds. How does he make me so paranoid?

"Get out of my way."

He leans over slightly, his lips morphing from a smile into a thin line. "How long are we going to do this?"

I huff out an irritated sigh. "Do what?"

"This back and forth." His eyes dart down to my supplies again. "Like we don't know what this is that's happening right now."

"Listen, Christian Grey." I glare around at the obvious irony of this situation. "Stop fucking stalking me."

He snickers and seems to understand the *Fifty* reference. "Yeah, you vandalized a twenty-five-million-dollar wall of mine, and I'm stalking you."

Shit. He has a point.

I shake my head. "Why are you even here? You live on the other side of town."

"So, you also know where I live? Seems like data a stalker would possess."

Ugh. I pride myself on being able to remain calm and rational, and this man makes me want to rip his eyes out. I take a deep breath and collect myself, then slowly move my gaze up to his. "What do you want?"

His eyes don't leave mine. "To get to know you better. What else?"

He didn't hesitate, didn't stutter, didn't show any signs of deception. He's being sincere. My heart races at his words, and maybe there's a little flutter in my stomach that's out of my control, but I have to keep it together. It's tough, though. I almost gasp a little in shock, then stare back at him. Not a harsh glare, but just a look of uncertainty. Uncertain as to what his motives could possibly be. "Why?"

He slowly walks around the cart.

It's the one barrier between us, providing not only physical distance, but safety in my mind, and it's evaporating in front of me. My heart beats louder in my ears, with each of the steps he takes coming toward me. It happens in a matter of seconds, but it seems like eternity.

I read his eyes, his reactions, anything for a clue as to what he's doing, but it's difficult. He has a look of pure determination on his face, the same way he did when he leaned over my desk the other day.

My body reacts the exact same way as it did then. My brain tells me to scream for help, berate him, do something that lets him know this is not okay. But I'll be damned if there's not a physical attraction there. Some pretty wild thoughts go through my mind as well, sexual thoughts. Thoughts of climbing him like a tree.

Finally, he bends over to my ear again, where nobody else around us could possibly hear. "I go to war against the smartest minds in this country every single day, and have yet to find a worthy opponent, until *you*. I don't like boring things." He leans back, and ever so gently pushes a wayward strand of hair back behind my ear.

I should cringe, shudder when he does it, but I don't. I stare back at him, letting him know I won't be intimidated by his ridiculous suits and his bullying, alpha male behavior. I'm not scared of him. Not of any man.

He says, "You are the furthest thing from boring I've ever found."

I should hate this. I really should.

But I don't. What just happened there? What does he mean? Finally, I say, "Sorry, I'm confused. Are you asking me on a date?"

"If that's how you want to define it, I won't object."

Why is my heart racing so hard? Why are my palms so

clammy? Why does my collar feel like it's strangling me? I hate this man.

Think, Meadow! Can you really do this? Do you want this?

A plan appears in my mind. It's not great, but it should do. Finally, I nod. "Okay, Covington." This time, I walk toward him the same way he walked toward me.

This time, it's he who looks nervous. I should've been on the offensive from the beginning. This is my comfort zone. It's always better to be on offense than defense. He tries to play it cool, but I can see the tiny twitches in his fingers, the way his tie seems to strangle him, the tiny beads of sweat across his brow.

So, the mighty Wells Covington is human after all.

I reach for his pocket, and his eyes widen. I smile right at him and rummage around for his phone, but it definitely looks and might feel like I'm doing more than that.

Part of me does want to reach down, see what he feels like, how big he is. But I don't. Making him think it might happen is far more effective, and I have to play this just right.

He knows better than to react. If he reacts, I win. We both know what's going on here.

I pull his phone from his pocket, then take his thumb and slowly unlock it, our eyes not leaving each other. Once unlocked, I go to his settings and look at his phone number, memorizing it, then I return the phone back where I got it.

"I'll text you a time and a place."

His lips curl up into a devilish grin. I know the look. It's the look on any man's face when they think they're about to get money, power, or laid. It's universal, no matter what their net worth is.

Not to be outdone, he gets even closer to my ear this time. So close I feel his breath play across my neck and shoulder. Involuntary goosebumps break out up and down my arms, and I know he notices. I would notice.

"See you then, *Meadow*."

He walks off.

I turn and say to his back, "How do you know I won't ghost you?"

He doesn't even turn around. "Found you once. Can do it again."

Without even realizing it, I bite my lip and stare at his ass in his slacks. What the fuck is wrong with me? I never bite my lip like some thirsty heroine in a romance movie, fawning all over the rich asshole. I mean, at least Ana got spanked and fucked. There was a legit reason for her behavior. This thing between Covington and me will go absolutely nowhere.

Regardless, I'm a walking cliché right now, reduced to a stereotype I detest.

At least, that's the impression I gave Covington.

If there's one thing I do know, it's that I don't have time for a relationship, and one with Wells Covington is right between lighting myself on fire and bathing in horse piss on a list of my greatest desires.

This just may be fun, though. What I have planned for him.

WELLS COVINGTON

THE SECOND I walk into Alinea, an upscale restaurant that was a very interesting and adequate choice for the date with Meadow, I know it's trouble.

She sent me a text message earlier this afternoon, two days after our Home Depot encounter. I'm almost positive it came from a burner phone, too. I thought eight pm sounded a little later than she would've chosen if this date were real. She would've wanted to keep it closer to five-thirty, less formal, and Alinea would be anything but less formal.

You're an idiot.

Still, my hopes were raised. For the first time in my life, possibly, I ignored reality and hoped for the best. Lesson learned.

Now, I want her even more.

As I stroll through the dining room, the confirmation this was a set-up verifies itself right in front of me.

Oh yes, there at a large table in the center of the room is every single partner at The Hunter Group, and most of the other employees. Dexter's eyes widen when he sees me, then he walks over and shakes my hand.

"Hey, little late for the party, but I'm not surprised. No women on your arm tonight?"

Damn, I didn't even shout, "Fuckers," at them, like I usually do. Meadow Carlson is doing a number on me. Come to think of it, I haven't so much as looked at or thought about another woman since I met her.

I decide to embrace the moment and be honest. I shake my head at him. "Wasn't invited to your party. A date stood me up, orchestrated this encounter."

Dexter laughs, then straightens up when he sees the serious look on my face. "Wait, you're not fucking around?"

I shake my head, grinning. "Not even a little."

Meadow must have someone on the inside at The Hunter Group to know they'd all be here. "What are you guys celebrating?"

"Firm's ten-year anniversary."

That information wouldn't have been hard to come by. I'm sure Decker did a press run on it. They wouldn't announce the restaurant or the party, though. Still, I'm sure the information could've been gained with minimal social engineering skills. She probably just called the firm, pretended to be an employee, and asked to verify the time and location of the party with some secretary.

Well done, Meadow. You'll pay for this, trying to humiliate me in front of all my friends.

I downplay her achievement, but inside, I'm impressed. I've never met anyone as intellectually capable as her. Or am I just building her up in my mind because I want to bury my face in her pussy? Blinded by how attractive she is mentally and physically? There's just something. Something more to her, that x factor I've never experienced with another woman.

I have a seat at the firm's table, because why not? I'm here, and they have booze, and Decker will foot the bill. Everyone looks halfway to being hammered already. It's a fun atmosphere. I imagine working at The Hunter Group is a good gig for someone right out of law school. There's prestige and money. It's a good place to work your way up to a position of authority, plenty of opportunity for advancement, and there's always the Dallas option too, if you want a change of scenery.

"Hi, Covington!" says Abigail.

"How are you?" I give her a kiss on the cheek, and Dexter glares at me as I do it. These assholes are so protective over their significant others. It's hilarious. I'll never understand them.

Why would they want to be tied down? They're in the prime of their life, in their thirties, rich as fuck, can do whatever they please.

"Good, just planning the wedding. You know?"

I shake my head. "No, no I do not know."

Everyone laughs.

"I've already prepared myself for you to show up late to the wedding and make a fool of yourself. Don't worry."

"I never worry. That's guaranteed to happen." I cheers her with a water glass because I currently have no booze in front of me.

I sit there and hang out, having a good time.

But there's only one thought racing through my brain the entire time everyone jokes and laughs around me.

Meadow Carlson.

I need to figure out my next move.

* * *

THE NEXT DAY, I walk into the war room. That's what I call the bullpen of cubicles in the center of my hedge fund.

Lipsy materializes next to me out of nowhere, looking disheveled like he went on a coke bender all night long. I don't really care what he puts in his body, as long as he gets results. His eyes are fully dilated, and he looks like he could drink a gallon of water if one were provided.

I shake my head at him.

"Don't shake your head at me. The paranoia is warranted." He gulps. "Feds are in conference room A. I had to show them to their seats."

I pat him on the shoulder, trying not to laugh. "Maybe stay away for a bit."

He straightens up. "Don't have to tell me twice. On my way

to a VC meeting for those fucks who diluted their shares on the nanotech play."

"Kick them in the dick for me."

"Absolutely. Gonna light them up like *Apocalypse Now*." He sniffs. "Love the smell of napalm in the morning."

And just like that, he's gone.

I shake my head, snicker for a moment, and head up to the conference room. I swing the door open. "Boys."

Two men in suits shake my hand. "Mr. Covington, thanks for taking the meeting."

"Absolutely, where are we in concluding this little operation of ours?"

"Thirty-two arrests were made, a hundred and twenty-five women ages twelve to nineteen currently being identified and processed, hopefully reunited with their families soon."

I cringe, just thinking about what their future may have held for them, then shake my head. "Fuck."

"Hey, their lives are all changed, because of you."

"The government is also providing resources they need? To get them back on their feet?"

"Definitely. We'll take care of them."

"Good, I can set up a private foundation if it's needed, if your resources are spread too thin."

"Not necessary. This is good press for the Bureau and Washington. Makes it look like we're making progress on trafficking. We're trying, you know? But DC is all about optics, playing politics. There's no way they won't give these people everything they need. The political fallout would be too great."

"Beautiful fucking world we live in. I think politicians might be worse than me."

"Well, you actually helped people without being asked. More than I can say for them. Like I said, you changed these people's lives. Saved them from a dangerous situation."

I lean back in my chair. "Nonsense, what I did was easy. I just think about the others who aren't as fortunate."

The other suit leans in. "We have paperwork to wrap this up, but we wanted to talk to you about the PR on this. It's part of the job, as unsatisfying as it may be. We want to—"

I cut him off. "Absolutely not. No mention of my name. No mention of my firm."

Both their eyes widen. One of them starts again. "But—"

"You may need me in the future. It creates a million problems with clients and relationships I've spent years building. Some don't possess the same moral compass as me. And I didn't do it for attention. I did it to help. How many other trafficking rings operate in the world right now?"

They both concede and hold up their hands. "Fine, whatever you want."

One of them sighs. "Not doing yourself any favors though. You know how the world sees billionaires right now. This could help change public perception, if they knew a few people in the top income bracket actually give a damn and are actively helping."

"Fuck everyone else on Wall Street. They deserve their reputation, and so do I." I grin. "Most of the time. Still, I'm no saint. Not by a longshot."

They both nod along and seem to give up on the idea of publicizing my involvement.

I call my in-house attorney in and verify a few things, then sign their documentation. My attorney leaves. The two agents stand up and we all shake hands.

"At least come to the press conference, as a guest. Get a firsthand look at what you helped us do. It's later today. You can just blend in with the crowd."

I shake my head, but then think about it for a moment. Slowly, I grin. "You know what? Maybe I will stop by, unofficially."

They both turn to me. "We'd like that a lot. Seriously. There are a few other agents who want to say thanks. They know we couldn't have done this without you."

I nod. "Okay, I'll be there. But no credit. My name is need-to-know only. No name on the record or to the press. Don't even tell anyone I'm coming, or there will be no assistance in the future. Our relationship will terminate."

They shake my hand once more. "Fair enough. Thanks again."

I open the door and lead them down the stairs to the elevator, eliciting several glances from my analysts. I'm sure they're not used to seeing me in such a good mood when feds are in the building.

Once they're on their way out, I turn around and stare at my sanctuary, my empire, the one place in the world where my brain has no limits and I can see the matrix clearly. The only place that has ever made sense to me in a world devoid of logic and rational behavior.

This is my crowning achievement, and I had to learn some difficult lessons to mold this place into exactly what I wanted. It is beautiful, though.

What's even more beautiful, is the fact I know the next step in my plan.

MEADOW CARLSON

CAMERAS all around me snap pictures at the FBI press conference. It was recently announced a huge trafficking ring was infiltrated and over thirty arrests have been made. I'm covering the story for a few of my news blogs.

I can't remember the last time I was this excited. It's a big deal for such a huge problem that's largely ignored by society. Or at least one the media seems to ignore quite often.

Yes, you can remember the last time you were this excited. When you set Wells Covington up for humiliation.

Okay, this story is better than that, but it still doesn't mean it wasn't fun. I only wish I could've seen his face once he realized what happened. The one drawback was the fact I kind of wanted to go on that date with him, and I hate myself for feeling that way.

He's a rich, corporate asshole. I know the type, and yet something about him feels different. It doesn't mean he's not gorgeous, though. But the gorgeous ones are usually the worst.

There's pushing and shoving in front of me, reporters doing what reporters do, when a large man in jeans, a tee shirt, and a cap pulled down low over his eyes, rams into me, almost knocking me sideways.

"Shit, sorry about—" He turns to face me.

I scowl right back at him, clutching my phone in my palm so

it doesn't get lost in this borderline mosh pit of media, until my eyes meet his, and *oh my fuck.*

I freeze in my tracks, because what else can I do right now? I have to squint to make sure I see what I think I see, but my heart identified him immediately, judging by the way it thumps in my chest.

My breaths grow shallow, and a million emotions course through me at once—anger and irritation sitting front and center.

Hold it together!

Finally, I just smirk at him and roll my eyes. "Nice outfit."

The hair on the back of my neck stands at attention. Is he seriously following me around everywhere? Can he not take a hint? It's getting a little scary and creepy.

"Thanks." He adjusts the collar on his shirt. "Thought I'd see what it's like, dressing like a member of the proletariat, when I'm not lording over Chicago from above."

I almost want to laugh because I think it was a joke. He's such a narcissistic asshole, but it's almost like he's aware of it at the same time.

"It was a fail. But a valiant effort, *Covington.*"

He leans in next to me, as if he's anticipating the announcement. "So, what's the big scoop? Writing another one of your little hit pieces on the blog?"

"It's a reputable news source, not a blog. More reputable than the corporate-owned news doing their masters' bidding under the guise of actual journalism." It's still a blog, but I know he said the word just to discredit what I do, as if it's not a serious endeavor.

"Sure it is. How do you find the time?"

I shrug. "What?"

"Do your investors like you playing crusader on the clock?"

I snort, but inside my blood runs cold. There's no way he knows about the impact fund. It's impossible. Not that I really care that much, but I prefer to keep my business interests quiet. Not parade them around the country like conquests as members of the hedgie world like to do. I'll never understand a man bragging about destroying another company and shredding it apart to make money. It's like they're proud of putting people out of work and gutting institutions, using the country's laws to profit.

I shrug. "Not sure what you mean."

He scoffs. "Sure."

Finally, I wheel on him, because he gets under my skin like no man in history ever has. "What do you want? This is getting a little *American Psycho*, Christian Bale-style."

He starts to say something, when a few of the FBI agents spot him. He looks away from them, but they both smile and give him a thumbs up.

"Fuckers."

I look at him long and hard. He's genuinely embarrassed, or even ashamed. He's hiding something. "What was that all about?"

Quickly, he recovers as if nothing just happened. "What was what?"

I glance back and forth, from the agents to him. Those were the lead guys on the investigation, and I thought Covington was here because he's stalking me, but something is going on.

"Did you have something to do with this operation?"

This time his eyes meet mine, and it's almost like I catch a glimpse of the real him for a moment. Not the man he portrays publicly, the persona, but a small hint of what's really ticking under the hood.

"No."

I know what he's doing. He wants me to put the pieces of this together on my own, without him having to commit one way or another, revealing any information. I'm done playing his games, though.

So, I just shrug. "Okay. Then what do you want?"

It's like he turns into a brand-new person in front of me, morphs back to asshole billionaire. "Glad you asked. I'll tell you over dinner tomorrow."

Clammy palms again. How does he turn me into this? I don't get nervous like this. Fluttering stomach and all that shit. "Not going to happen."

He does that damn lean-next-to-my-ear thing again, and yeah, it's hot. Doesn't mean I don't want him to stop though.

"Okay, Carlson. Enough games." He sighs right into my ear. "I want to know how you knew my projections and the timetables on my projects, and exactly how to maximize the pain."

I'm pretty sure my heart just ran a three-minute mile. Literally, a cold sweat breaks out across my forehead. He knows way more than I gave him credit for. "I didn't—"

"Enough bullshit. We're beyond that." He sighs in my ear again. "Tell me how you did it, and tell me what you want with the place. If your answers are satisfactory, I'll hand it over to you."

My eyes widen even more when he says that. "What?"

"I'll scrap the project. If you have dinner with me tomorrow and satisfy my curiosity."

This time, it's me who doesn't think things through. Before I can stop myself, I whip around, all business when I stare into his eyes, shedding the fake clueless-activist routine. I point a finger right in his face. "Don't fuck with me about this. It's off limits to whatever bullshit back and forth flirting we have going."

He holds up both hands. "Easy, Ronda Rousey, fuck. I don't joke about business and money."

The mood lightens a little, but I keep my gaze pinned on him. "To be clear, you want to discuss this over dinner? Make a deal on the building?"

Covington sighs. "I don't see why not. The goddamn project is about to lose me a fuckload of money because of your bullshit. I'm not in the habit of keeping losers on my books and flushing capital for petty vendettas."

That gets a slight smile out of me. This could be huge. I have big plans for that building. Way better than filling it up with Russian oligarchs and the Saudi royal family. I nod. "Okay."

"Good. I'll send you the damn time and place this time."

I nod. My adrenaline is through the damn roof right now, and I feel like I could float away. Could I have been wrong about him? The original plan was to make him lose money until he was forced to sell at a discount. I'm not opposed to using other methods to achieve the same goal, though. That's the end game. To get the building. It doesn't matter how I do it.

I glance up at his smug face. No, I definitely wasn't wrong about him, but I don't care. I'd do anything to get my way on this. Anything. "One dinner. That's it."

He leans over in my ear, and this time, instead of making me nauseous, I actually welcome it a little and maybe even lean toward him. *Maybe.*

"You ghost me this time, the gloves come off. You don't want me as an enemy, Ms. Carlson." He turns and walks off before I can respond.

I don't care, though. Part of me is worried this is some kind of setup, but for some reason, I know it's not. I don't know how to describe the way I read people, but he's being truthful. It was one hundred percent the truth. I'm sure of that.

Shit, I want to hug someone, or an even worse offense, squee. I want to squee in the middle of these damn reporters.

At the same time, something could very easily go wrong with the whole deal. His last sentence rings in my head, over and over.

"You don't want me as an enemy."

It's true. I don't. It's not like I went and picked a fight with him for fun. I don't understand why I'm so drawn to him either. I know exactly how men like him operate. How can I be so attracted to someone who will do anything to win, someone who's so corrupted by the finance world and the power that comes with that. Men who will destroy anything in their way, just to get what they want.

It doesn't matter. I'll go to the dinner, hear him out, give answers, and make a logical decision.

Yep. That's exactly how this will work. I want to know the story with those FBI agents, why they were smiling at him. There's something going on there too.

WELLS COVINGTON

WHY THE FUCK am I so nervous?

I have two hours before the date with Meadow. I'm sitting in a gigantic mansion, in my own personal sports bar inside my house, with a walk-in, custom humidor attached, full of the rarest cigars in the world. I shouldn't have a hint of anxiety, and yet in my gut is this feeling I'm not accustomed to. It's not even anxiety, per se. It's more like a good type of worried.

Very eloquent explanation there, dipshit.

Usually, when I make an investment, I've done all the homework. I've worked the problem from every angle and verified the math. I've accounted for every possible risk, to the point there is no chance it will fail. Many times, there is guaranteed arbitrage, where it's impossible for me to lose money, regardless of any possible catastrophe that's not world-ending.

This, though. This is different.

I feel like an underdog. Like I'm entering into an arrangement where it's likely the outcome won't be favorable. One would think I'd be bothered by this, but on the contrary, it's a rush. A dopamine spike. The uncertainty is intoxicating, floods my veins.

Orson walks in with two options for me to wear.

I take way longer than I usually would to select a fucking set of clothes. I pride myself on my appearance and efficiency in achieving it, but it shouldn't matter *this* much. It does, though. I don't like to lose. I won't lose, and I want to look perfect for her.

Meadow Carlson will be mine.

This whole scenario is the reason. I've never felt this with a woman before. They usually bore me. I just want to fuck them, see what they'll allow me to do, then it's just dull afterward. I'm not an asshole about it. I treat them right, do polite things. I don't just roll them out of bed and tell them to get lost, but it still doesn't make them interesting to me.

Meadow is different. She's the opposite of boring. I want to know more about her. I want to know where she got that brain of hers, what makes it tick. She's like fine art. You want to get inside the artist's head, understand what led them to create in the manner they did.

Dominic got back to me earlier. Said she runs an impact fund, but keeps it hushed. That didn't surprise me. It made some sense of how she calculated and sabotaged my project. Which leads me to the next thing. Normally, if an investment goes bad, which is rarely, I lose it. I have to check out for a day or two, get upset, drink, put Lipsy in charge, and go wallow in despair. Then I review everything a million times until I find out where it went wrong and ensure it never happens again.

I look up and realize Orson is standing there, staring. I've been ignoring him.

It's not unusual. I've been described as hyper-focused on more than one occasion by more than one psychologist.

"What's going on with you, Orson? What's new in your world?"

He quirks up an eyebrow. "Sir?"

"You heard me." He must think I'm batshit crazy right now. We never do the small talk thing, even though I care about him more than just about anyone in the world. Orson, Lipsy, Dexter, and Cole Miller. That's about it, as far as a social support system goes. I tend to despise almost everyone else. "What's going on with you?"

He walks over and takes a seat next to me. "You all right?"

"Yes." I shake my head at the same time.

Orson laughs. "It's okay to be nervous, sir."

I start to deny his accusation, then stop myself. "She's different."

"So it seems." He leans back, regarding me with amusement.

"Well, are you going to give me one of your pep talks? Or say some British shit that helps me succeed tonight?"

He laughs again. "Afraid I'm not much of an expert on relationships. How is she different?"

"She fucked up a half-billion-dollar investment the first day I met her."

Orson nods. "Well, that *is* a bit of a difference from the usual women you accompany."

This time I laugh. "Yeah. You could say that." I sigh. "She's smart. Fucking genius level smart. Never met anyone like her."

"So, you recognize yourself in her a little?"

"Yes, exactly."

"Well then, I think I would advise authenticity on your part. If she's anything like you, she'll sniff out deception a mile away. Maybe that's another reason you're drawn to her. She holds you accountable, forces you to be yourself. Demands the truth."

I sit up straight. "You're right. Fuck, she keeps me guessing nonstop. Impossible to read. Usually, I know exactly what people want from me, then I make sure the transaction is advantageous to my needs. I can't do that with her. I fall flat on my face if I try. She sees right through it."

"Well then, seems like you have a game plan figured out then."

I stand up and pat him on the shoulder. "Good talk. We should do this more often."

"I'm always here, sir. For whatever you require." He walks to the door. "Let me know when you're ready. I'll pull the car around."

"Okay." I think for a second. "Wait."

Orson turns around. "Sir?"

"I think I'll drive. Take the night off. Do something fun."

His eyebrows quirk up for a split second, then he levels me with his gaze and nods. "Very well."

"And give yourself a five-thousand-dollar bonus this week. Call it a counseling fee."

"Already did that this morning. Good luck on your date." He walks off before I can say anything else.

Old prick. I bet he really did it too.

I get dressed, chuckling in the process, and stand in front of a full-length mirror. Hair is good, outfit is great, dark jeans and a button-down, sleeves rolled up. Slightly casual, but still classy. Usually, when going out, my number one goal is to fuck someone that night.

I stare at myself in the mirror and realize, I don't even care about getting laid. In fact, I'd level the odds at ninety-nine point nine nine percent I won't. I just want to know her better, make her like me.

That's the one thing that scares me; craving her acceptance. It also excites me.

* * *

I PULL up to Meadow's building in my Tesla Model X. I figured it was the best choice, even though I wanted to drive the new mid-engine Corvette that was delivered yesterday. I mean, for fuck's sake, her name is Meadow. If she doesn't care about the environment, nobody does. Not to mention I can still go zero to sixty in two point nine seconds if I flip it to Ludicrous mode, and it has cool bat wing doors on it.

I ride the elevator up to her floor and, fuck me, the feeling in my stomach. It twists in knots by the second. You'd think I was back in the sixth grade, all tall and gangly, trying to impress a girl with calculus. I laugh at how far I've come in my mind, only to circle right back to that nightmare.

The entire walk to her door takes forever. This building is far more modest than I would've imagined. It's nice, middle-class, but I know Meadow is wealthy. She might dress like a chic hippie, but she runs an impact fund. Her media outlets, of which I've been featured in many times, always unflattering, have to pull significant ad revenues. She's not broke is what I'm saying.

I mumble to myself, "The fuck does she do with all her money?"

When I get to the door, I focus. I debated bringing flowers during the forty-minute drive here, but I don't want to look like that big of a pussy. That's way more lovey dovey than I think I'm capable of, even if I do like her. Plus, Orson said to be myself.

I hover in front of her door for a moment, staring down at her doorbell.

Push it. What the fuck?

Here's the thing, though. It scares me how much I want this woman. I know I'm not an addict. I can do drugs, then not do drugs. I can drink and not drink. I've forced myself to refrain from investing for a month, just to see if I could do it, to manage my impulses. I know I'm not addicted to those things.

With Meadow, I'm uncertain.

I'm not sure I can let this go with her if she rejects me. I've never wanted anything this bad.

That's what scares the shit out of me. Because I may be able to win her over, date her, fuck her, fall in love with her, all that stuff. But what are the odds that it all works out in my favor, that we grow old and die together, everything just as it should be? Astronomically bad. She's a bad investment, and yet...

I push the button.

"Just a second!" The words sound like they came from the other side of her apartment.

When I hear footsteps, my heart matches them, thumping in my ear.

First date. This is an important moment, this right here.

I focus my mind on remembering her, how she looks, the second she opens the door. For whatever reason, I want that locked in my memory forever. The whole moment, this entire thing, it just feels significant to me.

I would never wager on a gut feeling, but my gut is rarely wrong, and it's telling me this is the start of a new chapter of my life. This is a defining moment, some kind of transformation from within.

When she opens the door, all the breath sucks out of my lungs. I pride myself on not showing reactions, not giving away any emotional intelligence to opponents, day in and day out. It gives me an edge.

There's no stopping it here, though. It's the second I see her smile, her honey eyes locked on mine, lashes slightly fluttering, cheeks slightly pink. She's the most beautiful woman I've ever seen. There's nothing special about her outfit or the way she's dressed—light makeup, summer dress. It's not designer. Her hair color is her own. No plastic surgery or augmentations. She's the exact opposite of every woman I've ever been physically attracted to.

I think it's mostly the eyes. They're so disarming and I just get lost in them.

"Hello."

I blink a few times, and my mind blanks on me, like I've forgotten how to speak. I'm such a bumbling idiot around her, just seeing her face.

She grins at me, in that sly way of hers, like she's going to play dumb but knows exactly what she's doing to me.

My throat closes off, but I manage to get out a, "Hi."

"Want to come in for a second? I need to grab my bag."

Finally, my brain decides to possess an electrical signal and I say, "Sure."

I take a few steps inside as she walks off to a room, and I look around the place. It's very minimalist and cozy, I guess. It's the exact opposite of anywhere I sleep. There's a sofa, bookshelf, a few pieces of art that look like something you buy at a store and not Sotheby's.

Meadow returns with a small handbag.

"There's no TV."

"Smartest man in the world, ladies and gentlemen." She laughs.

I don't even dignify her little dig with a response, but I do grin.

She looks at me like *is that a serious observation that requires a response?* Finally, she says, "I read. When I'm at

50

home. I like to minimize distractions. Something tells me you don't watch much TV either."

I take a step toward the door and continue the conversation as we walk down the hall. "CNBC, that's about it. And *Peaky Blinders*."

"What the hell is a Peaky Blinder?"

I scoff like I can't believe she doesn't know of the Shelbys. "Cinematic excellence."

"Where are you taking me?"

"It's a surprise. I'm sure you've never been there."

We walk up to the curb, and Meadow turns to face me after she sees the car. "Nice choice from your garage." She nods at the Tesla.

I shrug, knowing nothing will get by her. "Charged it with solar. Not to worry, it'll be a carbon footprintless date to ease your worried little soul."

Meadow laughs as I open the door for her. "Know your opponent, Covington?"

"I prefer to think of us as an alliance now."

"Yeah, I bet you do." She buckles her seatbelt as I walk around to the driver's side.

After pulling down the driver's side door, we take off down the streets of Chicago.

"Figured you'd have a driver."

My eyes roll over to hers then back to the road. "I usually do."

"So you can be more efficient with your time?"

I flip the switch to Ludicrous mode on the Tesla. It's time to make her a little nervous. "No. It's more of a safety concern."

Meadow's eyes widen as she processes what I just told her.

Too late.

I punch it and we blast down the road. No sense in being able to do zero to sixty in under three seconds, unless you actually go zero to sixty in under three seconds. The force of acceleration throws us back into the seats, and Meadow's hand flies out and grips my forearm, her small, manicured nails digging into my skin.

Fuck, it feels amazing too. I don't want to stop, but I know she'll demand to be let out of the car if I push my luck.

"Goddamn it, Covington!" Her eyes are wider than I've ever seen them.

I try to hold in the laugh building in my chest as I bring us back down to the speed limit.

She gives me a little backhand to the shoulder and glares over at me. "Way to start off a date, asshole."

"Hadn't tested it out yet. Figured you'd appreciate the transference of all that electrical energy to the wheels." I smile and continue before she can respond. "So it *is* a date?"

She blinks a few times. "About to be the shortest one in history."

"Nonsense, I've already had shorter than this."

She tries to hold back a grin and just shakes her head at me while I keep my eyes on the road.

"Was just testing the power of solar—"

"Just… stop, okay?"

I finally laugh. "Fair enough." I glance down at her fingernail marks on my skin. Fuck, I'd love to have her put some of those on my back. The funniest thing is, I really don't even care if I get laid tonight or not. I'm just, happy. Happy being near her. When she's around me, I don't feel like myself. I'm a better version, if that makes any sense.

It's dangerous because I have to be a certain way to run my business. You can't show weakness, empathy, in the hedge world.

There's just something about this, though. This whole moment. Her in the passenger seat, me driving, in control of the situation. It's so foreign, yet I don't want to be anywhere else right now.

Finally, I pull up to the place, far sooner than I'd like.

Meadow's eyes light up when she sees the sign, but she says, "Seriously?"

"Seriously."

Her eyes dart around for a second; no doubt she's trying to think of how to approach this. "Al's Italian Beef?"

"That's what the sign says."

She turns in the seat to face me. "I want to hear your methodology for this selection."

I shrug. "Easy, it's the story behind it, with which I'm sure you're familiar. The business came about during the Great Depression when Al Ferrari needed to stretch a roast to serve a wedding reception. So, he sliced the meat thin and served it on thick Italian bread. It's right up your alley. Finding value out of little, to better the community in time of need."

Meadow stays quiet for a moment.

"Or it could be that I saw several Al's Italian Beef containers in your trash can when I surprised you at your office last week. Either works."

That gets another smile out of her. I'm making her smile an awful lot, for someone who purports to not enjoy my company all that much.

This whole date is a lot like playing chess against a grand master like Kasparov. She has not brought up the big project downtown, even though it's her entire reason for being here. She hasn't even alluded to it. She's playing her opponent, and I have to respect that. She's building empathy, making me think she's enjoying this. But I can tell. It's not working how she wants it to. She wants to loathe me. Her brain screams it at her, but this magnetic attraction between us, it's pulling on her the same way it is on me.

Interesting.

I'm sure she'll wait until we're approximately fifty percent through the meal and will mention the project, if I haven't brought it up by then. I don't see her holding out longer than that.

I raise up the Tesla wing door and step out, then walk around to get her door for her. I hold out a hand, but she gets up by herself. I'd expect no less from Meadow. She doesn't need a man's help to get out of a car. Secretly, she likes the chivalrous gesture, even if it feels like a manipulation.

This may be the first time I've felt a hint of control when it comes to her.

Her phone rings as we walk inside. Meadow silences it immediately.

"You can take that if you need to."

"Thanks for the permission, Covington." She stuffs her phone back in her little clutch bag.

"You're welcome."

She shakes her head as we look up at the menu. Which is a meaningless gesture, because when you go to Al's, you're getting the beef sandwich. Everyone knows this.

Meadow keeps smiling, probably more than she wants to. But I can't help but notice I'm doing the same. I'm not much of a smiling person. Definitely not at work, unless Lipsy and I are behind closed doors. The only other time is when I hang out with Dexter and Cole, or when Orson cracks one of his dry jokes.

We both order our sandwiches and I pay. Fortunately, Meadow doesn't throw a fit about that little detail. We opt to stand near each other, next to the window.

"You've had one of these before?" she asks.

"Of course. I'm from Chicago."

"Wouldn't think you like getting your fingers all messy."

If she only knew what I could do with my fingers. I'm quite capable of making her say my name repeatedly. My cock starts to harden, just thinking about making her squirm underneath me. I have to bite back the low growl that catches in my throat.

"I don't mind. But thanks for the concern."

Her phone rings again. She takes it out and looks at it. The screen flashes an unknown number. She sighs and silences it again. Has to be someone she doesn't want to talk to. I already told her she could take the call, which I'm positive she would normally do to get out of talking to me.

"Who is it?"

"Nobody." She doesn't even look up as she says it, and it's pretty harsh, confirming my thoughts.

"Sorry, didn't mean to—"

"Yeah, you did, Covington. Cut the shit. It's someone whose voice I have no desire to hear at the moment."

"Fair enough." I pause, still wanting to phish for information. "So, you have family around?"

She tenses the second I say it.

Must've been family on the phone.

Meadow sighs, as if she knows she just gave herself away. "My mom, that's it. You?"

"Are you close?"

"Yeah, though not as much as I'd like to be lately."

I ignore her question about my family.

She turns to me. "Riddle me this, Covington." She takes a huge bite, then turns and stares at me for a long time, chewing, thinking.

I set down my sandwich, wipe my fingers on a napkin, then turn and match her stare, waiting for her to finish chewing.

Finally, after what feels like forever, she says, "What makes you tick?"

It's a simple question. To the point, yet still vague and wide.

"In what sense?"

"What captures your attention? Drives your decision-making every day. We're all just carbon. The decisions we make define us as individuals, separate us from other animals. What force, what variable, drives yours?"

I answer immediately. "Things that are interesting. I despise anything boring, mundane, repetitive, predictable."

"Do I meet your criteria?" She doesn't blink, doesn't look away.

Those honey-brown eyes sear into my skull, like she can read every thought I have.

"Absolutely."

She stares for a long time, and I see the spark in her eyes. I know she feels it, whatever this is between us. This woman is everything. How has she been in this city, existing in this world even, and I never knew about her?

Eventually, she turns back to her sandwich. "Glad to know I'm not boring." She grins at her food and starts eating again.

"What about you?" I ask.

This time she doesn't look at me. "Same. Except I have an additional filter. A conscience."

"And I don't?"

She smiles through another bite and doesn't bother to finish chewing this time. "Maybe, on occasion."

Her words sting a little, but I don't show it. Sure, I've had my part in some questionable ethical decisions, despite always being inside the law, but overall, I feel I try to do the right things. I have to make money. I have employees who depend on me. Their families depend on me.

I just helped the authorities bust a human trafficking ring, but I have no desire to prove that to her. I didn't do it to win her favor or anyone else's. As much as I want her to think I'm a good person, words are cheap. She should know this better than anyone. All you have to do is flip on C-SPAN to see a bunch of people patting themselves on the back constantly. She'll find out about me, eventually.

If she knew what I've been through, what it took for me to break into the hedgie world, she'd change her tune. There will be time for that, though. I'll prove myself to her if I have to, the same way I did to Wall Street and the world in the past ten years.

"I was joking." She elbows me playfully. "You're not as bad as I imagined."

For the first time, it seems our conversation turns somewhat human. I don't believe for a second she believes what she just said, but I think part of her needs me to be the villain, even if it doesn't match her actual observations. Idealists need something to feed off. They need this cartoon caricature of a billionaire stereotype to rage against, separate themselves from, to feel good about their station in life. The stereotype exists for a reason, but it's far more nuanced than that. Context matters. Not to mention, the anti-hero and anti-villain are always the best characters, so I'm not too worried. Her bar is set low and I'll crush it. Nobody wants something black and white, cut and dry. It's boring as fuck.

She portrays herself as a hero, but I want to know about her being tested, what dirty things she's done. Because everyone has done dirty things, no matter how far they shove those skeletons back in their closet and pretend to be upstanding citizens, while pointing their fingers at the troublemakers. Everyone has regrets.

We finish our sandwiches, and I still haven't brought up the real estate project, the entire reason Meadow is even here with me right now.

She keeps glancing over, waiting for it. Admirably, she's made it past the roughly fifty percent mark of our date and still hasn't broached the topic.

"Mental stimulation."

She blinks a few times. "Sorry what?"

"The rest of the answer to your question. What makes me tick. That's what drives me." I hold out a hand. "Come on, I want to take you somewhere."

She glances back and forth, between my outstretched fingers and my eyes, like she's both scared and intrigued. Finally, after looking into my eyes, she reaches out and takes my hand.

We walk over, get in the car, and I start driving. "You've done well, holding out for information."

She exhales a huge sigh. "No shit."

I laugh. "I want to take you someplace special to me. While there, I will discuss the specifics of our arrangement. If you're too uncomfortable with the setting when we get there, I understand, and we don't have to go inside. But I hope you'll take your time and consider it."

"Okay." She wipes her palms down her dress.

I know she's read every tabloid article about me, studied me relentlessly, the same way I sent Dominic Romano to gather intelligence about her. She may even have people working for her, doing the same, though I don't hide anything about my personal life.

After about a ten-minute drive, we pull up outside the place.

"Covington, I don't—"

"Please?" It's the first time I've actually been vulnerable in front of her, showed any kind of weakness. I should not be doing this. It's a horrible, horrible idea. I want her to know the real me, though, and I don't know why. Okay, maybe I do know why, but it's reckless. "I'll surprise you. Just give me a chance. I've never done this, let someone into this part of my life."

She glances over at the building, then back at me. This is the big moment. This is where the foundation of trust is built.

I can practically hear her heart racing, her pulse speeding up on her neck. It's the most nervous I've ever seen her, even though I'm sure she supports anyone, with words anyway, who would frequent such a place. People talk a big game until they're put to the test.

She sits there, warring with herself, then finally looks at me, nods and says, "Okay."

We get out and walk toward the entrance to the building.

It's a BDSM dungeon.

MEADOW CARLSON

Holy shit.

I don't know why I'm so nervous, but I am. In my mind, I know it's not rational. There's nothing wrong with people living their best life, doing whatever they want to do. I know this instinctively, these are my principles, and I know this is some kind of test he's running on me. Some experiment to see how I'll react. It's his MO, and I knew this about him. I should've seen it coming a mile away, but he always manages to distract me one way or another.

My palms start to sweat as we stride toward the entrance.

I'm so not into this kind of thing. Not that it matters. A relationship with this man, sexual or otherwise, will never happen. I'm here for him to make good on his promise, then I'm done with him.

Still, my pulse speeds up, knowing what this place is, imagining the types of things happening inside. Maybe it's just fear of the unknown that's the catalyst for my internal reactions.

"You don't have to go in if you don't want to." Covington glances over at me, and I can see he's telling the truth.

Now, it's like a challenge to myself, and I don't want to lose. It's one of those moments where you really see if you believe what you preach. Will you face something uncomfortable to you and your way of life because it's the right thing to do?

I do my best to play it cool, but I know there's no way in hell he buys it. "I don't mind, seriously." The insecurity in my voice gives me away. I'm sure of that. This man is a hawk. He'll pick up on the tiniest of clues.

"Let's do it then."

Each step we take is like slow motion. I realize I'm holding my breath and do my best to manage it.

Covington glances over. "Relax. You don't have to participate. I just want to have a conversation."

I nod, looking straight forward, focusing on getting from one point to the next. "Okay."

He must be loving the hell out of this right now. I can tell by that slight smirk on his face. He wants to see me rattled. Wants me to have some kind of reaction. I honestly don't know why he's so obsessed with me the way he is. I get he's looking out for his business interests; that's to be expected. This is different though. I didn't plan this whole thing going the way it is, and I need to adapt. Once again, I'm playing defense, and it's uncomfortable as all hell.

We walk through a door, and a large man who I assume is security, greets us.

"Mr. Covington."

Covington gives him a little nod. "Brought a guest with me."

"Welcome, ma'am. Enjoy yourselves."

I can't help my curious eyes. They take in everything they see. There are tables with big leather straps. Walls full of different instruments, their purpose I have zero clue about. Some people go up to private rooms. Some are out in the open. There's a man, in nothing but his underwear with a gag in his mouth, being spanked by a gorgeous woman in a full leather outfit.

Covington reaches down and takes my hand in his. Strangely, I let him do it and don't pull away as he leads me through the main room. It's weird. It feels very protective, and even more oddly, I feel safer when he does it.

Safety shouldn't even be a concern of mine right now. I'm not threatened; there's nothing to fear, and yet it still courses through my body, and I'm unable to stop it, no matter how many times I tell myself I'm being irrational.

Finally, he leads me over to a little area with a table and two chairs. There are no torture devices around us. Just a place for people to sit and talk. There's even a coffee machine.

Covington pulls out my chair for me, then walks around and takes a seat.

I sit down and look across the table at him.

"So…"

"So…" I say in return, as if I'm not surprised he brought me here.

He smirks. Usually, his smirk annoys me, but this time it's slightly more tolerable.

Fuck, is he wearing me down? Getting to me somehow?

"Let's talk business."

It's almost impossible to focus on him with everything going on around me. At first, I was apprehensive, but now that I'm inside, sitting down, I'm just curious. I find myself glancing at a woman berating a man who is on his knees. He's trying to fight back a smile, and when he does finally grin, she yells and punishes him even more. Every visual clue tells me he's elated, loves every second of it.

It's so—interesting. I see why Wells enjoys himself here. It's anything but what the public would consider normal.

"Right?"

I whip my head over and see Covington grinning right at me. "What do you look so smug about?"

"I just know what's going through your brain right now."

"Do you now?" I smile back at him. "I know you're into BDSM. Everyone in the world knows it. You make no effort to hide it in the press."

Covington relaxes in his seat. "I have a simple question that I require an honest answer to. Possibly the most serious question I'll ever ask you."

"Fire away."

He glances down, and he actually looks nervous, like he's

afraid to ask it. Finally, he looks me dead in the eye and says, "Are you a woman of principle?"

I stiffen a little at the way he asks the question. I can't give him a direct 'yes' because that would be a lie for anyone. "I've made mistakes, but I'd like to think so."

He glances away, avoiding eye contact.

He's struggling with something. It's not a business decision either, or something computational. It's like he's battling his soul right now.

Finally, he leans in, almost like he might whisper, but he only slightly lowers his voice. "I want to trust you with certain information. It's something very important to me, though. Something I've never told anyone, not even those closest to me."

Oh. Wow, this is heavy. I don't know how I feel about being his personal shrink. That's not what I signed on for, but I can't help but be intrigued. He's an intriguing man. Nobody could argue that. "Something personal?"

His eyes sear into mine and he doesn't falter, even for a microsecond. "Yes."

It's a simple question. A reasonable person would automatically answer in the affirmative. But do I really want to know? Will I really not use personal information against him? I don't want to be put in that position. If I did ever use it against him, I'd feel horrible, and he knows it. Somehow, he knows me, damn near as well as I know myself.

I sigh. "You want a hundred percent honesty? Fact is, I don't know. I don't know you all that well."

"I'm trying to remedy that."

"Sure, and this date has gone incredibly different than I imagined. It doesn't change the fact I want something of yours, and it's very important to me. If I don't get it, I don't know that I wouldn't use any and everything at my disposal, if I thought it might help."

Covington smirks again, like he's reading me for a book report due next week. Like I'm some kind of anomaly and he's amassing every bit of data he can on my soul.

"I'm good for my word, Meadow. I told you I'd scrap the project. I will."

I sit there, staring back at him for a long time. Not knowing if I should trust a single thing that comes out of his mouth. I know the world of investing, the way power and money corrupt. I know men like him, and rule number one is never trust a damn thing they say. "Did you really help with that sting operation to bust the sex trafficking ring? Or was that all smoke and mirrors? Some kind of manipulation to get me to go on a date with you?"

His eyebrows rise, then he says, "So you didn't want certain personal information, but now you do?"

"Maybe this was a mistake." I start to get up.

He reaches over for my arm, and the second his fingers hit my skin, electricity buzzes through me again. It's a biological response. I know this, deep in my brain. He's attractive, commanding—it's nothing but an evolutionary process to seek out procreation with the most suitable mate for survival. But damn it, the look in his eyes.

I can't imagine he's ever been so vulnerable in his life, and it probably seems like I'm taking advantage of that, by leveraging more and more information out of him.

"Please, stay."

"Why?" I respond, almost immediately.

He laughs. It catches me off guard, then he just keeps laughing, almost like he's having a breakdown in front of me.

What the hell? He really is nuts.

It's almost contagious, and I find myself looking around to make sure nobody is watching, because it's embarrassing, then I turn back to him and snicker. "What the hell is so funny? Are you okay?"

Through a laugh, he says, "I don't know. That's why it's just —funny." He manages to rein in the laughter after a few seconds, and says, "I shouldn't trust you with a penny stock pick. But for some reason, I do. I can't explain it." He pauses and holds up a finger. "But you were honest a moment ago. When I asked if I could trust you. Someone in your position who wanted to take advantage of me would've lied their ass off. And you didn't."

I shrug. "Maybe it's a double bluff. Maybe I knew you'd know that, so I did this to get you to trust me."

"Circular logic can make you a paranoid son of a bitch. That's a rabbit hole you never want to go down."

This time, I'm the one who laughs. "That's the fucking truth."

Covington's eyes dance around the room, then circle back to me. "I'm just going to say it then. What I wanted to tell you. Fuck it, I don't know why. Nothing about this makes any sense to me at all."

"I don't—"

"I'm not into this." He says it so quickly, I barely make out the words.

"Huh?" My eyes widen.

His shoulders drop a little, like a weight just lifted off his shoulders. "BDSM, it's not my thing."

I blink a couple times. "Wait, what? Is this some kind of mind fuck? What are you trying to say, Covington?"

He sighs. "I've tried it. Tried a lot of things."

The way his eyes sear into me when he says *that*—like he's picturing himself doing unspeakably dirty things to me—I'd be a liar if I said my chest didn't bloom with heat. I pray I'm not blushing. God, why is he so hot when he stares like that?

"It did nothing for me. No form of carnal or emotional gratification, in either role."

I shake my head slightly to pull myself from this sexual daze he just put me in with nothing but a stare. For some reason I really can't picture him being a submissive, at all. This whole revelation is just—perplexing as all hell. It makes no sense. "Why come here then? Why let the press run these crazy stories on you and spread all kinds of rumors? I know it affects your bottom line, limits some of your client base with the pearl clutchers."

Covington nods out to the room. "For them."

"Them?" I glance around at the people in the room.

"Anyone who lives this lifestyle. I have several acquaintances, here and in Manhattan, and elsewhere, who practice these things with their spouses, partners, completely safe and with mutual consent—and they live in fear of it being revealed. I'm trying to do my part to normalize it. Whatever I can do, anyway."

"Shift the Overton window?"

"Exactly." He nods as he says it. "Not to mention, I like to come here because it's fascinating to me. The power dynamics. The people. They're interesting. Remember when I said I don't like boring? *This* is not boring. And if I can help make it seem more normal and mainstream in society, then it makes their lives better. They don't have to hide in shame at what gets them off and makes them happy."

I take a second to process everything he just said. "Aren't you worried someone might find out you don't actually practice the lifestyle?"

There he goes, staring at me again. "Nobody will know unless you tell them. I participate in the clubs I frequent on occasion, so it doesn't raise any alarms with anyone here, make them feel uncomfortable, like I'm some kind of outsider. Plus, I like coming here. The people are the best. This is the only place I know that doesn't judge me as some billionaire corporate raider. Hence, the problem of whether or not I could trust you."

"Guess we'll find out, won't we? You didn't really give me a choice." I don't know if I should be angry or impressed that he dropped that on me.

"Yes, we will." His lips curl up a little at the corners, like our situation is what he derives gratification from; the unknown.

Am I the only person he's ever told this?

"So, what do you think? Interested in trying something out?" He gestures over to one of the tables.

Was that a joke? I'm pretty sure it's a joke.

Regardless, the same tingling rips through my veins again, every time he brings up something remotely sexual. It's like he's trying to prime me, flirting, teasing. To say I'm not aroused would be untrue. Fact is, I haven't had sex in a long time, and I'm pretty sure Covington would be up to the task.

Get your life together, Meadow. He's everything you hate. Despite this rather humane side of him.

"It's not my thing." I swallow a little. "But I agree with you, it is interesting. The power dynamic intrigues me too. It's nice to see females in control once in a while." I nod over at the woman spanking the man. "You guys kind of have it coming."

He looks at me in a way I can only describe as a look that says he'd like to spank me.

I shake my head, trying to ignore the endorphins coursing through my blood. "So what are you into then? If not this?"

What the fuck? Why did you just ask that?

Covington's tongue darts out just slightly and wets his lower lip before he starts to speak. I want to say it does nothing for me, but it does. I should *not* be having this conversation, let alone leading it. It's not my purpose for being here, but I can't help how curious I am.

"Honestly, I'm not really sure."

I lean back. It's about the most unsexy answer possible.

"I have an active sex life. I'm always safe. Get a physical release. I've never been drawn to a woman on an emotional level before. To be completely truthful, sometimes I wonder if I'm a sociopath because I rarely feel anything. I barely relate to anyone, and since I was a child, I've always felt like an alien, like I don't belong here. Like some kind of freak experiment being observed from afar. I rarely relate to people or their motivations and actions."

"Bullshit."

He blinks. "Excuse me?"

"You heard me. You're not a sociopath."

"What makes you so sure?"

"The FBI thing. The modesty about it. The reason you're here. Those are emotional courses of action. It's related to having feelings, whether you admit it to yourself or not. You're wired differently—that's for damn sure—but you're not a sociopath. You long to do the right thing and justify the shit things you do, just like anyone else on the planet. There's no doubt you're anything but normal on the intelligence curve, but you're more *normal* than you think, on a human distribution."

Wells stares back at me for a long second. "I like you, Meadow."

He's getting to me. He's so getting to me, and I don't know if I can put the brakes on this thing, because let's face it, I want him. I'm not going to kid myself into thinking there will be a long, happy relationship and we'll fall in love and have kids. But I'm attracted to him. Not in a million years did I envision this night going the way it is, but I don't want to be anywhere else in the world right now.

My brain fights itself, trying to reconcile how he does what he does every day, yet seems to have a heart for people. Some kind of moral code guiding his principles.

"I will concede on the real estate project. Not because I want something from you, but because I know you care about it. You came here. You listened to me with an open mind. That's all I wanted. I'll get with you to work out a deal, and have my lawyers begin on the paperwork." He stands up.

What the fuck? I'm so excited I could jump up and down, but I have to get a grip on myself. It'd be inappropriate on so many levels.

As best as I can, despite my body trembling with elation, I get up and follow him through the place and out the same way we came in.

When we get to the car, I stop Covington and look up at him. The moonlight holds his features in sharp relief, and I could kiss him. I really could.

Finally, I say, "Wells?"

"Yes?"

"I like you, too."

"I'm glad."

Our eyes lock as he says it. I don't even know what I'm doing at this point. All I know is I want to live in this moment a little longer, and surprisingly, I want to know even more about him. I want to see where this goes. It feels wrong, like I'm clinging to him because he just did something nice for me, but that's not it at all. The feelings were there before the revelation.

"I should probably get you home. It's getting late."

I shake my head at him. "It's still early. Take me to your place. I want to see it."

What the fuck did you just say, Meadow?

WELLS COVINGTON

I KNOW before we've driven two blocks that I'm not getting laid tonight. There's no way it's happening, and to be honest, that's fine by me. She said what she said in the moment, and she has forty-five minutes to talk herself out of it on the drive. Once she sees where I live, those old reservations will boil to the surface, and it's not going to be pretty.

Sometimes I hate being able to anticipate the future in advance.

My pressing concern is how she disarmed me tonight. Taking her to the dungeon wasn't in the original plan, nor was revealing one of my deepest secrets. Jesus fucking Christ, I barely even know this woman. I thought we'd go to Al's, have a nice, fun meal, learn about each other, like a normal first date. I'd give up the real estate deal, and we'd make plans for a second date, if things went as planned.

The real estate deal.

Fuck, I'm almost happy that's off my plate. It's a loser now, and I hate to lose. She wants it. That's a win-win situation, everyone gets what they want in the end.

No, the alarming thing is how much information I just gave her. The FBI sting, the BDSM revelation, those things, as altruistic as they are, could hurt me. It could hurt my business, bad.

The media would spin the fuck out of it. I've made plenty of enemies there.

I glance over and think *she's worth it* to myself, but I'm still unsure. I really *hope* she's worth it. I've just taken on more risk in two hours than I've ever stomached in my entire life. Yeah, she's beautiful, and fucking smart. I've never had someone who seems to get me, and I'm making irrational decisions because of it. Fucking reckless. I've never felt a pull like this before, and about now I'd walk right off the edge of a cliff chasing after it, and not even worry about hitting the goddamn ground.

"How far away is it?" Meadow grins.

Glad one of us is still happy and thinks they're getting fucked tonight.

"Forty-five minutes. Right off the lake. We could go some-where else in—"

"I want to see your place." She pauses and takes a deep breath. "This isn't something I usually do. I want to know you, not be taken to some hotel room."

I look straight ahead at the road. "Fair enough." She's going to get to know me, all right.

While she sits in the seat, eagerly anticipating what's to come, my brain goes into overdrive, trying to figure out exactly how the night took this course of action and why.

It doesn't take long to analyze.

I know myself.

I agreed to take her to my house, knowing the outcome, because it will create conflict. Conflict and competition get me off, spike my dopamine levels. They're what drive me. Some-times, when I go up against someone, be it a company or an indi-vidual, I create an entire narrative in my head. Stories that may or may not even be true, but then I use it for fuel to make sure I destroy them and their business at all costs, just to get the outcome I want.

It's the same principle here. Conflict makes life interesting. It will make this situation with Meadow interesting. I'll sabotage the whole damn thing, just to see if I can win her back over.

Fuck me. I need to go see my shrink, bad. I can't believe I'm doing this with her. I just put billions of dollars, other people's livelihoods, my relationships with my friends and colleagues, at risk. For what? For one night of impressing Meadow Carlson?

The entire drive out to my place, it's quiet. Too quiet.

Meadow is thinking, so it's understandable. I know she's playing out the new information she received from me a thousand different ways. Permutations, variables, she'll run through every scenario like a human supercomputer.

I wince when we pull down the private drive that leads to my gate. I already know what's going to happen.

"Open gate." I give the command to the Tesla, hoping the gate opens before we get there.

It doesn't. I have to stop and wait.

I can't even look at Meadow to gauge her reaction to it.

It's gaudy as hell, with a giant golden "WC" right in the middle. I did it on purpose, just to fuck with people. Don't get me wrong, I love my house. It's my sanctuary. But it's over the top like no other. I did the same thing I do to other hedge funds when I moved into town; established dominance. Solely so a bunch of rich pricks didn't think they could push me around. I built bigger and better.

Maybe it was foolish, in hindsight. I don't need anything remotely close to this size, but it's an investment. I'm a human being, and making mistakes is what we do. It's what you learn from them that gives you an edge.

The gate hasn't fully opened when I turn in.

I glance over, knowing I shouldn't, and watch her eyes widen as we pass through. Then, slowly, a glare forms on her face.

I'm so ridiculous I actually welcome the argument that will take place when we reach the house. I look forward to it. As much as I bared my soul to this woman earlier tonight, I like seeing her fiery. I want to push her buttons, get her riled up.

I snake around the golf course, past the helipad, and I damn near laugh, because I can feel the powder keg brewing next to me. Everything my house represents is everything she hates.

I think she made me take her here on purpose too. I think

secretly, she wanted this to happen. She wants me as bad as I want her. That advantage shifted to me earlier. She's going to fight it tooth and nail, and I'm going to love every goddamn second of it. I don't buy her *not going to a hotel, I never do this kind of thing* spiel. If all she wanted to do was fuck, she'd have been perfectly fine with that arrangement. Truth be told, I don't want to just fuck her, as fun as it might be.

By the time I park, she's already out of the car and has her phone out.

She hasn't made a call yet, but she will.

The evening is done in her mind.

Finally, she looks up at me. "Nice place."

I nod and smirk. "I like it. Ready to go see my room?"

Fuck, the fire in her eyes. Her standing in front of my gigantic mansion, looking like she wants to burn the place to the ground, it couldn't be more perfect. Yeah, she knew exactly what she was doing, asking me to bring her here.

Her fingers begin to tremble. I start toward her, loving how her cheeks redden with every step I take.

"I thought you were different somehow." She shakes her head. "Fuck, I don't know why. That was a hell of a presentation back there, during our meeting."

"Thought it was a date?"

Her jaw clenches. "It was *not* a date."

"Pretend all you want, Meadow. You enjoyed yourself."

"Briefly." She nods, but with purpose. "Briefly. Until I had time to think."

"Maybe you should think about this." Before she can respond, I yank her into me and plant my lips right on hers.

She practically melts in my arms, both of our hands roaming. I lick and explore her mouth, and she reciprocates. Goddamn, she's perfect.

I've kissed many women, but none like this. There's some-thing here, something not even my brain can quantify. A magnetic attraction, binding us together, and simultaneously trying to rip us back apart, searching for some kind of balance.

In the middle of the kiss, Meadow pulls away. "What am I

doing?" She glares up at me. "What the hell are you doing to me?" Her eyes dart around, like she can't believe she just said that out loud.

I can so relate to her right now, because I don't know what the fuck I'm doing either. But I want to keep doing it.

She then swipes angrily on her phone. "I'll call an Uber. This was a mistake."

I take a step toward her, and she has to take two in retreat to match my stride. "Mistake or not, you felt that kiss. Right down into the tips of your fingers and toes."

She backs away a few more steps, putting even more distance between us, sneering at my house, punching buttons on her phone.

Now, it's time to really piss her off. "Don't be ridiculous. I'll have my driver take you home, save you some money."

Her entire body stiffens. "I don't give a shit about saving money. I'm not having your personal driver parade me around town in one of your cars. What's wrong with you?" She glares right at me.

All I can think is how I want to kiss her again. As much fun as it'd be to take her up to my room and fuck her so hard she can't walk straight tomorrow, I'm already looking forward to the chase. Pissing her off then going after her. Winning her over. Not going to lie, it stings a little, the way she seems to abhor my lifestyle, but I fucking love how frustrated she is.

I shrug. "Just being practical."

"Practical?" She fakes a laugh, then turns around and starts walking down the driveway. "Nothing about you is fucking practical."

I snicker to myself.

She's not wrong.

"Let's do this again sometime. Maybe next week."

All I see is a middle finger fly up over her shoulder, and she never turns back.

Fuck, I've got it bad for this woman. Real bad.

MEADOW CARLSON

I can't believe I almost fell for Wells Covington's bullshit. That's what happens when you do things on a whim, buy into someone's story. The entire ride to his house, I thought through everything. What's his angle? Men like him don't just write off investments. I know them intimately. Some of them literally kill people to make money, only they do it mostly legally. I've seen men like him buy pharma companies and jack up the cost of life-saving medications, own factories where the conditions are so bad it causes depression and suicides. It's legal fucking murder.

He's playing some kind of game with the Parker project. Something is off. Something that will make me look like an idiot in the end.

Don't even get me started on his house, from the giant gold initials on the gate, to a fucking golf course for one. The man is everything I stand against. The exact opposite of anything I'd look for in a potential life partner.

The worst part is, no amount of rational feeling changes the fact I'm more aroused than I've ever been in my life. The way he kissed me, then described it perfectly. I wanted to punch him in his smug face. Because yes, I did feel it all the way down to my damn fingers and toes, and I hate him even more for knowing he had that effect on me.

Ugh!

Men.

I need to regroup. I need to focus and have a plan. Flying blind is not how I live my life.

My phone rings while I wait for the Uber. It's my mom. Maybe she can bring me out of this funk I'm in. I haven't heard her voice in what seems like forever.

We used to be close, but we've drifted apart the last few years, with how busy I am. I still check in on occasion, go out for lunch, hang out on the weekends. I love her to death, it's just hard for me to be close to anyone. I chalk it up to my personality. I don't feel deep connections to people and I think it all comes from, well—I don't even want to talk about *him*.

"Hello?"

"Meadow?"

My blood goes cold the second I hear the voice, and I can't believe I was just thinking about this asshole and then he calls from my mother's phone.

It's my father. How the hell is he calling me from her number?

Despite the fact I hate him with every fiber of my being, I'm actually kind of glad, because now I can take all this frustration out on him and not feel an ounce of regret, because he deserves it.

"One of the smartest men the world has ever known, yet you fail to realize I don't want to fucking talk to you, ever. Haven't you gotten that message yet? Processed the data? I ignore every one of your calls, smile as I hit that little red button on my phone. Nothing makes me happier. How the hell did you mask this to look like mom was calling me?"

"Meadow, it's important. I didn't mask the call. This is your mother's phone."

I laugh. It's not a real laugh though. It's the kind when you hear something so utterly absurd it's all you can do.

"What game are you playing?"

"I'm out on temporary parole."

I scoff. "No. There's no fucking way." I shake my head as I say it. "What is this? And even if that's true, why the fuck are you at Mom's? She wouldn't allow it." I know that's not true, but I'm so goddamn furious I just want to hurt him any way I can. He deserves it.

"They let me out for spousal support. To take care of my wife."

"Take care of your wife?" I bite the inside of my cheek hard enough to taste copper because I could murder this man. "She doesn't need you. She has me. There's no justice in this world for white-collar crime, is there? Bribed your way into a sweet deal, didn't you? Fucking unbelievable."

"It really is for your mom. She's sick."

"Bullshit." I shake my head again. How much worse could this night get? First Wells, now this asshole. "Why didn't the doctors call me? Why didn't *she* call me? You make no sense."

"Your mother wanted you to hear it from me. I've been trying to get hold of you for a few days, but you wouldn't accept the calls. I just got here."

"You're at Mom's house?"

"Yes, I can't go anywhere else. I have a, umm, monitor."

"Wonderful." I sigh the most sarcastic sigh of all time. "I'll be there in thirty minutes. Don't fucking touch her or even look at her." I hang up before he can say anything else.

Suddenly, Wells Covington and that situation is the furthest thing from my mind.

I pace back and forth on the side of the road, just waiting for the Uber driver, worried, upset, angry. I don't know if I've ever been this pissed off in my life. Part of me wants to run back to the mansion and see if I can take him up on his offer with his driver.

As much as I want to do that, should do that, I just can't, and I know the reason I can't show weakness is the stupid fuck that just called my phone. He made me this way, and he's about to hear about it.

* * *

77

I BLOW through the front door of my mom's house, straight past my dad, not even bothering to look at him. I say, "Stay the fuck out of here and away from me," as I walk into my mom's room.

She's in bed but doesn't look much different from how she normally does.

"Mom." I don't mean to, but I sprint to the bed and take her by the hand. "Is everything okay with you?" I look her up and down. "You look okay." As I say it, I feel the rage burning in my chest, and my eyes narrow on her. I grit my teeth. "Why the hell is *he* here?"

"I look better than I am. Sit down, Meadow." She pats the bed like I'm still a six-year-old child.

I want to yell, scream, punch something, but I don't. Instead, I take a seat next to her. "What are you talking about? You were fine, what? A month ago, when I saw you? We went to the Chinese place around the corner."

"Meadow?"

"What?"

"It's been three months since we went to lunch."

The air sucks out of my lungs, and I shake my head. "What?" I do my best to play it off. "No, that can't—"

"It's true. And I'm not trying to make you feel guilty. I know you're busy." Her hand reaches out and she smothers my forearm with it.

Has it been that long since I saw her? Fuck, I'm the worst daughter ever.

I think for a minute. I know what she just said is true, I just lie to myself about it. I know I get laser-focused on singular purposes, and time slips by around me, I just didn't think it could possibly be that long. My eyes dart down to the ground, and I can't even look at her.

Her hand reaches up from my forearm and she puts it on my cheek. "It's okay. It's who you are, and I love who you are. Do you understand me?"

I nod against her hand. "What's wrong? He said you're sick."

Mom nods a little and looks like she's more worried about

how I'll react, than how she actually feels. She's always been that way. She might be the strongest person I've ever known, always protecting everyone else instead of herself.

Finally, she says, "Glioblastoma. Stage four."

"Brain cancer?" My heart squeezes so damn hard I think I might have a heart attack. My brain goes into overdrive, doing the math on everything I know about glioblastoma, like I can see the Wikipedia page in my mind. It's the most aggressive type of brain tumor. My mental image scrolls to the prognosis section. She probably has twelve months, maybe a little more, but possibly less. A tear streams down my cheek. "Wh-why didn't you tell me? I could've gone to the doctor. I could've stepped away from work." I do my best to hold back, be strong in front of her. She once told me the only thing that could hurt her was seeing me in pain.

"I didn't know it was going to be this. I was just having migraines. Thought I had a sinus infection that got out of control, but it didn't get any better."

I'm angry at the world for doing this to my mom. I definitely don't want to be angry at her, for having him call me like that, especially when she's going through this, but what the hell? I shouldn't ask the next question. I think part of me already knows the answer, but I do it anyway. "Why did you tell *him* first?" I already regret it. How fucking selfish can I be right now? I can't believe I had the balls to hate Covington over his house, when I'm behaving like this, having the thoughts I'm having. I just don't know how she can still love the man out there in the hallway the way she does.

"Because I thought—" She pauses, as if collecting her thoughts to make sure she explains appropriately. "I thought I might get one positive out of this situation. If I can get you and your father to reconcile, then it would make the best out of a bad situation."

"A bad situation? Mom, you're dying." I try to bite my tongue, but I've never been able to hold back. Not about something like this. "We can talk about this more, after we come up with a plan. We'll do every single thing that's right for you, and I will be by your side no matter what, doing whatever you need. But I'm telling you right now, I will *never* forgive him for what he did to us. I just won't. Now, let's put that to the side and just focus on you for a bit." I crawl up in bed, so I'm sitting next to her, and I take her hand.

For the next fifteen minutes, we just cry together. I don't think the news had really sunk in until I was up in the bed with her. She had to feel like she was living in a dream world, just walking in a daze, and the whole time she was struggling this week I was out and about, doing whatever I usually do, worried about Wells Covington and other insignificant shit.

I'm so self-centered. I'm everything I hate right now.

When we're done, Mom looks at me for a moment, then surprisingly, she smiles.

"What?"

"Thank you. I needed that. To do that, feel sorry for myself for a little while."

"You deserve it. If anyone does, you do." I wipe my eyes and try to smile for her. "This still doesn't feel real to me. I don't get it. You're the healthiest person I know."

"Things happen, sweetie."

I try not to lose it again when I look her in the eye. I want to hold it together for her, but every regret in my life bubbles up to the surface. All the wasted time, all this activism, trying to change the world with my impact fund. I could've spent that time with Mom. I have a ton of money, more than I could ever need, and I give most of it away every month. We could've gone on trips, had lunches, spent time together. Yeah, it'd be awkward for me, doing those things. I'm not that great at them. But that's what daughters are supposed to do. Those were my obligations and I blew it. I always thought I'd have time to settle down, maybe even meet someone, have a family. Dropping grandkids off at her house for weekends, her being over for family dinners. I don't know. We'll never have any of that now.

I always saw "normal" being right off on the horizon some-where, after I accomplished things I wanted to accomplish, and then I'd do all that. It's all gone now.

"Sweetie?"

"Yeah?"

"I have a request. It might make you a little upset."

I shake my head, intent on doing whatever she asks without protesting. "Whatever you want. I'll do it." I say the words without even thinking it through.

"I want to spend some time with your father."

I frown, remembering he's still in the damn house.

"You don't have to be in here for it. But I don't want you to leave yet. Do you mind?"

I look at her for a long time, then finally nod a little. "I'll do my best to be civil. For *you*. Only for you. But I'm done with him, Mom. I'm sorry. That's just the way it is. He did this, not me."

She looks away, then back at me. "He still loves you, just the same as he did. You were two peas in a pod." She laughs a little, as if she's recalling happier times.

I've blocked all those memories, stuffed them somewhere deep and dark where I won't want to ever retrieve them again.

"*Were* is the keyword there, Mom. *Were* two peas in a pod."

She pats my hand, still managing to smile after everything she's been through. "Okay. Well, please don't go anywhere yet. I like having you both in the house again, even if it's in different rooms, under these circumstances."

Fuck me, the guilt. It's bad. "I won't go anywhere. I promise. Right outside in the living room."

"Okay."

I get up and walk out of the room. Dad's sitting on a bench in the hallway with his head down, holding it in his hands.

I glare. "She wants you." I walk right past him and don't even look in his direction.

Once I'm in the living room, I plop down on the couch, and I think I might hyperventilate. It feels like the walls are closing in on me and I can't breathe. What the fuck? How did my life take this turn? Everything, all at once. It started with Covington at his place, and then escalated like a damn rocket into the stratosphere.

I turn on the TV, something I never do, just for a distraction. Just to pull me out of the moment for just a second and give me a chance to breathe.

I try not to yell, but I cover my mouth and scream, "Fuck!"

* * *

"MEADOW. MEADOW."

Someone pokes me in the arm, saying my name.

My eyes flutter open, and I smile for a second as I wake up, then my whole body constricts at once as I recognize the face in front of me.

A glare slowly forms. "The fuck do you want?"

My father smirks back at me. "Such civilized language."

I spring up from the couch, right in his face. "I'll show you civilized, asshole."

He holds up a hand. "Calm down, please. I'd like to think we've evolved past this primitive behavior."

I take a few steps away from him then turn around, putting distance between us. "Is Mom done with you in there? She send you to come get me?"

For a moment we both glare back and forth at each other. It's so hard, seeing him. We're so alike, and so painstakingly different at the same time. He's my biggest fear in life. That I'll end up like him, go down that path.

My childhood was spent watching him transform from hero to villain.

I shake my head at him. "What promises did you make to get out?"

"That's not your concern, Meadow. My wife, your mother, is the concern here. So, we're going to have to work out our differences. We owe it to her."

I point a finger at him. "I don't owe you shit. And I'll take care of Mom. You can go on back to your little cell, where you belong."

"That's not going to happen, and it's not up to you."

I stand there, practically shaking, because I know he's right. I have no control over this and it's going to consume me from the inside out. I hate myself for being this way. I hate being like him, needing to control every single variable and account for every single action. It's like nails on a chalkboard, a hammer banging a wall over and over, everything racing through my head, nonstop.

I walk toward Mom's room but stop next to him on my way. "I'm done with this conversation. I will do each and every thing Mom requires and be there for her. But there is nothing left between us, and that's *your* fault. Not mine." I shoulder past him and head to the hallway.

"You've never made a mistake before, Meadow?"

I turn around, and it looks like I just crushed him, like he finally realized how ridiculous he's behaving. I shake my head, not falling for his pity tactics. "Not the kind you did. Not the kind you haven't owned up to or apologized for. I didn't leave my family behind to clean up my mess."

"I've admitted I made a mistake. I thought I was doing the right thing, creating a legacy for the family name." He scoffs. "Not that our name will carry on, anyway."

"Fuck you and the family name."

"So pure. Always out to save the world, aren't you? I'm going to be here, whether you like it or not. So, make peace and get on board with that. I won't abandon your mother again."

I sneer at him and turn around and head to Mom's room.

The worst part is, I know he means every word of what he said. I know he loves my mom, more than just about anything. I know he'll help take good care of her, but I want nothing to do with him.

Nothing.

It'll be a miracle if I don't kill him.

WELLS COVINGTON

I sit in the meeting with Penn Hargrove at The Hunter Group, but I can't stop thinking about Meadow. In fact, she's really the reason I'm here. She's been dodging my calls for days, and I haven't had time to track her down in person.

For someone who wants my real estate development for whatever reason, she sure doesn't act too interested. I thought it meant something to her, but apparently not.

Can't believe she wrote me off like that, summed me up all just by looking at my house, after the things I told her, the way I exposed myself to her. Oh well, chasing her down will be the best part. That's the real fun.

The hunt.

"I think I'm a little confused on why you wanted to meet with me, Mr. Covington. What exactly are we doing?"

I lean back in my chair and play dumb. "I want to know about impact funds."

He cocks his head like *you're paying me a grand an hour to tell you something you should already know more about than me?*

"I mean, I'm just a lawyer. I work with impact funds. It's really no different than a hedge fund, they just look to make a positive change with their investments, be it social, environmental, or some other altruistic objective. I'm not active in the management of any. What's your goal here?"

"Thinking about adding one to my firm, in-house, actively managed by me. At a high level of course. Curious to any additional administrative overheads I may not be including in my calculations. Are there any additional regulations I'm not aware of?"

"The main problem is how you market the investments. It's appropriate to use correct terminology to avoid any bad faith arguments of greenwashing dollars. I would advise to keep everything independent of your other operations, and to have internal processes in place because determining which investments provide positive social change and the impact you want can get murky during selection. If you want contacts, I can put you in touch with people. The best in the business, really."

I was already aware of a lot of this, so it's not groundbreaking news. I'm not sure what I thought I'd get out of this meeting. All I can think about is Meadow and that kiss, and how I know she runs her own impact fund. Maybe I just felt I'd be more connected to her, discussing these things with my legal representation.

"You could handle the legal work and entity structuring, though? If I were to organize a fund like this?"

Penn's eyes light up, like he just saw dollar signs. "Absolutely. I can handle any of those needs."

"You looking for a new job?" I grin at him.

"Like I said, I'd be better off here. I'm not an investment guy. It wouldn't be worth the hassle to hire me for in-house legal work, not for something this size. It won't even be full-time work for one employee, and your options will be limited."

"You mean a limited pool of investments? Impossible to scale."

"Exactly. There are a much smaller, finite amount of investments that can change the world, depending on the criteria you decide on. Then, you're not only competing with other impact funds, but every other hedge fund in existence, like your own, who might not care if it's good or bad for the world, but they want the return. It's a tough egg to crack."

I bet Meadow thrives under that kind of pressure. No wonder she's so formidable, all while trying to keep it hush hush. It makes me want her even more.

I stand up and shake his hand. "Thanks, Penn. I appreciate this."

"Any time. Just holler at me if you decide to make a go of it."

"Will do."

I walk out of the conference room and catch Dominic Romano sneaking away from Mary's desk. We lock eyes, and he motions with his head over to the hallway.

Once we're out of earshot, I say, "Anything new?"

He shakes his head. "Mostly the same stuff I already gave you. She runs the media outlets we discussed, has an impact fund that she keeps very quiet. Didn't really find anything on her prior to 2010, not that it matters. She'd have been a teenager."

"So you've got jack shit?"

"Pretty much."

"Can't believe this cost me a night on my boat."

"A weekend, bitch. And it's because I got everything for you so fast already. The information trail dried up."

"Fine, fuckface." I laugh. "Enjoy the weekend with Mary. I think I'm satisfied with the transaction and we can conclude it. Until I need something again."

"Until you need something again? I swear, you hedge fund assholes are worse than the actual mafia."

I raise an eyebrow.

"Don't ask." He laughs, then says, "And I don't owe you anything now. But I'm always willing to hear proposals for my services."

"Yeah, I bet you are." This time it's me who laughs as I walk away.

I have a lot to think about, planning my next move.

* * *

BACK AT THE OFFICE, and I still can't concentrate. It's that fucking kiss. It's etched into my memory. I have to taste her again. I just need to be near her, feel her against me. An emptiness consumes me, like I'm hollow now when she's not around, even if she's pissed at me.

I miss that connection.

A PM walks into my office with a junior analyst. They look like they've been fighting with each other.

"Someone better be bringing me a good idea, or they're getting fired. Which one of you will it be?"

They both freeze and stare at each other like I just put the fear of God into them. Where else in this city can these guys make a couple million bucks a year for sitting in front of a computer? They perform or they're gone. I have a list of smart people who want a job here. It's more than a mile long.

If I thought my social skills were lacking, these mathletes are even worse.

They stand there, both stammering and stuttering.

I stand up. "Jesus. Nobody is getting fired."

They both relax.

"Yet. Now what's the issue?"

The analyst finally speaks. "We've had our eye on this Chinese manufacture play."

Fuck my ass. There's nothing easy about investing in China. There are a million bad optics, plus an authoritarian state in charge that likes to interfere with business. It's definitely an area of growth though. Lots of opportunities there.

"And you want to hold it long?"

He nods.

"Tell me about it." Maybe this is just what I need to take my mind off a certain someone, a problem to solve.

He glances around. "Speak freely? Here?"

What the hell did he just bring into my office? I arch an eyebrow. "You worried about compliance? Do you have research to back this position?"

He nods. "I can make the research work. It's a manufacturer. I also have a source—"

I hold up a finger. "Stop right there. Don't say another word about that. Think clearly before answering any of my questions."

He nods, hastily.

"What are the concerns?"

"That the information might not be reliable, and that we *may* have it prematurely."

"For fuck's sake, make some sense. Forget the information you have from your source. The fundamentals. What's the problem with the business?"

"They should experience a boom in growth over the next few weeks, even before a certain announcement is made. We won't have any way to monitor that, to show it's why we made the investment. And the, umm, s-word I'm not supposed to talk about, might be full of shit."

I lean back in my chair. "What kind of signs would fore-shadow the growth before an announcement like this. What would that look like?"

The PM has stayed stone quiet, but says, "It's a bad idea. I tried to tell him. It's risky and borderline—"

I hold up a finger. "Enough. I want to hear. Maybe we can solve this problem without exposing ourselves."

The PM paces back and forth, glaring at the analyst like he can't believe he got him into this shit.

"Usual signs before expansion, umm, hiring more workers, maybe some renovations to the factory building."

I stand up and walk over to my window, staring out at the Chicago skyline. Solving problems is what got me into this busi-ness, and it's the only thing I enjoy. Right now, the only thing that makes me feel alive even close to the way Meadow does, is this. "How is their relationship with the government?"

"Favorable, but that's hearsay and can change at any moment. Can't be guaranteed."

"Sure." I nod. "It's high risk and they like to manipulate numbers over there. Less regulation. What's the market cap on this company?"

"Projected five billion in the Chinese manufacturing sector, lots of room for growth."

Then, the plan all comes together at once.

I point at the portfolio manager. "BM Satellite."

"What?" He looks at me like I'm nuts.

"We have a fifty-five percent stake in the private satellite company."

He looks around nervously, then says, "Okay? I'm not seeing—"

Lipsy walks in just as I start to say something. "What's up, boss?"

"Perfect timing." I point at him. "Someone who will get it. Chinese manufacture play, big news coming in next few weeks, should be growth activity before a large announcement we're not supposed to know about, BM Satellites. Take it from there." I wave the other two off with a flippant hand.

Lipsy blinks for a second, then opens his eyes and a Cheshire smile forms on his face. "Fucking genius." He turns to the other two. "Get your goddamn heads out of your asses and get the satellites pointed at the motherfucking factory so we can monitor the parking lot for an increase in truck activity, cars in the parking lot, and renovations to the building." He puts an arm around both their necks and leads them out of the office. "We're about to be some fucking voyeurs looking up Chinese skirts, then we'll bukkake profits all over the firm's bank account. Talk to me about capital acquisition strategy."

I try not to laugh. Fucking Lipsy. I've never met anyone like him.

My phone rings and I answer.

"Covington."

"When you coming back to Manhattan and leaving that Podunk Midwest shithole?"

Bennett Cooper. I don't mind him as much as my lawyer friends do, but he's too entrenched in sophistication and the old way of doing things. Never been my style, even if I leverage him to keep the Collins brothers motivated to keep my business.

"Cooper. When are you going to get with the twenty-first century? You're analog in a digital age." Most people would get pissed if I said that to them. I don't know if Cooper ever gets angry, he just gets even.

"If you say so. We'll see."

"Look, you know the deal. I have personal ties to the Collins brothers, and it's not like your legal representation offers me any advantages. Plus, they're in town. I can go get in their face if they fuck up."

"True. Just think about it. You're always welcome back here at the firm."

"We've been down this road. I'm worth more than just my business. Remember all those people who would flock back with me? That's worth more than an occasional phone call and ridiculous posturing."

He pauses for a moment. "Things are in play. I'd hate for you to be on the wrong side of it."

Interesting.

I'm sure he's up to something. I don't really have time to deal with petty law firm beefs, but I've told the Collins brothers a million times to keep their heads on a swivel, and to worry about this man. If they don't listen, it's their own fault.

Regardless, I need to make a few things clear to this pompous asshole. "I hope it's nothing that would affect my bottom line. That might upset me more than a little."

He laughs like he doesn't have a care in the world. "Of course not."

"Well then, you know the deal. Offer me better services at a lower rate, and we can set a meeting. If not, I have shit to do."

"Just giving a heads up. I know the Collins brothers are your friends, but they stole from me. You know I can't allow that."

"First, I'm not your property, and they beat you at capitalism. That's not theft. Personally, I don't give a fuck. I've made myself clear. Don't give a shit what goes on between your firms unless it affects my bottom line. If you cost me money, I will fuck you up. I don't give a shit what name is on your building, or how old it is. I'll reduce it to ash. That's not a threat, it's a promise." I hang up the phone.

Fucking asshole.

I do my best to clear my thoughts.

Now, let me think of how I can piss Meadow off even more. I need to force her to come talk to me.

As a plan begins to form, Lipsy walks in with his usual ornery grin.

"The Chinese play should put our fund at ten billion by third quarter. I've got a dick harder than DC Henry Cavill."

I try not to laugh, but it's impossible. "*Man of Steel*, nice."

"Indeed." He walks to the window and says, "Fuck, almost forgot why I came in here. The Parker project high rise. What do you want to do with it? Someone said we were scrapping. Need to make arrangements."

Just then, it comes to me. "You know what—" I pause and rub my chin. "Stall it for a few days to create an air of uncertainty."

He whips around. "You're thinking about keeping it on the books? It's a fucking money pit now, bringing down numbers. Let's dump it. You know I like my book virgin fresh, without blemishes."

The cost is immaterial to me, even though it might fuck up a couple portfolios downstairs. Those are bonus-based for the employees. They won't be happy. I'll make it up to them, even though they won't like it. "Do it how I said. I have reasons. Ensure people the metrics won't affect their comp."

"Done." He walks off down to the bullpen.

This will definitely piss Meadow off.

As far as I'm concerned, she deserves the stress after her little outburst at my mansion. I'll still give her what she wants, she's just going to have to work a little harder for it. Most importantly, she's going to have to come see me.

I lean back and kick my feet up on my desk.

Now, it's just a waiting game until I get to see those honey-brown eyes again.

MEADOW CARLSON

I STORM into Wells Covington's hedge fund offices on a mission.

This goddamn son of a bitch. I've about had it. I don't have time to be dealing with this distraction, no matter how good he looks in a suit. He made a verbal agreement, a legally binding contract, and he's going to honor it, or I'll rip his fucking head off and go bowling with it.

An incredibly attractive brunette in a designer dress stands up at a receptionist desk.

"Where is he?" I borderline growl the words at her before I can stop myself.

"Ma'am I'm going to call security if—"

"Let her up." Covington looks down from over a balcony, smirking right at me like he's been waiting for this.

My face goes red when I look up at him, leaned over a railing like he's lording over a bunch of serfs from on high. The visual in front of me only heats my blood more. It's the perfect representation of this country. A rich, oligarch, ruling elite sitting up on another level, away from all the working-class people, toiling away to create more wealth and power for himself.

The woman in front of me looks pissed but motions to the stairs with her head.

I fly past her to the steps. Why does he have such a beautiful woman as his receptionist? Does he have something going on with her?

Oh my God, who are you right now?

I know these problems are all compounding right now, and I need to take a step back, assess, come up with a game plan. But between my mom and this, I'm about to lose it. Every hedge fund I've been to has a model receptionist, because that's who rich white men love to be greeted by when they come to do business. I know this, but still. Everything feels like some conspiracy with Wells Covington, and I can't tell if it's rooted in reality, or just my own bias at play. It eats at me every time I'm around him, because reality and the things he says are so contradictory from everything I've experienced in life.

I get to the top of the stairs, ready to lay into Covington, and he walks off, toward a conference room, turning his back on me. I huff out a sigh and chase after him, trying not to run because he has such freakishly long strides.

Goddamn it. It's like he's trying to piss me off on purpose.

The door barely shuts behind me before I'm up in his face. "What the fuck?"

"Just breathe." He holds a hand up and mocks me with a condescending tone.

I know he doesn't know about my mom or any of my personal issues, but I can't help myself. "Did you just tell me to calm down?"

He retreats and takes a tiny step back, but it looks like he wants to smile as he does it. "I didn't say *those* words, I merely suggested you—"

"Perform a bodily function that's involuntary, you smarmy prick."

"Smarmy prick?" He feigns innocence, then smiles. "Well, that's a new one to add to the list."

I point a finger at him. "Don't do that. Give me my building. We had a deal."

He walks off and pours himself a glass of water from a little pitcher on a table near the wall. "I will. It's in flux."

"In flux?"

He shrugs. "Limbo. Purgatory. You know how this goes. Legal matters. I don't have to explain the intricacies of real estate transactions to you. They can be very tedious." He stops, like a thought just occurred to him. "Actually, you used these same tactics to cost me money on the project you're about to take ownership of, did you not?"

"You son of a bitch." I start toward him, teeth clenched.

He holds up a hand. "Where's this coming from?"

"What?"

He sets the water aside and waves a hand up and down, as if he's scanning my entire body. "*This.* It's a gross overreaction."

"I'll show you overreaction." I hate that I'm doing this, acting defensive. It's not in my DNA. I want control and I want to go full bore, always have the upper hand. I really do need to calm down, but he doesn't get to say it. *I* decide when I calm down. Not him. Especially after everything that's happened this week.

Staring at him only makes it worse. He's so broody and ridiculously hot in the suit he has on. He looks—intimidating. I'm not afraid of him and the way he conducts business, though. I'm afraid of how much I like him, despite everything else. I don't want to, but I do.

It only pisses me off more. I'm on the edge of a breakdown. I feel it looming on the horizon, just waiting for an opportunity to strike, and when I crack, I'm going to crack hard.

I'm emotional. You should never get emotional about money or an investment decision. That being said, just sitting there, staring at Covington—rage consumes me. It mostly has nothing to do with him. He just lit the match with this stunt, pulling me away from my mother's side to deal with it.

"Never get emotional about money or an investment decision." The words ring through my head, reminding me of the man who gave me that advice, and how much I hate his guts—and now he's showed back up in my life.

The boiling point hits, and I just snap.

I take two hands and shove Covington against the table.

White-hot anger fills my veins. My father I hate just showed up, I'm about to lose my mom, now Covington's threatening the building that means everything to me. I can't take it anymore.

He stumbles back a few steps and hits the table, jarring him a little.

Shit. Shit. Did I really just do that?

His eyes go wide. It wasn't anything that could hurt him. He's six four for crying out loud and a million times stronger than me.

His shock doesn't last long. His eyes narrow on me. Fucking good. He's off his game now. I'm finally back in control of the situation.

Not to mention, it felt good. Really good.

He recovers, and I go to shove him again because I want to feel an ounce of that control again. I want to take everything out on him, use him as a damn punching bag.

This time, he catches my wrists and our mouths fuse together.

The moment it happens, a warmth spreads through my limbs, and I latch on to him.

The kiss is amazing, and ten times hotter than the other night. I kiss him as hard as I can, doing whatever I can to transfer everything, this huge weight on my shoulders, into him. He bites my lip, maybe hard enough to draw blood. I don't care. The pain, the pleasure, it all distracts me from reality, and it's just what I need.

I just want to feel good, for a few moments longer. I need a break, some kind of release from reality, even if it's for a few seconds.

His hand goes to my ass and he squeezes hard and thrusts his hips into me. I feel his hard dick up against my stomach, and I dig my nails into his shoulders through his suit jacket.

What the fuck am I doing? I'm supposed to hate him right now.

I don't know, but I can't help but think about the fact it feels right. This. It makes sense. In a world of chaos and walls crumbling down around me, right here, for a few moments, I feel safe, protected.

My brain finally wins out, and I shove him away from me and wipe my mouth with my wrist, as if it erased what I just did.

We stand there, glaring at each other, two intelligent people who don't know what the hell they're doing.

"I'm tired of these fucking games. You want the truth? Why I want this so bad?"

He starts to say something, but I cut him off.

"Be at five hundred west Fullerton. Seven pm." I storm out of the conference room before he can say anything else.

I shouldn't do this, but I am. He needs to know, so he'll stop this childish crap. Deep down, I know he deserves the information after everything he confided in me the other night. He told me some big secrets.

Plus, I think part of me wants him to have some kind of leverage over me, so I won't be tempted to use his information against him.

Deep down, somewhere in my heart, I know the real reason I'm doing this. The truth. It's because I like him. I like him a lot.

WELLS COVINGTON

WHAT KIND of shithole did Meadow bring me to?

I look around before walking in. The building is dilapidated, surprisingly not condemned, and I'm pretty sure it smells like animal piss, just from looking at it from the curb. Everyone has been in a building like this before. You know what it smells like. None of the lights seem to work on the outside, the door is cock-eyed. I walk up the small stoop to the entrance, praying this fucking thing doesn't collapse on me.

Don't get me wrong, there are opportunities in things that are broken. I haven't written off what she has planned—yet. It's just not my idea of a good time to go traipsing through death traps. Part of it is the uncertainty. I don't know what she's up to. What I do know is she shouldn't be in a goddamn place like this during the day, let alone when the sun is about to set on it. Chicago is dangerous at night.

I plan to let her know exactly how reckless it is, no matter how pissed off she wants to act toward me. I make my way through the slanted door with paint all stripped off.

"You're five minutes late." The words come from the shadows.

It startles me a little, but I play it off and look around the hall. Thank God there are a couple of functioning lights, even though Meadow chose not to stand in any of them. I know it's purposeful. This whole situation is of her design.

I crane my head around. "Lucky I stepped into the fucking building."

She emerges from the shadows, and immediately my adrenaline spikes. What is it about being in a room with this woman that drives me insane? Action potentials fire across my synapses, reminding me of every minute detail of our kiss, how her tongue felt, her ass in the palm of my hand, her ragged breaths when she pushed away from me, the undeniable look in her eyes.

She smirks, not taking the bait. "Follow me." She walks with confidence.

Instinctively, I take off after her, realizing the effect she has on me in the process. It's psychological warfare on a scale unimagined with her, but I don't mind the games. I welcome them. My life hasn't been boring for one second since I met her. I feel alive for the first time in forever. It used to be investments, wealth accumulation, outthinking opponents, that held one hundred percent of my attention.

Now it's Meadow Carlson.

We turn a few corners and walk through a door into an office.

A man and a woman sit there, fidgeting nervously with their hands.

They're a thousand times easier to read than Meadow. Both lean in when I walk into the room. This is a huge opportunity for them. I'm about to hear some kind of pitch.

My eyes narrow on Meadow when she turns around.

Is it really just about money with her? Is that all she wants? Use me for my capital for whatever this is? I told her she could have that damn building; I'm just using it to frustrate her a little. It's impossible for me to think she's misread our situation. The probability is less than one percent. So what the fuck is happening?

Before I can get a word out, she says, "Just hear me out. Don't be an asshole."

The other two pairs of eyes in the room widen.

"This is Martha and John Freeport."

I turn to them. "Nice to meet you." My eyes dart back to Meadow. "What is this?"

"The reason I want your building. I want you to know the purpose, so you'll stop fucking with me."

She has my motives confused. I want to fuck her. Fucking with her is a means to achieve that. I don't say it, of course.

"You had no problem fucking with my money, but now, I'm supposed to what? Show some kind of mercy? Sympathy? Understand?"

Martha and John glare at Meadow this time. A surprising turn of events. So, they didn't know what she was doing to secure the property? Interesting, but I'm not surprised. I can tell they're philanthropists and not investors. They both have dirty fingernails, calloused hands. They're honest, hardworking people who would never do the types of things Meadow and I are capable of.

"What's he talking about?" Martha asks.

Meadow, for the first time since I've met her, looks somewhat ashamed and almost trips over her words.

"It's nothing. Water under the bridge." I stare at Meadow the entire time I say the words.

Meadow seems to thank me with those eyes of hers and doesn't miss a beat. "This place is theirs."

I turn to them. "Congratulations." I don't hide the sarcasm in my voice.

"Look, Covington, they built this from nothing. So, while it may not seem like much to you, it's everything to them."

"Is someone going to tell me exactly what this place is?"

John turns to me. He looks like an honorable man. When you deal with enough assholes trying to rip you off at every turn, get some kind of edge on you, you learn to recognize genuineness the second you see it. He says, "It's a shelter. We provide subsidized housing and services for low-income families."

"Section eight?"

"Yes, but we've managed to secure funding from our donors that cover the costs one hundred percent."

"They want the building you're trying to turn into high-rise condos." Meadow's commanding voice takes over the conversation. "I have investors and philanthropists on board. Everything is on track. But you came in and paid above market value for the property. We couldn't compete with the price."

I'm sure they couldn't. That's the problem with philanthropy. It can't compete with profit-seeking entities at scale.

I understand Meadow is trying to save the world with venture capital, but the market works how the market works. I have a feeling if these people knew half the shit she's pulled, they'd drop her in a heartbeat, but fuck me if I want to spare her that. I want to tell myself I don't know why my behavior changes around her, my entire existence, but I know. I both hate and love that about her. She's the only person who has ever made me behave irrationally, and it's kind of refreshing in a weird way. It humanizes me.

"So, you want me to scrap my high rise so you can convert it into a shelter?"

Meadow hands me a packet of information. "A state-of-the-art shelter. It's never been done before. It'll be the nicest and largest of its kind. Read the mission and projections. The math all works out, I did it myself. Investors are on board, grants are lined up. This will help reintegrate struggling people back into society, get them on their feet. Help working-class families who are economically displaced feel like they have worth again. Help their children—"

I stare at her, effectively telling her to stop pulling on my heartstrings, as if that would possibly work, then thumb through the pages, scanning. Meadow's lips curl into a smile, most likely surprised I'm even looking at it.

My brain immediately shifts from lovestruck mode to investment mode. "Most of these people have probably been let go because jobs have become automated or outdated. The next five years might possibly be worse than the industrial revolution. This creates enormous risk for something of this magnitude. It's a scale only the federal government could impact, not a private enterprise. Not to mention the elites downtown who don't want a bunch of poverty-stricken people clogging up the city more than they already do."

John and Martha's heads drop, as if they know this is true and want to give it a try anyway. Meadow's eyes harden. I didn't mean to be so blunt, but someone needs to acknowledge risks. You can't sugarcoat investment strategy. The market will eat you alive on passion projects like these.

"We already have training and education services in line, networks for jobs set up."

"It's a loser, Meadow, and you know it." I cringe a little at my words. I would never cringe like that if my own people brought this to me. It's one of the drawbacks of impact investments. You get emotionally involved.

"We have to try." John looks up at me. "What does this say about us as people if we don't try to make things better. You look like a man who has taken on risk before. You had to, to get to where you are. Tell me this isn't a worthy risk."

I glance back and forth at the three of them. "I'll think about it. That's the only promise I can make." I turn and walk out of the room.

Three steps into the hall and I can already hear Meadow's footsteps pounding after me. Fuck, I love her tenacity. How can I channel that energy and focus onto me? Onto us?

When I get to the front of the building, about to walk out, I hear, "We had a fucking deal."

I freeze in my tracks and smile. I finally have her alone again. Slowly, I school my features and turn back around to face her. "I said I'd think about it. You're lucky you're getting that."

"Why are you such an asshole?"

I step toward her and lean down so we're eye to eye. Normal Meadow is amazing, but pissed-off Meadow is intoxicating. "Because I can be. You know that."

She regards me for a long moment, then something changes. Her entire demeanor. She folds her arms across her chest and pushes her tits together. I don't think she realizes she does it, but my dick damn sure does.

"You're in."

"Excuse me?"

"You knew before you walked in here, that you were going to say yes."

There she is. She knows, but I'm still going to make her work a little more for it. "I've never taken a loss on a project because it was the right thing to do."

She takes a step closer. "You're about to take that risk, though. I can see it in your eyes. In every one of your actions. Your mouth runs on and on." She takes another step, so she's dangerously close to me. "But your actions, they speak much louder."

Since we're getting everything out in the open, perhaps I'll hit back just as hard. "You're right."

Her eyes pop open, like she hadn't expected the admission.

"But before I commit, I want to know something in return."

She relaxes a little, as if she's letting her guard down for the first time around me. "What do you want to know?"

"What's going on with you?"

Her eyes dart around. "What do you mean? This project. It means a lot to me."

I shake my head and take another step to close the distance between us, because I want to be closer to her, and I don't like that she backed away from me. "No. There's something else." My eyes rake up and down her. "Something that has nothing to do with this. Something personal."

Meadow looks away.

I reach over and with a finger under her chin, I turn her head back to face me. I see it in her eyes the second they land on mine, and a rage builds inside me. A rage I didn't know I was capable of, that I've never felt before. There's sadness there, and I want to punish and destroy whatever has caused it. "Tell me."

She shakes her head and her eyes well up just slightly. "Don't. It's not part of the deal."

I push a few strands of hair behind her ear. "Of course it is."

"What?"

"None of this other shit matters to me. That building is

immaterial. I could lose that money a thousand times over and be fine. It's all just a means to get you. *You* are the deal for me."

I lean down to kiss her, but she stops me.

Our foreheads meet, and I stare into her eyes. "I want you." My hands slide down and find her hips. I dig my fingers in, letting her know exactly what I want. The only goddamn thing I want. "I'll do anything to have you. Tell me what's wrong."

Her eyes close then open again. "I said it's off limits."

"You don't understand, Meadow." I pull her over into the shadows on the side of the building, and my hand hikes up her skirt. I cup her pussy in my palm, and I can feel the heat radiating through her panties. She can glare at me with those eyes all she wants, but she can't hide how turned on she is right now, how much she wants this too.

Her chest heaves up and down. She's both scared and excited. I can see it in her eyes, feel it vibrating through her body.

"I don't just want this." I squeeze her a little harder.

She gasps against my lips.

"I want all of you. Your problems, your laughter, I want it all. And I'll do anything to get it. I'll buy a thousand shitty buildings if that's what it takes."

Meadow's brows knit together, and she stares straight into my eyes. "I don't want to talk about what's bothering me, *right now*."

I start to let go of her, but her hips surge, grinding her pussy against my hand. It's almost unbearable, the urge to take her right now, in front of the world.

"That doesn't mean I won't open up about it later. It's new, and I just want to forget about it for five minutes."

My heart comes alive. She basically just said she wants to share with me when the time is right. That's fair.

I move in to kiss her again, but she starts to speak.

"One other thing."

Our lips are inches apart, and I nod a little against her forehead as if to say, *go on.*

"Business and sex is separate. You don't use your wealth to get what you want with me. I'm not a whore."

This time I mash my lips against hers. It's even hotter than the kiss in my office. I slide her panties to the side and take two fingers deep, then kiss up the side of her neck to her ear. Her pussy is hot and wet and constricts. I think about how good it would feel to have it wrapped around my dick as she comes over and over.

In her ear, I whisper, "Understood." I circle her clit with my thumb and a shiver rips through her body. "But I have two conditions of my own."

"Making unproportionate demands. Why would I expect anything less? What are they?" Her words come out on ragged breaths.

Exhaling in her ear, I say. "This is mine." I circle her clit even harder.

Meadow nods and looks like she's about to pass out but manages to whisper, "The second?"

"You're right, you're not a whore." I take my fingers deep and curl them up to hit the ridge deep inside her.

She gasps, audibly. "Shit."

"But the second we get home, I'm going to fuck you like one." I slide my fingers out of her and take her by the hand, leading her to my car.

She follows.

WELLS COVINGTON

MEADOW'S PLACE IS CLOSER, so that's where we go.

The drive seemed to take forever, even though it was approximately five minutes through downtown. We pull up to her high rise and it's still fairly modest, like I remember.

I park in the garage and we're both out of the car, hands all over each other on the way up to her apartment. I don't want her to think about what we're doing for a second longer than she has to. A million things could happen in the span of the next three minutes that could keep me from fucking her. I won't allow that.

I know Meadow wants this as much as I do, but there's still something going on with her. Something unrelated to this shit going on between us. Honestly, I don't even know why I give a fuck. I shouldn't. Still, it bothers me. I don't like to see her hurting.

Sex has always been a transaction with me. A very fun, exhilarating one, to say the least. But I never give up a part of myself. There's no real connection.

This is different.

I'm one hundred percent on a mission to make Meadow come all over my face, multiple times. As far as I'm concerned, this is all a test. It's evolutionary biology in its purest form. I need to show her I'm the most suitable mate possible for her. I need to perform at my peak, to let her know no other man could ever satisfy her the way I'm about to. There can be no doubt left behind when we're done.

I glance down, and our eyes lock as she leads me to her front door.

There won't be.

I'm going to ruin her for any man that dares to come near her after tonight. If something goes south between us, if it doesn't work out, she'll still think about me any time someone else is around. I will be the benchmark, and nobody will ever measure up.

Her Bluetooth door unlocks when we're about five feet away, and I yank her up against the wall, effectively pinning her against it.

Before she can react, I take both her wrists and shove them above her head, then trail kisses down her neck. "Last chance."

She knows exactly what I mean. I'm offering her an out. I've never done this before, but I want no doubt left that she chooses this willfully. That she chooses *me*. Wants to be with *me*.

"I made my decision a long time ago, Covington, before tonight. You know this."

I smile against her neck. Fuck, she has no idea how happy those words make me. Humans are weird. We can know something with almost one hundred percent certainty, feel it in our bones, but when it comes to things like relationships, emotions, you still have to hear the other person admit it out loud before your soul will accept it. We're all illogical creatures scrambling to figure out life.

I work my way to her ear. "Just so we're clear, when I walk through that door, I'm in. It's more than sex." I push my chest harder against her and damn near growl my words in her ear. "You're mine." I bite down lightly on her ear lobe the second I say it. "I'm not just someone you fuck."

"Holy shit." She exhales the word, then nods lightly. "Okay." That's all I needed.

The second she gives her consent, I pick up her petite frame and toss her over my shoulder, then walk through her door.

"Oh my—"

I step into her entryway with her. "Which way?" The commanding tone of my voice even surprises me a little.

Meadow immediately points down a hallway. "First on the right."

My heart races at how quickly she responded with the words, like she couldn't get them out fast enough.

I take huge strides, power walking with her over my shoulder until I reach the door and take her inside. My eyes scan the room, taking in every detail. Single Queen bed, art print on the wall, dresser and mirror. She's definitely a minimalist, but I'll make it work.

The furniture is super nice, but sleek with clean lines and only essentials.

It's crazy in a way. I never thought I'd meet anyone with a mind for quantitative analysis like mine. In that respect, I'd say Meadow and I are almost identical. However, I see stories in everything. On the surface, my possessions look like excess, and some are. But everything I own has a story behind it, a history that I know intimately. Meadow is all about functionality. I think that's where we contrast the most. That's what I love about her. We can be so alike and so different, as to remain a mystery to one another.

I walk over and toss her down on the bed. I think it damn near knocks the breath out of her because she gasps. She doesn't have time to react because I've hiked her skirt to her hips and yanked her legs apart.

There's no need to say anything. I want my mouth on her pussy, and that's what will happen. Meadow's eyes are huge when I glance up to them.

I've always maintained eating pussy is a forgotten art form, and I pride myself on being the master of it. Like any art, it must tell a story, follow the structure. There's intrigue and mystery in the beginning, as the action slowly builds. The climax is well, the climax, then the conclusion. What she doesn't know, is I plan on this being a series. When one story ends, the sequel begins, because I plan on fucking her until I can't breathe.

I take my time, staring into her eyes as I remove both of her shoes from her feet and toss them onto the floor. Fuck me, her legs are soft and smooth. I want to wrap them around my face, feel them squeeze around my head as she comes undone.

My cock has been rock-hard since she chased after me at the building. If I don't fuck her soon, I might need medical attention. I'm already worried I'm going to blow in a matter of seconds as it is.

As I work down her legs, kissing, licking, I watch Meadow's reactions, her body language. I want to know every single thing she likes, and what she doesn't, log every bit of data possible. I work my way between her legs, teasing up next to where I know she wants my mouth, so much her fingers rake through my hair, tugging me closer to where she needs me.

I fight back against her hold, even though I can feel the heat from her pussy next to my face. It's almost unbearable, the urge to rip her panties in half and fuck her with my tongue.

Right when I finally graze her clit, I rise up and take my shirt off.

Meadow's eyes roam up and down my torso.

I reach down and slowly remove her skirt first, then come back and remove her panties too.

She's perfect.

I get the first glimpse of her pink pussy, her legs spread apart, moonlight filtering through the window illuminating it perfectly.

My nostrils flare. It's going to take an act of sheer willpower to refrain from shoving my dick into her until after I get her off with my tongue.

Repeating the process from earlier, I work down her legs again, with a little more urgency this time, allowing the tension to build inside her. Once I'm almost there, I grip the backs of both of her thighs and shove them toward her shoulders, angling her right up to where I want.

"Hold your legs."

Both of her hands fly forward, like she's given up trying to fight any of this. She's a damn ticking time bomb, and it's going to be glorious when she goes off.

When she has her legs held in place, I grab each side of her hips, lean down, and graze her clit with the tip of my tongue, just to see what happens.

"Shit." She draws out the word, and her legs already start to tremble.

She's so close already.

"I could exhale across your clit right now, and you'd get off, wouldn't you?" I use my thumb to barely stroke it this time.

Meadow's head rolls to the side, and she bites down on the pillow, like she's doing everything she can to hold back. "Mmh-mm," she groans while nodding her head up and down.

Without warning, I push two fingers inside her, even deeper than before.

Meadow's eyes fly open, and her entire body constricts. I don't know what it is with her, but I almost don't even need to see her reaction to know what it will be. It's like I'm already living inside her brain. Like I already know every single thing she likes and doesn't. I can sense it.

My tongue flicks across her clit as I work tiny circles around the ridge deep inside of her. She fights back every bit of plea-sure, because, well, she's Meadow. Slowly, I work small circles, increasing the tempo as I go, incredibly aware of how close she is to her orgasm.

"Holy shit." Her hips buck against my face.

I push her so close, I worry if it may have gone a little too far. When she starts to convulse, I bite down on the inside of her thigh, hard enough to leave a mark there.

"Fuck." She draws out the syllable, and her nails dig into my scalp.

It's amazing how responsive she is.

"Not yet." I growl the words against her leg.

For the next few minutes, I do the same things I did before. Push her right to the brink, then bite down on the other side.

This time she tenses even harder, but I can tell she loves

every goddamn second of it. Her body is practically humming with energy, damn near nuclear.

"I'm so close. So fucking close, Covington. Don't stop." She groans as she says it, short of breath, biting down on the sheets again.

I reach around, shove her blouse up, and grip both her tits in my palms. It's the first time I've felt them, and like her, they're perfect. I want to bite and mark every inch of her body, tell the whole world she's off limits.

I focus my tongue on her clit, pushing her higher and higher, tweaking her nipples when she gets close. She's so fucking wet I can barely stand it. My hips grind against her bed, dry fucking her mattress, just to mildly satisfy the need to fuck her. I'm not sure how much longer I can hold out.

It's time.

I ready myself, because I want to remember every minute detail of the first time I get Meadow Carlson off. My arms wrap around her legs, fingers digging into her thighs to hold her in place as I work her clit. She tries to squirm, anything to give her some kind of relief.

I don't fucking think so.

I hold her in place, my mouth capped over her clit, tongue relentless.

"Oh God, Wells."

She seizes up, body convulsing, and both of her hands bunch the bedsheets up in her fingers. Her chest heaves up and down, but I hold her legs in place, riding out her orgasm with my mouth sucking, licking, stroking her every way possible.

Her hips try to fly up from the bed, and it takes a herculean effort to keep her pinned down.

"Fuck. Fuck." Finally, after several long, beautiful waves, she exhales a giant sigh. She tries to say something but can't. Her legs are like Jell-O, goosebumps pebbling all over her body.

I don't even give her a chance to catch her breath. With one smooth motion, I flip her over onto her stomach and pin her down with my chest to her back.

She starts to say something, but she can't.

My mouth in her ear, I say, "Nobody else can make your body do that. And nobody else will ever fuck you the way I'm about to. Remember that."

"Holy—"

I unzip my pants, and the second she hears my zipper, I know her heartbeat spikes even higher. I yank my pants down halfway, freeing my cock, and I don't think I've ever been this hard in my life. I lean back from her, but she doesn't move. She wants this just as bad as I do. I know it in my heart, feel it in my DNA.

The connection between us is undeniable. This is what we were meant to do.

I stare down at her pussy, barely peeking out under her ass, and my nostrils flare again. I've never wanted to fuck someone bare so bad in my life. I want to shove into her and come deep inside her, mark her as mine every damn way possible.

Somehow, my brain can still function, and I pull a condom from my wallet and roll it on. Parting her lips with the head of my cock, one last time I say, "You sure?"

I want the confirmation. I need it. It would be so easy to just fuck her, no questions asked, but my heart needs to know she hasn't changed her mind. Eating her pussy was phenomenal, but fucking her changes everything. I'm about to feel things I've never felt before, and not just in a physical sense. It's out there, swirling around the room, this magnetic field between us.

"Yes."

The second I hear the word, I push into her.

Fuck. Fuck. Fuck.

It's even better than I imagined. Meadow's walls squeeze tight around me and I'm already so fucking close. I don't even care. Time stands still in this moment, like it could go on infinitely. My brain etches the data in, piling it all away somewhere, specifically for Meadow. Every memory, every sensation. She owns a part of me now, a part of me that will never go away.

I push in deep, then pull back, then push in once more. If there is a heaven, this is it. This is fucking it.

Once satisfied I won't hurt her, I lean up over her, and clamp one of my hands down on her collar bone, digging in my fingers.

Meadow constricts even harder around me.

In her ear I say, "I made a promise. I always keep my word."

"Holy fu—"

My hips surge forward, crashing into her ass as I fuck her deep and hard.

She reaches back and digs her fingernails into one of my thighs, pulling me even harder into her. Her nails threaten to draw blood.

It speeds my hips up even more, as wet skin slaps on wet skin, the sound echoing through the room.

"Fuck, Meadow." My words come out on a groan, her nails fueling me even more.

"Shit, W-W-Wells."

I fuck her so hard her words vibrate.

Right when I don't think I can hold off any longer, I slip out of her and flip her over onto her back. I struggle with my pants, wanting to rip the fucking things from my legs. I don't want to be apart from her for a split-second longer than necessary, but at the same time, it helps stave off the load building in my balls.

I roll to my back and yank my pants down my legs, taking my shoes off in the process. Once I'm free, I flip back over, and my mouth is on her pussy instantly.

"Oh God." She gasps.

We both know I'm stalling, trying to hold off and keep myself from coming early, but she doesn't say anything.

Once she's close again, I lean upright and angle my dick down to her pussy once more.

I reach down and lightly wrap my fingers around her throat, her eyes widening as I do it. She must see the look in my eye because I feel her pulse speed up against my palm.

"You're coming on my dick this time." It's not a question. I flat out tell her that's what's happening.

Her eyes flutter closed, and I push inside her once more. Immediately, I'm about to blow.

Fuck, how does she do this to me?

Both her hands fly back to the headboard, looking for anything to grab onto. I release her throat, and take her hips in my hands, yanking her into me as I thrust back against her. Her blouse is still wrapped around her shoulders, and her firm tits start to bounce loose from her bra.

"That's it. Fuck me, Covington." She bounces herself back into me as I thrust into her.

I do exactly what she says. So hard her headboard crashes against the drywall and vibrates the wall. I don't give a single fuck about any noise we make at this point. My focus is singular; feeling her come all over my cock.

I take one hand and circle her clit as I pound into her.

"Shit." She looks like she's about to come so hard it puts her in a coma. Her legs wrap tighter around me, her hips grinding up and down uncontrollably.

I take my free hand and grip her chin, squeezing her cheeks so hard her mouth forms a big O. Her eyes fly open and she stares right at me. My finger circles her clit even faster as I fuck her harder and harder.

"Look at me when you come."

She nods against my hand and clamps down on me so hard my eyes squeeze shut.

It feels so fucking good it's almost unbearable. My balls tighten, and I do everything in my power to hold it off.

"Oh my God, Wells." She convulses and her words trail off.

I shove into her as deep as humanly possible, groan, and blow into the condom, wishing I was coming inside her. It's the most intense orgasm of my life. It comes in waves, and I groan and grunt, over and over, until she's milked every last fucking drop possible.

Fuzzy stars dance in front of my vision, and I'm in a daze. A pure euphoric daze, like an out-of-body experience. When some semblance of consciousness returns, I hear myself mumbling, "Meadow. Meadow."

I shake my head and look down at her. Her eyes are locked

on mine, her chest rising and falling in huge waves as she catches her breath. Finally, I bend down and stare into her eyes, for what feels like an eternity, before our lips meet. It's not a passionate kiss. It's just a recognition.

It's a recognition that something just happened between us that neither one of us can explain, that will probably set us both on a course for a massive collision, but we don't care. We'll run headfirst into it, heads down, no caution, because the universe is strange like that. Humanity is illogical, and as smart as both of us are, we can't stop it. Nothing can.

Neither of us say a word, just have an entire conversation with our eyes.

I look down at her. She's the most beautiful thing I've ever seen, and I'm pretty sure I've seen every beautiful thing the world has to offer. At least I had, until I met her.

Finally, I slip out of her and walk off toward the bathroom. I can feel her eyes burning into my skin the whole way. I dispose of the condom, then walk back and lie down next to her in bed, spooning her with my left arm.

We both lie there, wondering what we just did, what it means. I know every thought going through her head right now. It mirrors my own.

How will this work? What is this connection? Do I have time to do this correctly?

It doesn't matter. It *is* happening.

Eventually, I break the ice. "A bit hypocritical, don't you think?"

I can see her smile in my mind before she turns her head and shows it to me. "Can't wait to hear this."

I laugh and push a few sweaty strands of hair from her forehead. "Storming out of my place, when you're up here, living the good life."

This time she laughs, hard. "Like my place is anything like yours."

I glance around at the room and raise my eyebrows. "Still, you're not living in a cardboard box, and I don't have a Bluetooth lock on my door."

She gives me a little shove, but I yank her back into me, even closer than she was before. She nuzzles back against my neck, and it might be the most comforting thing I've ever felt in my entire life. "Yeah, you have a human to open it for you."

I smile again. "Doesn't matter. Nothing fucking matters but this." I kiss her on the back of the neck, and we both fall asleep.

MEADOW CARLSON

THIS DOESN'T MEAN ANYTHING. Not a damn thing.

I wake up in my bed and nobody is next to me.

Maybe it was all a dream.

No, it was definitely *not* a dream. I can still feel him between my legs, feel his arm wrapped around me, his fingers on my throat.

It was just sex. Just a way to release all this rage about Mom. That's all this was. You could've done far more reckless things.

I say these things to myself over and over, but I know they're not true. Yes, it was an escape from dealing with Mom's situation, and with my father. That doesn't make what's happening any less real, though.

What the hell?

I don't know if I'm upset about what I did, or the fact I left Mom's side to deal with Covington and made one horrible decision after another.

I'm pretty sure I hear singing. Did we leave a radio on?

I get up and wrap a sheet around myself, then yawn as I make my way toward the kitchen. The smell of frying bacon lands in my nose, and the singing grows louder.

It's Covington, and he's tone deaf. Honestly, it's nice to know he has at least one flaw.

I should record it on my phone and post it to Twitter. He'd never live it down. Would definitely make the news cycle or end up on TMZ. I sneak over to the corner so I can peek in at him. He sounds so happy, even if he can't sing for shit. Despite everything, I grin.

I love knowing I'm the one making him smile. He's always brooding, always on, nothing but business. This feels like a quick glimpse at another side of him, possibly his real side.

We all wear masks to shield who we are from society, and I've learned, the more money you make, the more famous you are, the thicker the mask. When I spy him around the corner, he's even happier than he sounded. Grinning from ear to ear, cooking on my stove.

It might be the first time it's been used in, well, forever. I can't believe he knows how to cook breakfast like this. I always had this picture of him as a kid, eating eggs benedict from a butler or something. Right now, he looks like he could hold his own working in an IHOP kitchen. He flips a couple pancakes at the same time without missing a beat.

"I see you watching me." He smiles but doesn't look over at me.

"Listening more than watching."

"Yeah, I never did master that art form."

I can't remember feeling this happy. Guilt slams into me because of Mom, but also because I can't really remember feeling this happy before I heard about Mom too. I shouldn't be this happy right now, it's not right, even though I know my mom would want me here and not in her house, moping around.

I'm just...

I don't know what I am right now, but I know if I don't find a way to order all these feelings, it's going to be bad. Really bad.

"Have a seat."

I don't hesitate and walk over to my little two-seat table, even though I never use it. It's literally there just in case I ever have someone over, and so the room looks like someone actually lives here.

I watch Covington, in nothing but a pair of boxer briefs,

continue to cook like he was born behind a stove. The food doesn't even register, because this is the first time I've gotten a really good look at his body.

He's tall.

Very tall.

But he's not weird and lanky or huge and bulky. He is long and lean, like an Olympic swimmer. His muscles flex and contract with the tiniest movements, and not going to lie, it's hot. *He's* hot, like something out of a museum. Like he was sculpted by an Italian master.

How the hell did his brains and that body end up with the same person? It's really not fair to the rest of humanity.

There's a cup of coffee waiting for me when I sit down, and I take a sip. Covington walks over after flipping a spatula around and filling up two plates. He makes a show of setting my plate in front of me.

"Fried pork strips, griddlecakes, and eggs ala Covington with fresh pepper for the lady."

I crack up because he's being as pretentious as he possibly can on purpose. It's regular bacon and eggs with some pancakes. I can see the package he must've gone to the store to pick up.

He sets his plate down in his spot, and says, "Same for the gentleman."

But then, he leans over, like he always does. He loves whispering things in my ear, and some of it last night was the filthiest things a man has ever said to me. What's worse? I liked it —a lot.

Covington exhales across my neck, and it sends goosebumps all over my body again.

"Though afterward, I'll be having your pussy."

He is so crude, and I'm not sure why I like it so much. The worst part is, I can't just sit there and act surprised. Oh no, I have to always hit back, even when it's to my detriment.

"Don't know if you have a big enough appetite." I turn my head and smirk at him.

In a flash, his hand is down the sheets I'm wrapped in, and his fingers are on me again. The way he looks at me, I'm not sure if he's ever going to let me out of his sight now. What have I gotten myself into?

You love every second of this.

"Trust me." He glances down at his hand and wets his bottom lip with his tongue, just barely. "I'll save room."

"Why wait?" I reach over for his dick and squeeze it over his briefs.

His jaw ticks, and I swear a groan catches in his throat. He hardens instantly against my palm, and holy shit, I'm still not sure how this thing fit inside me last night. I hadn't had sex in a long time.

Before he says anything, I adjust and reach down the front of the briefs, then pull his dick out. I don't know if I've ever been so forward with a man before. Something about Covington, though, it just feels like a giant sexual fantasy, where I can do whatever the hell I want. Isn't a good partner supposed to make you feel that way? Like this is how it should always be?

I stroke him a couple times, back and forth, and I start to lean forward to put him in my mouth, when a hand snakes up into my hair and pulls my head back. It feels phenomenal, and I don't think I've ever had a man pull my hair like this.

Our eyes meet, locked together, as usual. He looks like he's studying me for an exam, and then he just kisses me. It's not like a super-hot, passionate kiss either. It's like two people who have lived together for ten years kiss. It's an *I care about you more than anything, you make me so happy* kind of kiss.

It takes me by surprise, but it's really nice. It's emotional, even. My heart warms as his lips press to mine, and I just feel safe, and perfect, like everything in the world is going to be just fine because his lips are on mine.

When we part ways, he reaches up and lifts me out of the sheets and against his chest. My legs wrap around him as our bodies press together. I've never had this kind of view of my apartment, and wow, is this what the world looks like to him every day from way up here?

Covington carries me out of the kitchen and into the living

room. At some point I let go of his dick, but my legs wrap around his waist and I can feel it, right where I want it.

It pushes up against me, and for a second, the head of his dick slips in and out.

It felt even better than when he wore the condom, but I don't give a shit how right the moment feels. He's going to be safe.

Without missing a beat, as if he can read my thoughts, he sets me down on the couch and says, "Don't fucking move."

I grin a little, and I'm pretty sure once he's around the corner, he sprints to my room. Either that, or he cleared the distance in two of his long strides, because he's back in the blink of an eye.

"Sorry to kill the mood."

He reaches down and fists the back of my hair again.

"Mood's back," I say almost instantly.

Covington grins like the damn devil himself, I swear. There's something with him. Something about him. He's so damn alpha, but somehow, it still feels like I'm in control, like I could do whatever I wanted.

Most guys, in my experience, just kind of flop around for a few minutes then roll over and fall asleep. Even the promising ones are not that great in bed, they just have other qualities that allow you to overlook the shortcoming.

Not so in this case.

"You think you can just pull my hair whenever you want to?" I pretend to glare at him, hoping this is how he wants me to react. Hoping he wants me to pretend to put up a fight.

Covington flips me over, so my ass is in the air, and it's a little ridiculous how fast he can do it. My heart pounds the second he does it, and my breaths become shallow. My adrenaline spikes off the charts, and I'm wet for him. No denying that.

Good God, when he went down on me for the first time... I've never had an orgasm like that. The one when he was inside me too. Never. I've never even given myself one that good.

"Let's make quick work of this, before breakfast gets cold."

"So romant—"

I can't finish the phrase because his mouth is on me from

behind. I've never had a man want to go down on me this much, ever. The tip of his tongue teases my clit, and my legs already start to tremble.

He rolls his tongue back and forth, then licks everywhere. Then, he sits up behind me, and lines himself up.

I strain to turn back a little, just to get a look at him. "Protection?"

He smirks right at me and turns so I can see he has a condom on. When the fuck did he do that? While he was licking me? No way any man on this planet has that kind of a skillset, can do two things at once that quickly.

It's the only explanation, though.

I turn back around and wait for him to fill me again. Last night his hand clamped around my collar bone when he fucked me from behind. Today he seems fixated on my hair, because he maneuvers it into a little ponytail, then grips it just hard enough to pull on my scalp.

It's incredible.

"Food's getting cold." I don't give a shit about the food. I just want his dick.

I expect him to say something back, but he doesn't.

Crack!

Oh. My. God.

His hand connects with my ass. Hard. Hard enough to definitely leave a handprint, and it stings like crazy as the blood rushes back into my skin. I gasp out a sigh.

"What the—" I start to turn around.

Crack!

He does it again.

This time, I tense up and start to turn around to let him have it, even though I think I might like being spanked. "You fucking—"

His cock slides into me, just as I'm about to let loose on him.

"Oh my God, yes."

He's turning me into a sex addict. I know it's what he's doing. He's conditioning me with his dick. I quickly find myself throwing my hips back into him as he thrusts forward. One of his hands slides around my hip and he strokes my clit with his fingers while he pounds into me.

I can't help but notice Covington is different than any man I've been with. I have no doubt he enjoys being inside me, but he's constantly trying to make sure it's just as good if not better for me. It's almost like he's in it more for me than for him.

I reach back and shove him away. His eyes get a little big.

I stand up guide him forcefully so he's sitting on the couch, then I straddle him. He's been in control enough and I haven't been on top yet.

"You're so fucking beautiful, Meadow."

I ignore his words and sit down on top of him, taking him as deep as he'll go. Holy shit.

The look on his face tells me he feels the exact same. His eyes close, then they open back up and we stare at each other.

"You have no idea what you do to me." His hands come up and his palms are on both my cheeks as I slowly glide up and down on him.

It's different than last night, but no less intense.

His big hands reach around, and he splays his fingers across my ass as I rock up and down on him. His mouth surges out and he takes one of my breasts in it.

I hook my arms around his neck, and I think I could get used to this every day, doing this with Covington. I'm already close.

"Fuck." Covington groans, and I'm pretty sure it means he's almost there too.

I grind my hips in a small circle on him, doing my best to get off before he does. He takes notice, and his hand slides down and strokes my clit.

"Shit." My head tilts back to the ceiling.

Our tempo speeds up, until I'm bouncing up and down on him, and another giant orgasm rocks through my body. Covington grunts, then shoves me down on him as he takes me as deep as humanly possible.

We both convulse a few times, finishing simultaneously, which I always thought was bullshit. I thought it was something people joked about happening or was only possible in fictional stories. Nope. We just did it.

After a few moments, Covington picks me back up, his dick never leaving me. He carries me all the way to the table, where our food still awaits us. He kisses me full on the lips, then slips out of me and sets me down as he goes around the corner, presumably to get rid of the condom.

I've already eaten a strip of bacon when he returns, and it's like heaven, even if it is a little cold.

"Thanks for waiting."

I take a huge sip of orange juice. "My pleasure."

He laughs.

"This food's amazing. Thank you."

"No problem."

He doesn't eat, just sits there, watching me eat like a weirdo.

Finally, I say, "What?"

"Nothing." He cants his head slightly to the side and says, "I'm taking you somewhere later."

I shake my head. "Can't." I stop and finish chewing, trying to apologize with my eyes. "Sorry. I just have places I need to be today."

"Please." He takes my hand. "Just an hour, later in the evening."

I look at him. How the hell am I supposed to say no? I *have* to say no. "An hour? Tops?"

He laughs. "Yes. Take it easy. It's just an hour."

"Sorry, I don't mean to be rude. I really do have some things going on though."

"Didn't take it as rude. We'll figure this out. I'm a great problem solver. I'm sure we can figure out an hour."

I look at him for a long time, knowing I shouldn't, but maybe I can make it work. I have no desire to be around Dad, so it would be a nice break so I don't murder him. Nothing would make Mom more unhappy than that, and I know she would want this for me. "So, where you taking me?"

His eyes light up. "Somewhere special."

WELLS COVINGTON

My stomach tightens as we head up the sidewalk. Never in my life did I think I would be doing this. My hand slips down into Meadow's, and fuck, it feels good. It feels so right, and it scares the living shit out of me.

I pride myself on making reasonable decisions, using objective data. I'm anything but objective when I'm around her. Emotions I didn't know I was capable of, flood my veins.

Usually, I get single-minded on an investment track. I see the goal so clearly, and I'm relentless until I have what I want.

All of that has faded.

All I want is her, and I know I won't stop until she's mine. The thing at the back of my mind, driving all this uncertainty, is the one thing that is as constant as the earth moving around the sun. What goes up, always comes down. Everything is a cycle, and right now, with Meadow, I'm on the upswing. We all know what happens with relationships, it's inevitable. Do we have what it takes when things go south? Even worse is half the equation is out of my control.

I think that's just it. I usually control everything, and I can't control what Meadow thinks, what she feels. I can't make decisions for her, and that is exactly what haunts me right now.

Meadow glances up and smiles. "Where we going?"

I do my best to hide my uncertainty about us. "Patience."

"Patience." She mocks me in a deep, serious voice. "Seriously, tell me."

"We're almost there."

When I reach the door of The Gage, the bar of choice where the entire Hunter Group firm always hangs out, I open it for her.

She glances around, surveying her surroundings, and raises an eyebrow. "A bar?"

She's teasing me and expects me to grin, but I'm so damn nervous I can't bring myself to fake one. I tell myself over and over I shouldn't do this, it's too soon, I'm caught up in my feelings. Yet my feet keep taking me whatever direction they want with her. It's like I'm outside of my body, and some other force is acting upon me.

"It's not about the location."

She regards me for another few seconds, studying me like she always does, trying to figure out what my end game is. "When you said somewhere special, I thought it'd be some big romantic gesture or something, or something meaningful to you. You do know how to date, don't you?"

"Nope," I say as she walks inside.

Once she's a few steps past me, she stops.

I fill the empty space next to her and look straight ahead at the bar, but more importantly, at the people sitting in front of it. "Some things are more significant than big romantic gestures."

The people at the bar turn and smile at me when they see I'm with a single woman. I'm going to catch more shit for this than I ever have in my life. Part of me wants it to happen, I think. Meadow is worth it to me, a lifetime of ridicule from these assholes. I'll do anything to have her. Anything.

"So what's significant about this?" For the first time ever, I think, Meadow appears confused, like she doesn't understand.

"Those people at the bar, staring at us." I look down to her.

"Yeah?"

"Those are my best friends. My only friends."

"Okay?"

I smile at her and then shrug. "I don't bring women to meet

them. Not women I'm serious with, anyway, because I've never been serious with a woman."

Meadow tries to hide it, but her lips curl into a slight grin. Finally, she nods, and I think I've made her happy. "Okay."

As we walk over, I can already see everyone running their mouths, snickering to each other. It's time to eat some humble pie. I've given them so much shit, ridiculous amounts of shit, the last two years as I've watched each of them fall in love and get engaged. There has been relentless mocking and teasing about how I would never settle down, how I could never be with one woman.

This is deserved, and Meadow is so special to me, I want her there to witness all of this. Plus, I just want her to know the people who are most important to me, the only people I value more than my business.

Dexter, Abigail, Cole Miller, and Harlow Collins stand up as we approach.

"Hello everyone."

Meadow walks right at my side, eager to greet them. I love how she stands front and center, doesn't shy behind me. This woman isn't afraid of anything. If she only knew the viper den of sarcasm she's venturing into.

"Wells, is that really you? We waiting for one more?" Abigail smiles and doesn't even give me a chance to respond. She goes straight for Meadow, as women do. "Hi, I'm Abigail."

"Meadow." They shake hands.

Harlow, who has never met a day she smiled upon, frowns and says, "Harlow."

I pray she doesn't crush Meadow's hand when she shakes it. I'll admit that woman scares me a little.

"What's up, fucker?" Dex shakes my hand.

"What do we have here?" says Cole as he shakes my hand as well.

And just like that, they all turn their backs on me and focus their attention to Meadow.

"Dexter Collins."

"Cole Miller."

"It's a pleasure to meet you," says Dex. He grins his ass off right at me, the entire time he shakes Meadow's hand, like *oh, you're about to catch some shit, sir.*

Finally, after all the introductions are made, we all have a seat. The women pull Meadow away from me and surround her on one side of the bar, talking about shit women talk about. The guys yank me to the side. It seems like it's some kind of divide-and-conquer tactic they all thought up on the fly, or perhaps it's some social norm I'm not aware of.

I'm not sure how I feel about it. Not the fact that they'll be interrogating Meadow or giving me shit. I don't give a fuck about that. It's the fact that when Meadow isn't right next to me, I get this empty feeling in the pit of my stomach. She's four seats away at a bar, and I miss her.

I glance over and can't hear much of what they're saying, but Meadow is grinning and laughing, chatting up a storm like she's having the time of her life, possibly getting dirt on me. There's no telling. But she glances over at me, her cheeks slightly pink, and smiles.

Not a normal smile, but a smile that says she's happy. Like this is how she'd love to spend this hour. Like it's something that's important to her.

My heart warms at the thought. I have plenty of time to romance her, take her places, surprise her with flowers and dates and all the shit you do with someone you care about. But this right here, I hope she knows how big of a deal it is for me to let someone in like this. Judging by the look on her face, I believe I knocked this one out of the park. Which I'm not surprised about, either. It was a big risk bringing her here, but that's how I live my life. Big risks, big rewards.

"Something's different with this one." Dex smiles. He knows damn well it's different.

The women I usually bring around when we meet at a club all have huge fake tits, fake smiles, and are worthless for conversation. I think that's why I used to enjoy them. They didn't even attempt normal human interaction. They wanted some money and some dick, and I supplied them with both.

Finally, I smile. "Just get it over with, you motherfuckers. I set myself up for this, purposely. Let's not skirt the topic."

"So direct." Cole grins. "Why can't you let us take our time and slowly enjoy torturing your ass?"

"Do what you must, gentlemen."

Dex nudges me with his elbow. "Naw, I don't want to ruin this."

"Ruin what?"

"Your high," says Cole.

"My high?"

They both laugh. "Never seen you look the way you do right now."

I scoff. "I get that it's a big deal, but it's *not* that big of a deal. Let's just slow down a little and not get carried away."

"Pick out a ring yet?" Cole laughs.

Dex laughs just as hard.

"I did, but your mom came over and now it's gone."

Cole's eyes get big.

Dexter dies laughing.

Nobody else in the world could get away with saying that to him, a former MMA world champion. Earlier in the year he reunited with his estranged mother, and she stole a bunch of money from his safe.

"Such a fucking asshole." Cole's shoulders start bouncing, and eventually he laughs as hard as Dexter does.

"They're having way too much fun over there." Abigail's voice carries over and lands in our ears.

The three of us turn, and all three women stare at us, shaking their heads, as if we shouldn't be enjoying ourselves as much as we are.

"Billions of dollars of net worth between the three of them, and you put them in a room and it's like a bunch of immature middle-school boys." Harlow snickers at us.

Dexter straightens up. "We can be mature, when we need to be."

"Sure you can," Meadow says in the most conde-scending mom voice I've ever heard. Didn't even miss a beat. "Bet you're a real *roller coaster* of emotional maturity."

Harlow and Abigail die laughing.

I freeze up for a second, because I have not said a single word about the roller coaster proposal between Dex and Abigail.

Dexter looks like he's about to have an aneurysm, staring at her, trying to figure out how she knows. He turns to me. "What the fuck? You told her?"

I hold both hands up while everyone else laughs, and I try to keep a straight face. "I swear, I didn't." My brain goes into overdrive trying to figure out how she knows that.

Finally, Dex just shakes his head. "Oh, she'll fit right in. Fucking ruthless." Dex smiles at me and knocks his rocks glass into mine.

The women go back to their little chat, Abigail and Harlow looking at Meadow like they're impressed.

"Still drinking water?" I ask Cole.

"Yeah, man. Trying to see how long I can go stone sober. At first, I was just trying to see if I could go a month. But I got there, then two months, and now it's like a challenge. Gone so far I don't want to break the streak."

"Can't even do sobriety without having to compete. Do you wear the same underwear nonstop while your streak is alive?"

Dex and I share another laugh at Cole's expense, despite the fact he could pummel both our faces if he wished.

Suddenly, Dex's eyes widen, like he just had some kind of epiphany. He glances over at Meadow, then his gaze returns to mine. "Wedding's coming up."

I lean in, doing my best to keep my voice down so we're not overheard. "Oh yeah, how's the planning going?" It's impossible to mask the teasing tone. If these women catch a whiff of this conversation, they'll be all over it, and it will not be enjoyable. There's nothing worse than a bunch of chicks talking about wedding plans.

Suddenly, we're surrounded by all three women.

Fuck. It's amazing how well they can hear. Equally amazing

how they can show up like a swarm of bees when they hear wedding talk taking place among men.

"Actually, Dex has been doing most of the planning. Taking care of everything." Abigail is so sweet and naïve. She deserves so much better than the man sitting before me, who's now cowering because he knows she just handed me an arsenal of ammunition to fire at him.

"I have no doubt that he has." I smirk right at Dexter, and he won't even look at me.

Abigail continues while Harlow and Meadow can clearly see what's happening.

"He gets so excited about things when he finds a good price or sees something he really likes. He Googles coolest wedding ideas, or points things out that happen in movies, and sends me links to articles to see what I want. It's super sweet."

I clap a hand on his shoulder. "Well, that's our Dex in a nutshell. Do you have a Pinterest page?"

Cole attempts to contain himself.

Abigail says, "Actually…"

I start to lose it. You can't make this shit up.

"I think it's awesome," says Meadow.

Dex's eyes dart over to her, completely ignoring me. "You do?"

Meadow nods. "Hell yes. There's nothing sexier than a man who's confident and takes charge, even with wedding plans. Wants to do whatever he can to make his fiancée happy. That's how it's supposed to be, isn't it? Why else would you want to be with someone unless you get excited about making them happy?"

I smile right at Meadow. I think that's the main difference between us. She's much kinder than me, likes to build people up. It's addictive, too. Makes me want to be better. Even I find myself admiring Dex a little after she puts it in that perspective. Before Meadow, I wouldn't have understood at all. Now, I find myself wanting to be that way with her. She's right. I'd do anything to make her happy. Including taking the lead on wedding plans.

Though, to be fair, I still feel it's my friendly duty to make sure Dex is thoroughly made fun of for it. That's also the natural way of good friendships.

"Thank you," says Dex. Then he flips me the bird right in my face.

Cole and I laugh.

I give his shoulder another squeeze. "I really am happy for you."

"Thanks, man."

"So—" Abigail pauses for a moment, then kind of looks around, like she's unsure about what she's about to say. Finally, she comes out with it. "Still need a plus two?"

Fuck me. I should've seen this coming, but I was too blinded by everything else; giving Dex shit, being mesmerized every time Meadow is in my presence.

Meadow folds her arms over her chest, the way she always does that's so fucking hot. "Plus two?" She plays it off like she's teasing, but I can tell it probably bothers her a little.

I do my best to be nice, because I know Abigail didn't mean anything by the question. I know exactly what she's doing, and what everyone else in this damn group wants me to do right now, apparently.

It's like they have shone a spotlight right on my fucking head.

But I don't mind. I have no reason not to do it. I want to do it.

I look right at Meadow but speak out the side of my mouth to Abigail. "Nope. Plus one." I know I said odd numbers bother me. They usually do, but not this time. There's only *one* I want.

Just. Fucking. One.

Abigail smiles, obviously reading the situation she forced to light, and it's working in her favor. "Do you—"

I don't let her finish her sentence, still gazing right at Meadow. "Will you go to their wedding with me?"

I don't think Meadow was quite ready for this when she started all the teasing. Her eyes remain locked on mine, but I know the look anywhere. I can see behind her eyes. A million calculations, permutations, every possible outcome, the significance of every event along the way. I know that feeling intimately and have never been able to relate to anyone else because of it—no one else, but her.

"For sake of clarity, you want me to be your date to their wedding?"

It's a stalling tactic, to give her more time to think. We both know what her answer will be.

I rise from the barstool and take a step toward her. Everyone else immediately backs out of our way.

Her eyes roll up to meet mine.

"Absolutely," I say, leaving no room for misinterpreting my intentions. It allows her to make the decision, but asserts that I'll go to the ends of the earth to get what I want if she tries to say no.

We do the stare down thing, everyone else fading off into the periphery, just the two of us standing there together. It's how it always is with her. Life just fucking fades away in every moment with Meadow, boils everything down to just us.

Finally, she nods and says, "Okay. Yes, I'll go with you."

I don't know if anything has ever made me as happy as I am right now. The plan was to just bring her to meet my friends, not this. But now, my night is even better than it was.

MEADOW CARLSON

THE PAST TWO weeks have been anything but normal. I don't know if my life has ever been tipped upside down like this. The fact I'm even somewhat juggling it impresses me. I think my father being out of prison is the only reason this is even working with Wells Covington.

That's what worries me, though. It feels so real with him, but I'm worried I'm just using him as an escape, even if I keep telling myself these feelings are real, that this could actually happen between us.

It may indirectly be the only nice thing my father has done for me, pissed me off so bad I can't stand the sight of him, which forces me to go out and do normal people things, like have a relationship.

I want to be there for Mom so badly, and I am most of the time. I just need a break every now and then.

When he's there, I want to yell, throw things, lash out, and that's not healthy for her. Of course, she's a champion through all of this. The guilt eats at me constantly when I'm away, but she made it clear she also wants time alone with him, which I kind of understand but don't at the same time.

How does she forgive him so easily? It makes me want to scream.

Loyalty and trust are probably the most important things to

me, which is why I feel a small pang of guilt every time I'm around Covington. He has no idea what I'm going through with my mom and my father. I haven't let him in on any of that yet. He introduced me to his best friends, let me into his world, and I really haven't given him any of my personal life in return.

To be fair, he doesn't ask, but I know he's serious about me. Serious as a goddamn heart attack. Every time he looks at me, touches me—I see it, feel it.

I do *not* have time to fall for a man, especially right now, not with all this going on. When Mom dies, and she *will* die from this cancer, it's going to put me out of commission for a while. There's no fucking way around it and it guts me to think about it. How bad it's going to hurt. I know Mom will forgive me for working so much, not getting enough time with her the past few years, but I won't forgive myself. I just won't.

I had enough money, and I could've made enough time. The world could've waited. I know I'm being irrational. She's fifty-seven and was in perfectly good health. We should've still had decades to come. Nobody could've seen this coming, yet I still should've gamed it out, should've had some kind of plan for this.

I hate that I'm like my father in that way. I hate that I got so much of him and so little of my mom. I don't want to be like this. I just want to be normal and not have a brain that constantly calculates odds and risk and possible outcomes.

There's no point in feeling sorry for myself though. It is what it is. Mom's going to die, I hate my father, and Covington makes me happy and is carrying me through the downtime, while my mom is with...*the asshole*.

I pull up to Covington's ridiculous gate, and I don't really hate his place as much as I once did. I don't think I ever really hated it that much, I just hated the idea that Wells could win me over, make me like him as much as I do. To be fair, I like the tension just as much as Wells does. I pushed back at him, just to see how hard he'd come after me.

There's also another thing that helped change my opinion on

the ostentatious mansion. The main reason is the man who answers the speaker when I pull up.

"Orson, it's me!"

"Very well, Ms. Carlson." The gate swings open.

I can't believe how at home I feel in this gaudy-ass place now, in a matter of weeks. Half the time I'm here, I just try to ignore the opulence and excess. Maybe one day I'll talk Covington into donating it or selling it off. I know he doesn't even want it that much; he just likes to piss off wealthy people, and I haven't figured out exactly why that is yet. I think he might hate his Wall Street colleagues more than I do.

The psychology would tell me something happened in his childhood, he had poor experiences with wealthy people, something. I don't know. To be fair, he hasn't given me much insight into his past, beyond his friends, which I use as justification for keeping my personal problems from him.

I weave around up his mile-long driveway, past the golf course and the helicopter pad and all that. I pull up to the roundabout, park, and head toward the door.

As always, Orson opens it right before I can knock or ring a doorbell.

I immediately give him a hug, probably against his wishes, but he never complains.

Instead, he politely pats me a few times on the back, and quickly gets some distance between us. "Pleasure to see you, Ms. Carlson."

"Likewise, Orson." I fake a frown at him. "Is he ready?"

"Ms. Carlson, I don't know if that dignifies a response."

I crack up laughing. "That's fair."

"Too right, ma'am. You can wait in the living room, and I'll have a go at getting him to get his act together. If you'll excuse me."

"Thank you."

He walks off, and I head for the living room.

It's crazy how every day, the moment before I see Wells, I still get the same butterflies in my stomach. I love how he can make me forget my other stresses with Mom's situation, issues with my firm, the big shelter project. I feel normal when I'm here, even though we are anything but a normal couple.

A few minutes later, Covington rounds the corner like he's been hustling to get ready.

God, he looks so hot when he dresses casual. Don't get me wrong, the man can wear a suit like no other. But I like it when he's dressed down. It makes him feel more—real.

Right now, he has on some dark designer jeans and a charcoal-gray V-neck shirt that clings to his chest and biceps. I want to rip it off him immediately.

"Don't pretend like you were ready. Orson sold you out."

"That old prick." He turns and yells, "Orson, you're fired!"

I fold my arms over my chest and shake my head. "You are not getting rid of him. He's the only reason I come over here."

Before I know what's happened, Covington's long arms reach out, and he grips my hips and yanks me over to him. His hands make their way to my cheeks, cupping my face in his palms.

"The only reason?"

I nod. "Mmhmm."

He bends down to kiss me. "Don't lie to me, Carlson. Or I shall have his employment terminated."

"I decline the offer!" Orson's voice carries into the living room, like he yelled it from the other end of the estate.

"Old bastard has some pep in him. I'll give him that."

"I could listen to you two banter in your formal jargon all day long. It's cute."

Covington kisses me, and that familiar tingling shoots into my fingers and toes.

I want to just float away, but I manage to open my eyes and say, "Where you taking me?"

"Romano Custom Tailoring."

I take a step back. "Wh-who? What?"

"I guess that's a no?" He laughs, clearly messing with me.

"No, it's not a no, dipshit. Massimo Romano's shop? That one?" I just want to make sure I have this right.

Covington shrugs. "Of course. Why?"

I realize I might be fangirling a little. His shop is amazing, though. I shake my head, trying to play it off. "Nothing. Why we going there?"

"You're excited about this." His fingers dig into my hips a little harder.

"You going to try to leverage that into some kind of deal?"

He nods. "Of course. You know how this works between us."

I grin and shake my head at him. "Seriously, what's going on?"

Covington breaks his little posturing act. "I need to buy a tux for Dexter's wedding. We're all going to wear similar ones or some shit. And we need to get you a dress."

My heartbeat pounds in my ears. I push away from him a little and look him straight in the eyes. "I'm getting a dress? From *Massimo Romano*?"

Covington's jaw clenches. "Not if you keep saying his name like that."

I laugh. Then I run my hands up Covington's broad shoulders and kiss him full on the mouth. As our hands start to explore, the kiss gets hot and heavy, and I paw at his belt, trying to get it undone.

I succeed, easily, and reach down the front of his jeans and grip his thick cock.

His eyes roll back a little when I stroke it in my palm.

He groans. "Who's gonna make us late now?"

"I'll make sure it doesn't take long."

Covington's eyes dart down to mine. "That a promise?"

I nod. "Of course." I fall to my knees and yank his jeans and briefs down his ass, freeing his dick.

I take my time, staring up at him because I'm pretty sure men enjoy it. That's something I learned a long time ago. They like acts of submission, someone kneeling before them, handing over some of their power. I don't mind, though. I find it to be an act of trust, and *that* I do value. He definitely goes down on me way more than I go down on him, so it's only fair.

I've never really done it exactly like this with anyone else.

I've sucked a few dicks, but not on my knees looking up all helpless.

With Covington, the dynamic is different than anything I've experienced. I doubt he ever purposely gives up a position of dominance or power with anyone else. It's not how to operate and be successful in the finance world. But he does it for me sometimes. Puts himself in vulnerable positions, like meeting his friends. He didn't have to do that.

So, I don't mind doing this for him.

The moment my tongue strokes the tip, he groans even louder.

A guttural, "Fuck," comes from deep in his throat, and it's so damn sexy.

I love that I can drive him as crazy as he drives me.

I start to take him into my mouth, when my phone rings. I'll be damned if my Apple Watch doesn't flash 'Mom' across it.

If it were anyone else, I'd ignore it.

I stop immediately.

Covington's eyes widen like *you fucking serious?*

I hold up a hand and try to apologize with my eyes. "I'm *so* sorry, but it's an actual emergency."

Covington glares for a second, then says, "Fine."

Now, I'm in a mad scramble. I need to figure out how to take this without him hearing anything. He's a fucking hawk. He'll deduce half the conversation and probably has a ridiculous security system all throughout the house. I bet he has videos of us fucking on them, but that's the least of my concerns right now.

I feel bad, but I walk outside before I take out my phone. She wouldn't call me if something weren't wrong.

And I'm forty minutes away from the city.

Shit. Shit. Shit.

WELLS COVINGTON

MEADOW DISAPPEARED when she took the emergency phone call, and now I can't get hold of her. I feel like I'm slowly going crazy, worrying about her, but I have to keep it together. I went and got the tux by myself, and made my best guess on a dress for Meadow, even though now I'm starting to doubt if she's even going to go to the wedding.

I know I'm probably being ridiculous. She wasn't mean, we didn't have a fight, she just said it was an emergency and bounced. I'm definitely worried. Who wouldn't be? I want to make sure she's okay. That is a rational thing, right?

I should give her a few more hours before going off the deep end. I know I should.

Now, I walk into The Gage to meet up with Dex, Cole, Harlow, and Abigail. The fucking fifth wheel. I've never been the fifth wheel in my life. I do my best to tamp down whatever this feeling is in my chest, this emptiness in the pit of my stomach that could easily turn into rage if I don't hear her voice soon.

To make things worse, Bennett Cooper keeps blowing up my damn phone. He does it again right as I walk up to them. There's no way I'll answer it in front of any of these guys. They all hate his guts, and I'm sure there are always conspiracy theories floating around that I'll go back to Cooper's law firm, and, inadvertently, a lot of their Wall Street clients would follow behind.

On a normal day, these things would be a top priority to address, but now, they're meaningless. I just want to know Meadow is okay.

How'd I go from about to get a blowjob from the woman of my dreams to jack shit in a matter of hours? I've never even lost on an investment this bad.

Dex's eyebrows rise when he sees me alone. "Where's your other half?"

Play it off. Don't let him know you're rattled. "How should I know? I have some independence, unlike the two boys in my presence who call themselves men." I fake a laugh, hoping they buy it.

Harlow rolls her eyes. "Yes, you're the epitome of refinement."

I give her a little nod, as if she meant it. "Thank you."

Abigail, surprisingly, seems the only one who has picked up on what's happening here. She reads people less in a business way, and more of an emotional way, I've noticed. In my experience, she's a decent paralegal and a hard worker, but nobody picks up on social cues like her outside of work.

Dex never knows when to shut up. "Seriously, where is she?"

Abigail nudges him with her elbow, and he gives her a look like *what?*

My eyes meet Abigail's, and I say, "It's all right, really."

"You sure?" She doesn't look convinced.

Finally, I just tell them everything that happened, sans the almost blowjob.

I don't know why I'm oversharing like this. It's so unlike me. I talk personal stuff with Cole and Dex on rare occasions, but definitely not in front of other women.

"I'm sure she'll call," says Abigail. "If it was an emergency, she probably just can't right now."

Dex and Cole look like they have no idea what to say, and Harlow looks oblivious, like she couldn't care less. I don't blame her. I would be too if I was gushing about these problems in front of myself.

I don't even know who the fuck I am right now.

"Uhh, yeah, man. She'll call. I'm sure there's an explanation," says Cole, and I can tell he really means it. He's trying.

Still, it feels patronizing. I feel pity, and I fucking hate it. I don't need anyone to pity me. I'm a goddamn billionaire with a fantastic life. My problems pale in comparison to a regular, working-class person. I'm blessed to have been born with an intellect and drive, and I don't deserve anyone's sympathy. I've done bad things, wrecked companies, destroyed careers, all to get what I wanted, just to amass more—shit.

If anyone has a front row ticket to hell for their time on earth, it's me, and I deserve it. Fortunately, I don't believe there's a hell. I believe we all end up nothing but fucking dirt one day.

I start to say something, when my phone rings again. "Excuse me," I say, much harsher than intended.

It's no secret I'm slowly morphing to pissed off every second Meadow is away from me, possibly hurting, and Bennett Cooper is pouring gas on that fire.

I walk outside onto the sidewalk, partially so nobody hears my conversation and partially because I need to breathe some fresh air. I'm sure they all assume it's Meadow, so no questions are asked.

That's what's pissing me off even more too. I'm waiting on a phone call from her, and this son of a bitch keeps getting my hopes up then dashing them when I see his name.

I swipe my phone and bring it to my ear. "The fuck do you want? I'm busy."

"Whoa, let's take about twenty percent off the top there."

"Fuck you, I'm waiting on an important phone call." I shouldn't have even given him that amount of information. Meadow is driving me mad. I feel so out of control, like I want to lash out at the world.

"Nothing could be more important than my phone calls."

He's such an arrogant prick. I know I'm not one to talk, especially with the company I keep, but he takes it to a new level.

"What do you want, Cooper? What's this game you're playing?"

"Not a game. It's simple. You know what I want. Stop fucking around and come home."

"Home? My home is in Chicago. Manhattan bores me. You bore me with your antiquated, stuffy, repugnant bullshit. You reek of desperation, unable to grasp the fact you may be aging out of the game, and you're what, thirty-eight? Flushing your family name down the toilet, first generation to not grow the firm's revenues."

He really didn't deserve all of that, but he's a big boy. Take a fucking hint.

All I want to do is text Meadow for the hundredth time and make sure everything is okay. I'd settle for calling her just to hear her voice on the voicemail. I'm mad for this woman. Everything was going perfectly, exactly how I wanted, until it wasn't.

Now, it's like bugs are crawling all over my skin. I'm obsessed with her.

"I see you have personal problems; your house is out of order. I won't contribute to that any longer. But just know one thing, Covington—"

I scoff. "What's that?"

"I wasn't lying. Circumstances are changing, and I'm giving you an opportunity. You'll be back."

"Knock sixty percent off my fee and we'll talk, Cooper."

He laughs. "Won't need to. You'll see." He hangs up before I can say anything else.

I glare at my phone. "Fuck you," I say to no one in particular.

I look around at the city, *my* city. The skyscrapers I've known since I was a child. The hustle, the money to be made everywhere I look. The promise of opportunity. Manhattan is fun, but this, this place is woven through my soul.

Then, I stare through the window at my best friends with

their fiancées. They're all just so—happy. It's a happiness that can't be found in wealth and excess. I never knew it until I met Meadow. Now, I want nothing else.

I'd give up my entire empire for a few more minutes of it with her.

I know I'm turning this whole evening into some existential threat, blowing these circumstances way out of proportion. My brain knows this, but my heart doesn't. I'm a fucking wreck.

It's right before the third act of a movie, and the tensions are amping up, the conflict is at a fever pitch. Usually, I would find this exciting, exhilarating. It would be a challenge. I can handle those things when it's a war against my brain.

My heart, it seems, is another matter entirely. It feels like it's too much and makes me wonder if I'm even worthy of a relationship with someone like Meadow. If I crack under this kind of pressure, how could I ever endure an actual relationship? How could she count on me in a time of crisis? Things are always great during the peaks, but what about the valleys? There are always valleys, and they're messy as fuck. What if I lose my shit at something like this before we're even serious?

That's the thing, though. I know it's early for her. But not for me. I'm serious about her; have been from the day we met, when she destroyed a twenty-five-million-dollar wall and completely turned my world upside down.

I stand there, staring through the window.

Dexter cracks a joke and even Harlow laughs at it.

The other half of the conflict boils up inside me even more. Bennett Cooper is up to something, and I can't see his next move clearly through the Meadow fog that clouds my brain.

I already know whatever he's up to will tear this family in front of me apart. In Cooper's mind, the Collins family stole from him. Stole his clients, his pride, damaged his ego. He's a dangerous man, and the Collins brothers started a blood feud, with me at the center of it.

There's no way I'll be able to dodge the battle as they rip each other apart.

That's all this is right now, with Meadow and with the brothers.

It's a calm before a storm.

MEADOW CARLSON

"Give me a fucking update." I should not be talking to the lady at the front desk this way. In my mind, I know she has no idea. She's just a clerical worker.

I think part of it is guilt. I wasn't there and I should've been. I was on my knees for Wells Covington when Mom collapsed into unconsciousness.

"Ma'am, she's in surgery with the best neurosurgeon in the country. That's all I can tell you at this time. They'll be out to update when they're finished."

I shake my head, trying to get out of the funk I'm in. "Okay, I'm sorry."

"It's okay. It happens. I understand, it's an emotional time. We'll do whatever we can to help."

Now, I really feel like an asshole when she's nice to me, but the rage returns when I glance over at my father, in his damn ankle bracelet as it blinks like crazy, pleading with someone on my mother's phone.

"It was an emergency, I swear. She went unconscious, and I was the only one there." He glances over at me when he says it.

Oh, fuck you, asshole.

The fact he's telling the truth pisses me off even more. I know I'm mad at myself, but I want to take it all out on him.

I look down at my phone, and Covington calls for the fifth time. I slam my finger down on the ignore button.

The worst part is I want to answer so badly. I want to let him in a little, but I just can't. Not to mention, I'm scared of what I'll say to him, how I'll treat him right now. Him and my father are the reason I'm in this position, one of them pushing me away, the other one pulling me close. I shouldn't want to be with Covington right now, and I hate myself even more for letting myself get entwined in whatever we are. Now, he's part of the shelter project and I *have* to work with him no matter what.

My life was so much simpler when it didn't involve two men.

Dad finally hangs up and our eyes meet.

He walks toward me. "I may need you to speak to my parole officer."

I let out the most sarcastic laugh possible. It's not even a laugh, more like a surprised gasp. "Right."

"Meadow, please?"

I try to hold back, but I don't see how I can. I just can't stop myself. I lower my voice so I don't cause a scene. "I should've been there. I would've been there if you hadn't fucking come home."

He glances around, as if checking to see if anyone can hear, then out of nowhere grabs me by the arm and pulls me over to a hallway.

I yank my arm away. "Don't fucking touch me or I *will* call your parole officer."

His brows narrow. "Stop acting like a child. This is serious."

"Me? I'm not the one with an ankle bracelet flashing and a goddamn parole officer."

He looks up at the ceiling, then his eyes land back on me. "We don't have time to worry about our petty differences." His eyes well up a little. "It was—" He chokes up for a second. "I'm worried about her. Really scared."

My emotions are all over the place right now. I'm scared too. Scared shitless, but I have no desire to share my feelings with the asshole in front of me. The man who let down our entire family and went away to prison.

"Fuck you. You gave up the right to care about us when you did what you did."

He can't even look at me. He just says, "I fucked up. Bad. But I'm not giving up. I'm trying."

I shake my head. I don't want to hear his bullshit excuses. "What the hell happened?"

He wipes a tear from one of his eyes. In another life, when I was a girl, I would've cared, but not now. I don't even know this man in front of me.

"I was getting her some water. She shrieked. Clutched her head. Like she had unbearable pain, then just went unconscious. She was still breathing, but it was like, like the pain was so intense it just made her pass out."

My heart pinches in my chest. "What'd you do?"

He stares at me like it's a ridiculous question. "Hauled her to the car and drove here as fast as I could. Called you on the way."

I search for anything I can to be pissed off at him about, even though he did everything right. He probably drove over a hundred and still managed to endanger them both by calling me on the phone, just to avoid me lashing out at him for not calling soon enough.

"So, she's in surgery?"

He nods. "They rushed her back the second we came in. Haven't seen her since." He looks like he's about to collapse, like prison has stolen his soul and the situation is about to take him too. He's pale, like a ghost. Just skin draped over a skeleton, barely holding on.

Part of me, in my brain, plays over and over on a loop, wondering why it can't be him, and why it has to be Mom back there. I know I shouldn't think that way, that it's wrong to wish that on another person. It makes me feel awful, but it's true. It *should* be him. He's the one who deserves it, not her.

I'm sure he would trade spots with her in an instant if he could.

"Can we just go sit down and wait?"

I glare at him, then glance over at the waiting room before I finally shrug and walk over there, leaving him behind.

He hurries after me.

The next three hours of my life are the most excruciating ever. It's like a nightmare.

Dad tries to make small talk a few times, then shuts up when I just stare at him.

His leg bounces up and down, the same nervous tic I had as a child but mastered. I thought he had too. He's the one who taught me how to beat it. You can't sit at a boardroom table and talk to investors with your damn knee shaking all over the place.

After the fourth time he attempts to make conversation, I turn to him. "We're not doing *this*. Playing catch up. Rehashing old times. I've spent years purging those memories from my brain."

He shakes his head. "I know I messed up. Really bad. But I kind of hoped you'd at least hold on to the good times, and remember that about me, even if you—"

"It's an all-inclusive package, Dad. You don't get to be the best, throw it all away, and then I just forgive and forget. That would be lying to myself, for your sake. It goes against everything you ever taught me."

He looks straight forward and nods. "I know. But I'm glad you remember the lesson."

I know exactly what he just did. Pointed out the fact I didn't purge everything, even though I told him I did.

I just look straight ahead. I should be worried about Mom, and I also know he's doing this to distract me, try to take some pain away. I'm sure it's for his benefit more than mine, though. Everything is a goddamn transaction with him.

Covington tries to call three more times, and sends me at least six text messages, leaving a voicemail every time. I want to hate him for it, but I can't. I listen to each voicemail and try not to crack because he sounds so worried.

The last one, I can hear the fear in his voice.

"Meadow, I'm really worried. Please call me back."

I can't.

I'll break down if I talk to him before I know if Mom's okay or not.

All I can think is what if this is it? What if she's gone? I wasn't there. I didn't hold her hand or talk to her right before she died. I was on my knees, staring up at Wells Covington with his dick in my mouth as she left the world.

How will I ever forgive myself for that?

I won't.

I just want to scream, punch someone, throw myself off a damn cliff.

As I work myself into a frenzy, a doctor walks out in his white coat, still scrubbed up for surgery in his PPE. He walks right toward us, and Dad and I leap out of our seats and run up to him.

He freezes in his tracks, like the fear of God just possessed his body.

"Is she okay?" Dad and I both ask at the same time.

He shakes his head. "I'm afraid I have some bad news."

Oh no, fuck! Please no!

WELLS COVINGTON

I T ' S BEEN twenty-four hours and I'm about to turn into a basket case. I'd forgotten all about this meeting with Dominic Romano, planned to cancel it even. Not now, though. I need a distraction and I need answers. I walk into the little coffee shop and have a seat across from him.

Despite the fact Meadow is clearly ignoring me, I still feel guilty for this. For having Dominic pry into her life to see what he can find out, but I want every advantage I can get. Plus, I have to know.

Romano fidgets with his cup a little. I've never known him to be nervous about anything. Usually he's cocky as fuck, confident.

Surely he doesn't feel guilty about doing his job.

"What'd you find out?"

"Nothing new, really. She has the impact fund which she keeps very discreet. You already knew that. All the money travels through a labyrinth of shell corps, dead ends. The blogs." He shrugs like *what the fuck, man? I already did this work.* "The traffic to her sites is ridiculous. Either she's a tech genius or has some serious money behind them. Her tracks are seriously covered on all of it. Domain names registered to different entities. Like I said last time, before a certain point, there's nothing. Literally nothing. Like she appeared in the world out of thin air."

"You didn't find anything on her mother? I know she has a mom who's still alive."

"Nothing. I can't even verify that her real name is Meadow Carlson."

I straighten up and ball my hands into fists. "You think this is worth taking your fiancée out on my goddamn yacht?"

This time, his jaw clenches. "I'm getting you everything I can, asshole. This is the best you're getting from anyone, trust me."

I know he's right. What the fuck is she hiding? Why do I care so much? I'm lashing out irrationally, something I never do.

Finally, I just nod. "Okay then."

"Yeah, thanks." Dominic gives me a dirty look, gets up, and leaves.

I sit there, contemplating. I'm frustrated, but there's more to it than that. That's the emotional reaction from my intimate connection with Meadow. There are other forces at play here. It's my curiosity. I have to know more about her. When someone tells me the information isn't available, I want it even more.

If there's one thing I love about Meadow Carlson, it's the fact she's not boring. She's the furthest thing from it.

Her pushing me away only ramps the intensity up to eleven.

I think about the way we fuck too. Never in my life have I experienced anything like being inside her, staring into her eyes, our hearts pounding against each other.

This whole goddamn thing is like driving in the dark toward a cliff, knowing I'm going off the edge at any second, but I don't care.

That's right. I don't care. Not one fucking bit.

She's mine. Maybe she doesn't think we should be together, but I'll show her, prove it to her, make her understand. When this is done, she'll know I don't give up, that I'll go to hell and back if I have to, as long as I'm with her.

She can't hide forever.

MEADOW CARLSON

IT'S BEEN days since the hospital incident. Dad and I are at home, and Mom is with us. They resected as much of the tumor as possible, inserted some radiation wafers, and want to start her on chemotherapy, but the doctor isn't hopeful. He kept saying the word 'aggressive' over and over. *"Too aggressive, very aggressive, aggressive and rapidly growing, abnormally aggressive."*

I wanted to claw his eyes out every time he said it.

Mom pulled through, barely, but hospice is taking over. She'll have a nurse here full time. She'll be on morphine and steroids to control the swelling in her brain.

It's not good.

She has a month, tops.

The worst part is, I feel happy about it. Happy that she didn't die while I was with another man, forty-five minutes away. I shouldn't feel happy right now, feel the relief that I do, simply because it eases my conscience and I've been given a second chance to get this right.

I should be doing everything she needs, every second of the day. That's what I owe her. That's what I *want* to do for her.

After they have her situated in a hospital bed in her bedroom, the nurse and techs leave the room, and Dad and I walk up to her bedside.

"I'm sorry, Mom."

She reaches out and squeezes my hand. "Stop saying that."

I shake my head and it takes everything to keep from breaking down. This shit is *not* fair. This whole situation, this world.

"It's okay. You have a life." Dad says the words from behind me.

I wheel around on him. "Don't!" I point a finger up at him.

He takes a step toward me. His brow furrows. "It's true. Stop beating yourself up."

"You're not my father. You don't get to tell me how to feel." I look at him and sneer.

"Enough!" Mom's voice booms through the room.

It must've taken everything in her to get that out, and I immediately feel terrible that she had to do it. That I can't just let this go with Dad. I just can't.

Dad and I spin around and rush to the bedside because she reaches up for her head and winces in pain.

"Mom, are you okay? I'm sorry."

We both lean over, probably too much, effectively smothering her personal space.

She waves us both back, then glares.

That's the thing about my mother. She never glares. This is serious.

Her eyes dance back and forth between us. "I am *tired* of you two fighting, butting heads, being the stubborn—" She pauses like she doesn't want to say it, but goes ahead anyway. "*Asses* that you both are. I am dying right now. *Dying*. I'm only going to get worse. All I want is for my old family—" She starts trembling, tears streaming down her eyes.

"Mom."

Dad and I lean back over. He grabs a tissue, and I take her hand.

She waves us off and continues through the sobs. "My old family to just get along. Even if it's fake, I don't care, just fake it for me, please."

The pain in her voice almost kills me on the spot.

"I want to remember what the best times of my life were like one more time before I'm gone. Then you can go back to whatever you were before all this."

I nod to her and my eyes drift over to Dad, and he has tears streaming down his cheeks. Our eyes lock, and in that moment, a deal is made. An understanding.

I nod at her. "Okay, I promise. I'm sorry, whatever you want." I squeeze her hand a little tighter, willing to say anything just to make her feel normal and okay for a few more seconds, to ease her pain.

"Me too, babe. Me too. Anything you want. I'm sorry too."

I don't think I've ever seen my mother this upset in my life. I think it speaks to her character. She has to be on her deathbed with her loved ones ripping her heart open before she'll lash out at anyone.

I think Dad and I secretly admire that she can control herself like that, forgive so easily, treat everyone with kindness. It's just not in the two of us, and this is going to be a real fucking struggle to do this for her.

She deserves it, though. I should've never lost sight of that fact. I should've been pretending all along, even if I told my father to fuck off the second we were out of the room.

Mom waves us off. "I want to sleep for a little while. And pretend I didn't just get angry at the two of you."

"Mom…" My word trails off as I reach for her.

"Go, please."

I glance over at Dad and it's that look that says, *yeah, we both fucked up badly.*

He nods, and we walk out of the room.

As we head toward the living room, my phone rings, and I don't think I can handle any more guilt than what I just went through. I need to answer. Talk to *him.*

I swipe the phone and answer. "Hey."

It takes a few seconds for him to respond, like he's surprised and expected it to be another missed call. Why does he have to be so perfect for me? I miss him so much. I never thought I could feel this way about a man. But how am I supposed to handle everything with my mom and be with him right now? I literally can't. She needs every second of my attention.

Finally, he just says, "Hey."

"Look, I'm—"

It's like he snaps out of his daze and is fully cognizant now. "Doesn't matter. Are you okay?"

His voice is so commanding, and his question says it all. The urgency in his words drives the point home even harder, and now I feel like an even bigger piece of shit for putting him through this. He sounds like he's done nothing but worry about me, twenty-four seven the last few days.

"Yes. I'm fine, and I'm—"

"Can I see you?"

I glance around. Dad is pretending to ignore my conversation.

"I can't—" My heart hurts so badly, the second I say it. It's like the walls are closing in and I can't breathe at all. "I just can't right now, I'm sorry."

Silence.

Deafening silence.

"Look, Meadow, if things are moving—"

"It's not that." I put anything I can into my words to convince him it's the truth. Why can't I just tell him? Why can't I open up to a man I clearly care about?

I feel Dad's gaze on me. I can sense him taking in every bit of information from this call that he can, filing it away in case it's useful at some point in the future. The same way I do and Covington does.

But it gives me the answer to my question. Why can't I open up to Wells?

I did that once before with a man I trusted, and he crushed me. I clearly still haven't recovered from it, and I clearly can't do this. I just can't.

"Look, I'm sorry about everything, and you can do whatever you want with the real estate project. I just can't see you anymore." I hang up the phone before he can respond, and it's like getting drop kicked in the chest. I have to be pale as a ghost, just anger and hurt ripping through my veins.

Dad starts to say something, and I walk into another room. I can't with him right now.

I won't lash out at anyone else. I won't hurt anyone else today.

I think I've done enough damage.

WELLS COVINGTON

I WALK through the bullpen when one of the analysts walks up to me.

"Hey, what do you think about—"

I freeze in my tracks and he stops his question mid-sentence at the sight of me. "What do I think about? More than you, apparently. If I wanted my own thoughts, I'd fucking ask myself, wouldn't I?"

This kid, probably a Stanford grad, damn near quakes in his shoes.

Doesn't matter.

I turn around, and everyone is staring right at me.

I point a finger at all of them and grit my teeth. "You will earn. Or you will get. The. Fuck. Out! Am I clear?"

About that time, Lipsy walks up and nudges me up to my office. "Hey there, boss, we got that thing, right?" He gestures over his shoulder up the stairs.

"What?" I squint my eyes and stare at him.

He repeats his little head gesture, urgently. "The meeting, with the fucking shit, c'mon man. You remember."

I glare around at all the PMs and analysts and other bullshit positions at the firm, then follow Lipsy up the stairs to the executive level offices.

Once we're in my office, I turn to him. "What the fuck is happening out there? Why don't you have the troops in line?"

He snickers a little and holds up his hands. "Okay, Mussolini, I never thought I'd say this, but let's ease up on the office fascism."

I stare at him blankly, so caught up in my own little world. I feel like a goddamn irrational zombie, walking around in a daze, lashing out at anyone in sight.

I have to figure this shit out. I've always had a course charted, where I was going, a goal in mind. Now, I'm floating aimlessly in a fucking boat with no sail, no wind.

"Lips?"

"Yeah, boss?"

I walk up and put a hand on his shoulder, like all that other shit didn't just happen in the office. "I'm fucked. My crystal ball is gone. You've gotta be my Dennis Hopper."

Lipsy's eyes widen, and pure panic spreads across his face. "No, no, no, I can't be the Scooter Flatch. I may be a drunk but we're not in Indiana."

"You have to be. I have things I need to do. I need some time."

Finally, he nods and heads toward the door. Once he's there, he stops in his tracks and turns to me, his eyes glued to mine, then he smiles. "Okay, Kemo Sabe. I'll be your Gene Hackman and measure the goal for the team. Just this once." He starts to leave.

I holler, "Lips."

He spins back around. "Yeah?"

"Thanks."

He tosses me a fake salute and heads out the door. I have to go see someone. I need to get my head right.

* * *

"THIS IS NORMAL. I know it will be hard for you to believe, Covington, but it's called caring for someone. And even you are capable of it."

I'm on the couch at Dr. Jenkins' office, staring up at the ceiling. Haven't been back here since I was a teenager. Never needed a shrink after that. It was the only place I could think to come that might give me any kind of answers.

I don't respond to her. I already told her everything that has happened in the past few months of my life.

"That emotion you're feeling—"

This time I interrupt. "Don't even fucking say it."

She laughs. "Okay, I won't say the actual word. But I don't have to. You're the smartest man I've ever met. You were the smartest man I'd ever met when you were eleven. I'm sure you can figure it out. And whether you say it or not, you know it's true. In fact, I'd be willing to bet you knew it before you came in here, and you were hoping I'd have a different explanation for you."

"Doesn't matter." I sit up and stare at her. "She wants nothing to do with me right now. I can't crack her shell. I've tried from every angle. Why do you think I'm here right now? Desperation. I thought I'd made my way in, got through her armor, but whatever happened, she's replaced it with something even stronger."

She stands up, walks over, and sits down next to me. She's aged so much, but I still see the same woman who helped me through my childhood, helped make sense of who I am. That I did in fact belong in this world.

"What would you do if there was an investment and nothing ever lined up right? They didn't want your money, no matter how hard you tried, how many good offers you made, but you just knew, deep inside, it was something special? That the potential there was unheard of. Something that would change the world. A once in a lifetime opportunity."

The light bulb goes off. I snap out of my daze because the answer is so clear and was always right in front of me. "I wouldn't sleep. Wouldn't rest. I'd think fifteen moves in advance, and be as patient as I needed to be, to let every single chess piece align exactly how I wanted them to, then I'd strike with full force until I'd pinned every person who told me no into full blown submission, and I wouldn't take my heel off their neck until they gave me what I wanted."

She lets out a small sigh. "Okay, well I *like* the intensity, but maybe, you know, adjust your approach to accommodate for a woman you care about. But I think you'll be just fine. This is all normal."

I look at her, and I want to believe her more than anything. I know I'm about to go all out, do whatever the hell I have to do. I will not fail in the effort department. I can't.

Only one thing bothers me about the approach.

Meadow is just like me. It's possible she might be uncrackable.

I guess I'll find out soon.

She puts a hand on my shoulder, and I stand up and give her a hug. "Thanks, doc."

"Any time. You know that. My door is always open."

I walk out with a renewed confidence. This is a ballsy play, but you either go big or go home. Live by the sword, die by the sword. Pick your idiom. I won't stop. I will never stop going after Meadow Carlson—ever.

MEADOW CARLSON

DAD DOES the dishes while I go over some work stuff on my laptop. I'm so far behind, I don't know how I'll ever catch up. I really need to hire someone to run things while I'm here with Mom, but by the time I train them…

The moment I think about how little time I have left with my mother, and all the time I squandered that I could've spent with her, tears stream down my cheeks. I always thought I'd go out and conquer everything I wanted, and then we'd have years to make up for it. My hand comes to my mouth as it all crashes into me when I think about the fact she'll be gone in a matter of months, maybe less.

I try not to have a breakdown in front of my father, but it all hits me at once, the finality sets in. The hardest thing is, I can't take any of it out on him, even though I want to. I made a promise. I hate the world right now, and I have to be nice to him, or at least pretend to be.

What makes things even worse is I want to let him back in so badly, the same way I want to tell Wells everything, let him be by my side too. All the memories from my childhood flood back every time I look at him.

He catches me from the corner of his eye, sets his plate down, and rushes over. He manages to stop himself before he puts an arm around me. It might be the way I glare right at him when he's about to do it.

He sits down. Just sits there next to me but doesn't say anything for a long few seconds. Finally, he just nods and says, "I know."

"No, you don't." The words come out of nowhere.

He nods. "I may have been in prison, estranged from you and your mom." He turns to face me. "But I still know. I still feel both of you with my heart, all the time. It didn't just go away."

I don't want to open up to him, but who else can I talk to about this? I need to get it out, purge everything from my system, so I can be there for my mom. "You don't understand. I haven't been here for her. Not the way I should've been."

He starts to reach for my forearm, then pulls his hand back. "Yeah, I *do* know." His eyes roll up to the ceiling and he lets out a sigh. "And it's my fault."

"What?"

"Come on, Meadow. We both know you ended up like me, even when I prayed every night you'd be more like your mother. I knew it the second you were born, though. You can't not work. You can't not go after everything you want. But it's my fault because I did what I did, and I went away. If I'd been here, you would've been here much more, spent more time with her. I soiled this house, this family. I shit all over this place and made it impossible for you to find comfort within these walls. I know you still came over, but not as much as you would have, and it's my fault."

"How do you know how often I came over here?"

He shakes his head at me. "I still talked to your mother all the time when I was inside."

My blood starts to boil a little at the thought, but I have to push it all back down because my mother is dying of cancer. She told me she cut him off. She lied to me.

As if he can tell exactly what I'm thinking, which is something else I hate about him, he says, "She wanted to tell you. But c'mon."

My brows narrow at him. "C'mon what?"

"You knew the whole time. You lied to yourself about it. I know how your brain works better than anyone. There's no way in hell you thought she'd cut me off. So don't get mad at her for lying about it when you lied to make yourself feel better. You did the same thing she did, theoretically."

"Theoretically." I mock him when I say it. He's such a fucking asshole. A brilliant one, but still a dick. Finally, I nod. "Okay, maybe I did know. Maybe I should blame you. You should've cut yourself off after what you did."

"Blame me if you want. I deserve it."

I sneer. "Don't do that. Don't fucking play victim when Mom is dying in the other room. Jesus."

"I'm not looking for pity. But, Meadow?"

"What?"

"I never stopped loving her. And I never stopped loving you."

I shake my head at him. "Really? Why'd you do what you did then?"

"I could apologize a thousand times and it'd never be enough."

"You're goddamn right it wouldn't." I lower my voice, so Mom doesn't hear, since I'm supposed to be playing nice. This needs aired out, though. Since he's here. I sit up straight and point a finger at him. "We were perfect. We were the best family. I was so h-happy." Goddamn it. So many emotions in this house. I don't want to look weak in front of him. I don't want him to know he still gets to me, but I've buried this pain for over a decade. "Why couldn't you have just kept being a professor? Why couldn't you just work at the college, then come home to us every night? Instead of starting that goddamn firm."

"Do you want the truth?"

I nod. "Yeah, what the fuck else would I want?"

"A lie, because the truth might be difficult to hear."

"When you want to help people, you tell them the truth. When you want to help yourself, you tell them what they want to hear."

He smiles the second I start saying the quote. "So, you do remember."

I scoff. "I remember everything. A curse you gave me, according to you."

"Thomas Sowell is a brilliant man."

"I know, I heard all about him constantly, when I *had* a father."

He winces at that. "Look, Meadow, I didn't feel alive when I was teaching at the college. I did briefly. But when I started that firm, it was magic. It was going to provide financial security for you and your mother and our family for generations to come. I just... I just became consumed by it. Had to do anything to win, anything to get an edge, take on every risk I could, just to see if I could beat it."

My hands ball into fists. "Why didn't *we* make you feel alive? Me and Mom. That should've been enough for you."

He shakes his head. "You did. It's hard to describe. You and your mother always held my heart. Every damn square inch of it belonged to you two. My brain... You know how it is. You know how it just goes and goes and never shuts off, and you have to constantly feed it data, information, events, then stitch them all together just for a few minutes of relief, just to get that rush when you break the code. That's what the firm did for me, something I couldn't do reciting theories to students who just wanted a grade to satisfy some degree requirements. It was mindless, dull."

I've never asked him what I'm about to. I never looked into it because I didn't want to know. It's a miracle I was able to distance myself from it to this day. It was in the papers when I was a teenager, but I avoided them like the plague. "What exactly did you do? To end up in prison?"

His eyes widen in surprise. "What?"

"I said what did you do?"

His eyes dart around, like maybe it's a trick question. "I-I, uhh, I don't understand."

"I don't know what you did. All I know is you were guilty and went to prison."

"How is that possible?"

I fold my arms over my chest. "I didn't want to know. But I do now."

He eyes me for a while, then swallows. "I got inside information on a few different trades. I learned one company was about to be rewarded a huge government military contract through an old associate who didn't realize I'd opened up a firm and spoke to me off the record. Another friend told me about a merger about to happen, a small tech company being bought up by a public one. Multiple arbitrage situations."

"It's not arbitrage if it's illegal. Fuck."

"The firm was young, and we needed capital. We needed a few big plays to really start moving major weight, to get respect on the Street. To bring in big clients. I was the only real name, and the other young partners were brilliant, but hadn't proven themselves. We were going to get crushed in a year if we didn't inflate our portfolios."

"So, your partners, they in prison too? Or did they just make an example out of you?"

He shakes his head. "They didn't know. I wanted to protect them in case there was blowback, but you have to remember, Meadow, this was before the mortgage collapse. This kind of thing happened all the time. Manhattan was trading on insider information daily. It was the only way we could compete."

"Sounds like excuses to me. Sounds like you would've been happier hanging out at the house and day trading. Wouldn't have lost your family." I can't believe he threw us all away, just to make money. "Why'd you end up in prison and not just pay fines? Isn't that what they do to you assholes when you get caught? You have to defraud old ladies out of their pensions to go to prison, and even then, half of them get released early."

"The DA was young and ambitious. Ran on a populist platform of ending corruption and coming down hard on billionaire investors, even though I wasn't a billionaire. Not even close. I was a big name though, in the economics world. Advised presidents. DA wanted headlines, to make a name for himself, and he used mine to do it."

I never saw any of that coming when I was younger. "I idolized you. You were my hero, even after you left the university. I had to watch men in jackets come into *this* fucking house, and perp walk you out the front door." I point toward the living room and do my best to hold it together. "Right through there." I point at the stairs. "While I hugged that post, watching it all."

His eyes move down to the ground. "I know."

"You were my best friend. I love Mom and she knows that, but I lost everything when I lost you. Do you know what it was like, at fourteen, to lose the only person in the world who could understand me? Who got *me*?"

A tear rolls down his cheek. "I'm sorry."

"Sorry is for being late to pick me up from school. You left me with nothing when I needed you the most. They took everything but the house. I had to set up some online businesses for extra passive income, just so Mom didn't have to work three jobs. We had to start all over. And you're *sorry*?"

The worst part of this whole thing is, I want to forgive him. So damn bad. If he only knew how many plane tickets I've purchased, telling myself I would go see him, then cancelled them at the last minute. The time I drove ten hours in the night planning to just hear his voice, then turned around and came back.

"I don't expect you to ever forgive me, or to stop hating me. I want to be here with your mother, and to help take care of you, and it eats me up inside, because I know how bad you don't want me around."

I shake my head, tears rolling down my face. "That's the thing, Dad. I *do* want you around. I want you around so bad. I always have. That's what makes it so hard, because you deserve my hate, and it's my brain making me treat you this way, because I stopped using my heart the day you went away."

That's not totally true, what I just told him. It *was* true, until recently. But it doesn't matter—circumstances, once more, are preventing me from using my heart *again*.

He stands up awkwardly, like he doesn't know if he should hug me or leave me alone. "Well, I really am sorry. And I'll only be here for as long as your mom needs me. And then I'll be out of your hair, okay?"

His cordial tone almost breaks me, as if this is just some kind of transaction. I know he's trying to just keep the peace and do whatever makes things easier on me.

"I'll do my best to make it easy on both of us too. Until, well, you know."

He puts a hand on my shoulder. It seems like just an instinctive move, like something a father would do.

It feels so good. For that split-second, I actually feel safe, protected, understood when he does it.

"Thank you."

Then, his hand is gone, and the emptiness fills me again.

* * *

MOM IS SLEEPING and didn't want to be disturbed. Dad is there, and I have no clue when I might get another chance to get caught up on some work, so I came into the office, but I'm literally ten minutes away and can rush home in an instant if I need to. I've been a machine the past hour.

Fifteen minutes to go over a list with my assistant, thirty minutes for Zoom meetings with several investors about the shelter project, and I've hammered out seven hundred words of a blog article in the last fifteen minutes.

This is the most normal I've felt in weeks.

I needed it, badly. A distraction, even if it's for an hour.

I finish up, apologize profusely to my assistant for being so absent and difficult to reach. I haven't told anyone what's going on because my family matters are private—and I'm out the door, heading back to Mom's before she wakes up.

It's a beautiful day, and I think to myself how it really would have been a beautiful day, walking out of the office and into this weather three months ago. Now, I'm not sure any day will ever be beautiful again.

No matter how hard I try to forget, how hard I try to focus on Mom, everything that's coming my way in the next month, I still can't stop thinking about Wells Covington. I can still feel myself wrapped in his arms. He's the opposite of what I should want, and yet I want more. Never in my life did I think a man would make me feel safe, like nothing could hurt me, but somehow, he pulled it off, even if it was brief.

I take the last step down the stoop and turn to head down the sidewalk.

"A rare sighting in public."

I freeze. Just stop in my tracks. I don't have to look. I know the voice, and I hate that the sound of him elicits that reaction from me.

It's like pure comfort envelopes me, but I have to pretend to be upset. I have to push him away, and I don't want to. It's just necessary.

As I turn, and he comes into view, my fingers start to tremble. It's not fear but pure excitement. Adrenaline floods my veins, shooting through my body at the sight of him. Why does he have to make this more difficult than it is?

Maybe you should tell him, so he understands.

Horrible idea. Maybe something vague, but I can't let him in right now. If I let him comfort me, which I know he would do, it'll just be another distraction. I saw how that worked out last time.

My eyes meet his, and my brows stitch themselves together. "I can't do this right now."

He's wearing a suit, and I want to smile so badly at his ornery, boyish grin in that five-thousand-dollar outfit, but I can't. It's not fair to lead him on, give him some kind of hope.

"What are we doing?" He takes a step toward me.

My heartrate spikes, like it does for him and only him. "Look, I'm sorry for just ghosting you. It wasn't fair."

"Damn right it wasn't. Social protocol would dictate I deserve some kind of explanation."

Maybe I've misjudged him a little, too. He's so calm and collected right now—mature. I thought he'd—I don't know, react differently. Be angry, be forceful, something. A small part of me is a little upset he doesn't seem to have a care in the world right now.

I know I owe him the explanation, and yet, all I want to do is make him go away so I don't want to kiss him. "I'm serious, Wells. I can't do this."

I need to get back home. I do *not* want my mother to wake up without me there, the same way I wasn't there when I should've been for the last several years. I won't do that to her again.

I start to walk down the street, and his hand shoots out and catches me by the forearm.

My reaction is threefold. First surprise, then a jolt of electricity fires through my limbs at his strong fingers clutching me. It's the anger that follows that wins out.

My gaze moves to his hand, then up to his eyes. I say through my teeth, "Let go of me."

This time, he's not cordial at all. All those things I was hoping for earlier, yeah, I misjudged him, apparently. He wasn't calm. His feelings were boiling up, and he was doing everything he could to suppress them, but one thing is clear in his eyes right now. He *will* get an explanation.

His jaw clenches and his stare doesn't stray from my face. "What happened?"

I yank my arm away from him. "Don't fucking grab me like that again."

I start to shoulder my way past him to get down the sidewalk, and he cuts me off, so my face is now inches away from his broad chest. I'm trapped. He's huge and there's no way I can boulder through him.

"Get out of my goddamn way."

He smirks down at me, like I'm some kind of pesky child, and it makes me want to punch his smug face. He makes a show of leaning down so his mouth is next to my ear. "Do I look like a man who will accept the shit you're trying to do right now?"

Jesus, his tone. I don't know if I've ever been so turned on and enraged at the same time. He's seriously holding me hostage, being a big stupid ape Neanderthal fuckface, and it's doing something for me. He's never been like this before.

Before I can say anything, he whisper-growls, "I'm owed an explanation. Let's have it."

I can tell butting heads with him will get me absolutely nowhere, so I look him in the eye and give him the bare minimum. "I had a family emergency. And I'm still dealing with it, and will be dealing with it for the foreseeable future."

"Family?" He scoffs.

Asshole!

The reaction I just received was not what I had expected. Why? My brain goes into overdrive. He scoffed at the word 'family.'

Shit, he knows.

I don't know how he knows, but he does. How much he has learned is the key variable. If he'd figured everything out, he would've said way more than that, and there's no way he could. I've covered my tracks on every detail possible.

"It's true." I do my best to sell him on that alone. It won't work, so I don't know why I do it, but I do. Why can't he be another dipshit who can be easily manipulated?

No, I bet he investigated me the first time he saw me. Got every piece of information possible.

"Okay, then." He pushes a few strands of hair behind my ear, and I want to melt into him so damn badly.

I just can't. This is not a time in my life to give in to what *I* want to do. I've done that enough already.

He plays with my hair, and I don't stop him because it feels so damn good. "I'm sorry for whatever happened."

Now, I just want to break down. Just so he'll hold me for two seconds.

You have to get back home.

I look away. "I truly am sorry for what happened. I've been a mess. But I really have to get going."

I start to walk past him, and suddenly his mouth is fused to mine. The second it happens, it's like heaven, and I kiss him back very briefly, before breaking free.

His mouth lingers next to my ear. "I'll be happy to help you deal with your family emergency in any way I can but, Meadow?"

He pulls back, and I stare up at him, still halfway stunned from the kiss.

"Fight it all day long, but you're mine. I want everything. I won't stop until I get it. We both know the universe is random chaos and fate is bullshit, but the two of us seem to be an exception. I'm here, and I will always be here, for however long it takes." He stares right into my eyes. "That is a promise." He turns away and walks off, disappearing into the crowd of people streaming past us.

I stand there, brainless, just staring in the direction he walked, and I lift a finger and touch my lips where he just kissed me.

Fucking fuck.

WELLS COVINGTON

THIS WOMAN IS INFURIATING, in the best kind of way.

I can do a Fourier series in my head, but I can't figure out Meadow Carlson.

Family issues?

Why the hell would she have family issues if she's hidden her entire past from public view? It doesn't make any sense. I need more information. I need goddamn data. Dominic Romano fucked me out of a weekend on my yacht. I know there's more to be had than what he has provided.

I stand up and pace back and forth in my living room. No, I know that's not true. It's not at all unlikely that Meadow has made the information impossible to find. I think she's the only person I've met who's more intelligent than me, and she's definitely more tech savvy with her network of blogs and media content.

My impulse is to think she's just afraid of whatever this is we're doing, afraid to commit. But I can tell from the look in her eyes. I could tell the second I kissed her. There's something going on, and I'm getting half-truths. I'll find out what the hell it is.

I have to. I'm drowning when she's not next to me. I can't breathe without her.

There's an emptiness inside me that makes me want to rage,

that depresses me, that reaches into my stomach and twists every time I think about her, and the reality we can't be together sets in. I refuse to accept it. It's not an option.

Orson walks in from the hallway. He quickly surveys the information laid out in front of him, me brooding around the room. "Everything okay, sir? Work issues?"

I shake my head. "No."

He remains completely still, but his eyes roam up and down. "Meadow issues?"

I nod, because there's no way in hell he doesn't know what's going on. He's a smart man. "I don't really have any—" I look away then back at him. "Experience with this kind of thing. You ever been infatuated with a woman?"

Orson walks over and takes a seat on the couch. "Once. A very long time ago."

I flop down on the sofa next to him and sigh. "It's brutal. I don't know why it bothers me so much."

"You're used to problems you can solve. Having all the variables, ordering them correctly, and making an assessment."

I nod. "Exactly."

He smiles. "That doesn't work here. You're dealing with forces that have no order, pure chaos. That's what makes it beautiful."

"So poetic," I say in a half-mocking tone.

He laughs. "Maybe it's because she shows your weaknesses, magnifies them, makes you vulnerable."

"Weaknesses?" I laugh.

He nods. "Yes, there's no doubt you're an outlier when it comes to analyzing investments, amassing resources, cataloguing a library in publication order. Love does not follow those rules. It's far more special than industry, buildings, politics, capital, intellectual property."

"Whoa." I hold up both hands. "Let's not get carried away with the goddamn L-word."

I expect him to laugh at the joke, but he looks right at me and just stares.

All the air leaves my lungs, deflating me in my seat. "I sound like such a pussy. I feel like one because I can't figure this out. I want to solve her."

"Maybe she doesn't need to be *solved*."

"What? Everything is a problem to solve. That's how the world operates, that's how life exists. It's how it evolves, solving problems."

"Then perhaps you need to boil it down, like you would with any other problem. I don't think you've been approaching this like you normally would with a problem, because *love*—" he stares at me when he says it, "—is irrational."

I stand up almost immediately and point a finger at him. "You may be on to something." I pause and stare at him, then draw a blank again. "All these damn feelings involved. What do I know? There's pain in her eyes. I can feel it every time I look at her. Something is going on, and she doesn't want to let me in. Says she has a family issue." I walk around and none of it means fucking anything. I have no clue. The answers don't come to me. My brain is just—idle, a blank canvas. I want to scream.

Orson says, "Is there something she cares about that you control? Maybe start with that?"

I freeze in my tracks, and the information highway in my brain opens up, full bore traffic, nothing but bandwidth. Just like that. My eyes widen, and I say, "Fuck me."

"I'd rather not, sir."

My shoulders bounce as we both laugh, and I finally compose myself. "I've been so goddamn blind. It was right in front of me. I know what to do."

MEADOW CARLSON

DAD and I have gotten along extremely well since our talk after Mom's stint in the hospital.

I tell myself I'm doing it for Mom, to make her feel better around us, but I know it's not totally true. Every time I look at him, he wins me back a little more. Maybe he *has* changed. Maybe he's not really the asshole he turned into before. Perhaps his investment firm was an addiction. I know it was. I try to rationalize letting him back in. I tell myself he was sick. He became obsessed. It's not so different from a drug addict relapsing, or an alcoholic or gambler.

He needed treatment, support, and I cut him loose and wrote him off because I didn't define his issue as a disease.

That's not how I would treat anyone else who suffered from addiction. I have charities and investments that help those very people, but when it came to my own family, I didn't see the writing on the wall.

Then, I remember how he crushed me. Crushed my mother.

Regardless, I'm starting to feel a little normal again, like a part of me has returned, completed what makes me, well, me.

We sit around the living room, waiting impatiently while the hospice doctor is in with Mom for a visit. We can't bring ourselves to even speak. I let out a deep breath I hadn't realized I was holding.

This is torture, and I know soon, Mom will be gone, and Dad will be the only family I have left. Then, he'll be back in prison, and I'll be all alone. I wish we had more time for this little experiment with him back in our lives, with her happy and healthy, instead of it being so forced. That's how it was supposed to happen, if it ever happened at all.

Dad and I sit there, trying to appear hopeful, even though we both know what's about to happen. Mom has been declining fast. Headaches, dementia-type symptoms, mixing up our names, sudden bursts of irritation. I think some of it is the steroids they're giving her, and some of it might be the tumor growing.

I've never believed in a higher power. It's always seemed silly, something us humans created to help ease the cycle of life and give us a sense of purpose. But like all humans, I succumb to that need and pray over and over I get some more time. Maybe we get a miracle, despite the odds I've calculated meticulously from the second I found out about her diagnosis.

The doctor walks out of her room, and Dad and I leap to our feet and stomp toward him. I almost feel a little sorry for the guy. His face tells the whole story, though, confirms every instinct I had and hoped against. I know Dad sees it too.

He shakes his head. "I'm sorry. Wish I had better news, but I don't think she has much time left. I've started her on morphine to help ease the pain."

Dad and I both do our best to hold back the tears.

The doctor takes a deep breath. "This conversation is hard, but my recommendation to you would be to go ahead, say good-byes, those types of conversations. If there's any end-of-life paperwork you need ironed out, I would get that done. I honestly cannot say when cognitive capacity may be gone, but my guess would be soon. Again, I'm very sorry."

I sniff hard and nod. "O-okay, thank you."

"Yeah, th-thank you," says Dad.

"I'll have some additional paperwork for you guys, but it can wait. Just be with her as much as possible, get every second you can. We'll make her comfortable." He gives Dad a pat on the shoulder, then walks past us to the front door.

Dad and I stand there for a minute, both dreading walking through that door. I know my mother has told me constantly not to beat myself up, but I'm seriously hammering myself like a boxing speed bag right now.

I always had this picture of us; me growing old, working less. This mental image of sitting on the deck, drinking wine, going to Italy or France and checking out the young waiters together, her living into her eighties or nineties.

Fuck cancer.

Dad hesitates for a second, and for the first time in a long time, I feel terrible for him. In my heart, I know how much he loves my mother, how he hasn't even looked at another woman since he met her. He looks like he's going to hang back and let me go in first, but I reach down and take his hand, and lead him into the room next to me. Even with everything between us, I don't want to do this alone, and I know he doesn't want to either.

The second he sees Mom his hand starts to tremble.

She rolls her head over to look at us and still manages to smile when her eyes catch me holding his hand. It's literally about the only thing that gets me through this moment.

"Hey, guys."

I sniff again and do anything I can to hold back the tears. Dad's a damn mess, trying to do the same. We make our way to the bed, and Dad walks around and sits next to her. Each of us take one of her hands.

"I'm dying." She says it like she's already at peace with it.

It's so crazy to me. Dad and I are the scientific brains, the ones who should be able to accept this, and we're struggling the most. Mom has always been this way, totally resilient, so accepting of whatever comes her way while Dad and I always fought against life, problems, the laws of the universe, no matter what.

I wish I could be more like her.

Even on her deathbed, she's so strong, stately almost.

"What did the doctor tell you?" I say.

"Everything he just told you, I'm sure."

Dad can't even bring himself to speak yet, so I try to do enough talking for both of us.

"I'm so sorry."

She lightly shakes her head. "Don't feel sorry for me. I have no regrets, and I'm not dead yet."

Dad pulls her hand up to his face and kisses her knuckles.

She stares at him for a long moment, like she's struggling to think, then says to him, "Don't blame yourself for this. I know you will, but what you did has nothing to do with this, okay?"

He looks away.

"Robert, look at me."

Slowly, he turns back.

"You are the love of my life. You were always the only one."

Dad's lip quivers, like his words are caught in his throat. "I would do anything to do it all over again."

"I know," says Mom. She looks at me, then back at Dad. "You still have time to make up for things. Please, both of you, that's the only thing I want. For you to forgive each other. I always knew my purpose was this family. I screwed up as much as anyone too. We all did. But the best thing I can do is use this situation to bring us back together before I'm gone."

What she's saying is so damn difficult. I hate the man next to her, and yet I love him at the same time. How is that even possible?

They both stare at me, as if this all rests on my shoulders, but what am I supposed to do? Mom could basically be gone any day at any moment.

I look at Dad then back at Mom and say, "I'll try. I promise." I don't want to lie to my mother and tell her everything will be fine. That's not fair, it's not who I am. I kiss her on the forehead. "I'll give you two a few minutes."

I know if I sit there, I'll do all the talking and Dad will be a pile of mush. This will force him to say the things he needs to say to her.

"I love you, sweetie."

I break down in tears and hug her. "I love you too, Mom."

I wait until I've stood up, turned around, and my back is to her before I cover my mouth. I just need to get through the door, then I can break down. The worst part is I feel so terrible for my mom, but I'm just so mad at myself. So angry at the world in general. This wasn't the plan. It wasn't supposed to happen this way.

I walk from the room and close the door, but I can't even move once it's shut. My feet are like concrete, like giant magnets attached to the ground, my legs too heavy to lift. I want to hit the wall so hard it breaks my fingers.

I stand there for a second, and I hear Mom start to talk. I shouldn't stand here. Shouldn't listen in on this moment between them, but I can't move.

"I never saw things playing out like this."

Dad's still a blubbering mess. "I kn-know. I'm so sorry."

Mom's tone changes drastically. "You should be sorry. Did you see your daughter?"

My eyes vault open the second it happens. Never in my life have I heard my mother speak to my dad this way. She never talked down to him, ever, anytime I was around. When he went away, she always defended him in front of me. It drove me nuts. Who is the woman in there? Is it the cancer?

"Do you know how many years I spent jealous of the connection you had with her? How close you were with her? I couldn't relate to her, be what she needed me to be. She was just like *you*. A mother is supposed to have that kind of relationship with her daughter." She continues through her teeth. "But I never got angry about it. I was happy. And you threw it all away. You destroyed us. I'm not even mad about what it did to me. She deserved her father. She deserved better. And if you don't fix the mistakes you made, right those wrongs, she's going to end up just like you."

I realize I'm leaning in a little close to the door. The tears are gone now.

"I know. I'll try."

"Do more than try!" Mom pauses for a moment. "You g-got her during the best y-years." Mom's voice cracks. "She adored you. Lived for you. No matter how much I loved her, she always wanted her dad. *Always.* But I never hated you for it. As long as she was smiling, had joy written all over her face, even if it was for you, it made me happy. All I want is for her to be happy. She works too much. She isolates herself from the world. You're about to be all she has left. You got the years when she was young, and you get the last years too, and it's not fair, but it is what it is. You've been given a gift, twice. So, if you *fuck* it up, I will come back and haunt you from the grave. Are we clear?"

I didn't realize my mouth could drop open any farther when Mom says 'fuck.'

It's one of the most emotional moments of my life, and I'm just stunned. In a daze. I never really knew she felt that strongly about me, or anything really. I always knew she loved me, that she tried as hard as she could, but I never really knew exactly how much she loved me, how much she sacrificed because of that love, until now.

Nothing she said is incorrect, either. I've always loved my mother, but it was always a different connection than with my dad. Mom tried as hard as she could to understand me, but she just never really did.

"I won't mess it up this time. I promise."

"Good." Mom sighs. "Sorry, that had to be said while I can still think and talk."

"Don't apologize. I needed to hear it."

"You're a good man. Cursed with too much intelligence and too much impulse, but I know you love us. And I know how much you love her. I'm sure you've punished yourself enough already, but she may punish you some more, and you will take every last ounce of it with a smile."

"I will." Dad pauses, and it sounds like he laughs a little, trying to deflect with humor like he always does. "You're pushier than I remember."

"Oh nonsense, I was the only one who could keep you in line. That's why you married me."

Dad sniffs a little. "It's true." He pauses. "You've told me everything I can do for Meadow, and I give you my word I won't fail again. I can't. I know what I need to do, that lesson has been learned. But what can I do for *you*?"

"Hold me for a little while. I want to remember what it was like when we were young and stupid and couldn't keep our hands off each other. The whole reason we have our little girl in our lives."

Dad adjusts on the bed, and I can't help but realize I'm smiling a little. It's like I just learned my mom is a whole different person. Someone she couldn't show me because it was her job to raise me. A strange feeling of comfort comes over me, but I walk away to the living room and sit down on the recliner, thumbing through my phone.

I should feel bad for listening in, but I don't. It was exactly what I needed. I needed to know that side of her. When I got older, moved out of the house, my mom did become more of my friend, but I know she'll probably never open up to me the way she did with my dad. I just—in this moment—I feel like I did when I was a kid, and I forgot just how goddamn good that feeling is, and how much I've missed it ever since he went away.

I want them to have their time together. She deserves it, to have a man who loves her hold her in his arms.

The only thing I've ever known that comes close to this feeling I have right now, as much as I don't want to admit it to myself, is when I'm with Wells Covington.

WELLS COVINGTON

I sit around a conference table with several fund managers and a few angel investor acquaintances I've met once or twice. They're all involved in funding Meadow's shelter idea that was once the Parker project. The couple who run the place flank me on the other side.

The investors all keep glancing over at me like I'm some kind of celebrity and they might ask for an autograph. It's awkward as fuck, but it'll be worth it.

Meadow's firm is as quaint and quiet as I remember. There's barely enough room to fit twelve people around a table. Hardly adequate, but this is how she runs her business. I imagine she avoids sit-down meetings as often as possible.

This shelter project of Meadow's is the reason we're all here. It's the one thing that has driven her since day one, why she vandalized my marble wall. I still can't believe I didn't think of this earlier. Orson was right, my brain works differently when she's around. Actually, it doesn't really work much at all. Hell, she doesn't even have to be around. I've been different ever since the day she came into my life.

Footsteps pound from around the corner, two pairs. One Meadow, I assume, and the other her assistant.

"What is this? I said I'm *not* taking meetings right now. I can't." Meadow does not sound happy—at all.

"They told me it was an emergency."

"*Who* told you that?" Meadow appears around the corner just as she barks out the question.

She freezes in her tracks. Clearly she was not expecting every investor on her project to be waiting in the conference room. Her eyes dance around, and then they land on me.

Oh shit.

I may have misread this thing. *Goddamn it, Orson!*

"You." She says the word right through her teeth.

The tension in the room amps up to, well—infinity. Anxiety rips through my body, but I can't help but smile, because fuck she's so beautiful. I miss her face every second of every day. Not even her face, just her personality, the way she carries herself, her confidence and intellect.

Just *her.*

Meadow glances around once more and does her best to compose herself. After a long few seconds, her jaw clenches tight, and she says to everyone else, "Give us the room, please."

She glares lasers so damn hot I actually start to get a slight headache. Who knew those honey-brown eyes of hers could be so lethal?

Everyone gets up slowly and after about fifteen seconds, they all walk out. Meadow apologizes to each of them individually, trying her best to remain calm and assure them this won't take long.

I start to get up as the last person leaves, to go over and talk to her.

"Sit the fuck down, Covington."

Jesus Christ.

Part of me wants to defy her, but I really don't know if I want to push back that hard at the moment. She can level people with a glare, but I've never seen her glare like this before.

"Any reason I should remain seated?" Fuck me, I always have to be an asshole. I just can't help myself. *You can't just be nice one time, fucker?*

She storms toward me. "So I can fucking look down my nose at you for once."

I do my best not to smile, but shit, these things happen. I love her like this. "Do you treat everyone who helps you out with such hostility?"

"Don't." She points a finger in my face, and there's definitely rage in her eyes, but there's sorrow too, hiding behind all the red, fiery anger. "I told—" She freezes to compose herself for a moment. She speaks slow and deliberately. "I told you I have family issues right now." Another pause. "They require my attention, one hundred percent of it, *twenty-four seven.*"

I look into her eyes, and she's a definite fireball right now, but this is different. It's like the anger is the only thing holding her together.

I try not to joke, and I adopt a serious tone. "Sorry, I really had the best intentions. That's the truth."

"By calling me away from where I need to be?"

Fucking hell, she's transferring all this guilt on to me? "By trying to help you."

"How is this helping me?" She yells the words at me. "Making me deal with meetings and paperwork right now?"

"Because you care about this shelter. Or I thought you did. It's been the number one thing that brought us together. And I thought if I could handle all this shit for you, you'd have more time for your family emergency."

She blinks a few times. "Wh-what?"

"I just wanted all the investors here to have you sign a couple things, giving me temporary managerial control over the finances and operations, to lighten the load for you. I didn't realize you couldn't spare thirty minutes. Probably because you won't tell me what's going on, so I have no idea. There's a broad spectrum of family emergencies, and I didn't realize this was DEFCON One."

She sits down in the chair next to me. It actually looks more like a controlled collapse than her merely sitting down. She looks straight ahead at the wall across from her, not turning to face me.

"I am, umm, I'm sorry." She sniffs a little, still staring at the wall.

I glance down to see her fingers tremble against the chair. She's barely holding it together.

"Meadow, are you okay?"

She plasters on a fake smile. Anyone in the world would be able to tell it's not genuine. "Of course, I'm fine."

I lean a little toward her. "Look at me and say it."

She starts to turn her head but can't do it. Her shoulders begin to shake, her nose crinkles a little, and she fights back some tears, but her eyes well up anyway.

"Meadow?"

She starts to turn, and then just crashes into me and buries her face in my shoulder. I wrap my arms around her, and she sobs, full body sobs racking her from head to toe. My eyes widen a little, because it has to be damn near end-of-the-world bad to crack Meadow like this.

I'm still not sure exactly what could be causing her this much pain, because this is the toughest woman I've ever met by far.

I squeeze her tight against me, and guilt rushes through my veins, because as bad as she's hurting, as horrible as I feel about that, I also don't know if I've ever been happier, getting to take care of her like this. It's all I want to do. I want to drive her to my house, put her in my bed, and hold her and give her whatever the fuck she asks for, whatever she wants.

After a few moments, she leans back and shows me her eyes.

"My mom, she's dying."

Oh, fuck. "She's sick?"

Meadow nods.

"How long does she have?"

"Weeks. Days maybe. They don't know how long her cognitive functions will last."

A searing pain tears through my heart. "I took you away from her. Calling this meeting. Pulling you away outside the building."

She shakes her head. "You didn't know."

I cup her face in one of my palms. "I should've known."

She leans into my hand, and I want to just keep her for

myself the rest of the day, but I know I can't. I stand up at the same time as her and pull her into a hug. It's incredibly intimate, and she holds onto me like she doesn't want to ever let go but knows that she has to.

I hold her in my arms and wish I could bear every ounce of pain for her. One of my hands caresses her back, and she nuzzles against my neck. Our mouths inch closer together, until we slowly morph into a long, deep kiss.

When we part ways, I say, "What can I do? Tell me what I can do to make your life easier. I want to be there for you."

She shrugs, just barely, still a little deflated but in better condition than she was. "Thanks. That, umm, it means more than you know. Aren't you needed at your work?"

I shake my head. "I'm sure it's getting pretty *Lord of the Flies* right now, but it'll make them stronger. They'll survive."

I get a smile, just a hint of one.

"What do you need? Anything."

"If you can make sure the shelter gets—"

"Done. What else?"

Her eyes roam up to mine. "That's a lot of work. It's a full time—"

I cut her off and put my palms on her face. "You don't get it, do you?"

"Get what?"

"You're mine. If my firm takes some losses without me there, so fucking what? It's all bullshit; just stuff. *You're* all that matters. I will support whatever you need, one hundred percent. Just tell me what you want done."

Her eyes dart around for a moment, then she nods a little. "Okay, yeah, the shelter. If you can just handle that, it will seriously make this all a lot easier on me, so I can be with my mom the entire time."

"Done. I'll support whatever you need. Do you want me to go with you? Be with you?"

She shakes her head. "No, this is too important. Too many families are impacted by it. They need to get construction going as soon as they can."

"*You're* too important. This shit can wait."

Meadow stares at me for a long moment, like she's looking at a man she didn't know existed in her life before right now. Finally, she tries to get some words out, and her voice nearly cracks again.

Fuck. I hug her to me before she can say what she's trying to say. It does kind of bug me that she doesn't want me to go with her.

As if she can still read my mind, she says, "N-no, it's not because I don't want you to go. She's about to slip away. She was so confused earlier this morning. I don't want to confuse her anymore." She pulls back and puts her palms on my cheeks this time. "I do wish I could have taken you to meet her, the real her. She would've loved you." She kisses me once more, then turns and walks away.

I stand there, wanting to run after her, chase her, make her let me do more. I can't, though. That's the hardest part about this. I have to share Meadow, can't be selfish and keep her to myself. She'd never forgive me.

She gets a few steps away, then turns back. "I don't think it'll be more than a week. But…"

I rush over there. "But what?"

"Nothing."

"Tell me, Meadow." I lift her chin with my finger, angling her gaze up to me.

She shakes her head. "I feel selfish asking for it."

"You can ask me for anything. I want you to ask me for anything."

"Okay, well, fuck this is hard. I don't like needing people."

"Trust me, Meadow. I understand completely. You know I'm the same way, but I want you to know you can always count on me. Just ask, and be specific with what you want, please."

"Okay." She nods. "Can I call you any second of any day? If something happens, I want to be able to call you at any time during the night, and you'll run as fast as you can to me. I know it's a ridiculous thing to ask."

"Done."

She looks up at me. "What?"

"Done. All of that. The second you call I'll be there, doesn't matter where."

I hug her again and drop a kiss on the top of her head. She squeezes her arms so tight around me it's damn near hard to breathe, but I don't give a single shit. I don't want her to go anywhere. Ever.

"I don't want to leave, but my dad's a mess and Mom, well, you know."

The last thing I want to do is to keep her from her family, even though I never want to let go.

"Go on. You need to get back to them." I kiss her one more time, then take a step back, giving her the necessary space to make an exit.

She walks toward the door, but glances back several times along the way, like she's torn because she's needed there, but doesn't want to leave my side either.

Once she's out of my sight, it's like the world cools off ten degrees, like colors are drab. Fuck, I care about her so much. I didn't realize exactly how much until just now.

I know it's still early, but this is a big deal. The stakes are raised. It feels like a gigantic, monumental test to see if she can count on me. It could have lifelong implications on our relationship.

That means I cannot fuck this up. Not if I want to be with Meadow for the rest of our lives.

Just like every other goal I've ever put my mind to, I will crush this. When this is done, she'll know no other man could ever be there for her in a time of crisis like I can. Can take care of her needs, give her the space she needs, but come running the second she calls, with whatever she needs.

She'll know I'm all in. I'll prove that to her.

MEADOW CARLSON

MOM SLIPPED into a coma two days ago. We have no idea how much longer she has, but probably not long. It is *not* fair how fast this cancer is moving.

They upped her pain medication to make sure she doesn't feel anything. It was so calm and serene, she was there with us, talking like usual, and then she just fell asleep and never woke up, like she was taking a nap.

Part of me is grateful for that. She's barely seemed in any pain, but I don't know how much of it she was holding in. I don't think I realized how much pain she was capable of bearing, until I heard her light into my dad last week. I've felt so selfish, knowing she harbored all those feelings and had the strength to never show me them because she didn't want me to feel guilty.

I've called Wells twice, the last two evenings, with updates. He's been ridiculously supportive, more than I would've ever thought. Part of me even feels a little bad for thinking he was just another trust fund billionaire type who doesn't care who they have to destroy to get what they want. I mean, I'm not naïve, I know he has that killer instinct, but it seems to evaporate when I expect it to flourish.

He caught me so off guard with everything. I have too many things going on in my life, and to be honest, it scares the shit out of me how much I care about him. Even more, how much I'm relying on him. Because when Mom goes, it's going to crush me, and I've put all my poker chips on Wells Covington being there to piece me back together. I hate myself for that, but I don't know if I can handle it all alone, and there's no way I'll ever trust my father. Not in the amount of time Mom has left, anyway.

I glance over at Dad. He's been by Mom's side, holding her hand, this whole time. I don't know how we're going to make this all work, how I can ever grow close to him again. But I have to try, for Mom. Knowing what I know now, I owe it to her to try. It's just going to be a long, arduous process.

I walk up and put a hand on his shoulder. "Dad, why don't you go take a shower, or get some rest. I can sit with her for a while."

He shakes his head vigorously, tears in his eyes, and grips her hand a little tighter. "No."

I use my own Mom-style voice on him. "Dad? Come on."

His head turns and his stare meets mine. "I left once. I *won't* do it again."

I give his shoulder a small squeeze and relax my features, knowing there's no way in hell I'll pry him away. "Okay."

I know he means every word of what he says, and there will be no changing his mind. He's as stubborn as I am. His parole officer showed up for some kind of visit last night, a surprise check-in.

Dad made the guy stand in the room and ask him questions while he held Mom's hand and never let go of her. It was about the most awkward thing I've ever seen, but honestly, it was really sweet too. As much as I hate to admit it, it made my heart happy, and despite the torturous circumstances with what's happening with Mom, it's the first time it has felt like we were a family again.

Slowly, I walk around and take a seat on the bed next to Mom, so that we're on each side of her. I lean over and kiss her on the forehead.

"I love you, Mom."

Dad pulls her hand up to his mouth and kisses her knuckles

again, like he does a million times a day now. "We both love you, so much."

Right as he does it, I look up at the monitor next to her. Her oxygen levels slowly start to dip, and my heart squeezes tight in my chest. Her heartrate speeds up so much the machine starts to beep.

It startles Dad, and the nurse comes in from the other room. Three of them work around the clock in eight-hour shifts.

We both know what's happening right now. She's here with us, can hear us, and it's time for her to go. It's like she was holding out, waiting for me to get here.

"I love you so much." Tears run down Dad's face as he kisses her hand over and over again.

My entire chest starts to shake, like my body realizes what's happening before my brain can fully process the moment. I lean down and hug her. I know I need to be strong for her, and despite how hard it is, harder than anything I've ever had to do in my entire life, I whisper, "It's okay, Mom. You can g-go rest. Dad and I will be okay. Th-thank you for everything. You m-mean so much to me, more than you'll ever know. I love you, s-so much."

As soon as I finish my shaky sentence, the heart monitor line goes flat, and the oxygen level slowly dips down further.

Dad hugs her close to him and kisses her forehead. He whispers something in her ear over and over.

The nurse stands behind him, trying to be respectful.

It lasts for about ten seconds, when I reach over and grab him lightly on the shoulder. "Dad?"

He sobs uncontrollably and more tears roll down my cheeks.

"Dad, we have to let her go. Just let her go. She needs to rest."

His eyes roll over to mine, a look of recognition, then he kisses her once more on the lips, then backs away. Instinctively, before I even realize what I'm doing, I walk quickly around the bed and nearly knock us both over I hug him so hard. Dad's arms tighten around me, and I can feel the tremors rippling through him.

I watch the nurse as she checks Mom's heart for activity,

presses a few buttons on the machine to silence it, checks the time and makes notes in a folder. Her actions are so simple, routine, but symbolic at the same time. The finality of what she does, a life concluded, my mother's life, it's too much to take in as the reality slams into my chest.

She's gone.

Mom is gone, and I'll never see her again. Never talk to her again.

Markets measure everything in dollars, but the truth is, time is the most valuable commodity on the planet. You just never realize that simple fact until you're out of it.

It's so surreal. She was here, and now she's not.

I bury my face in Dad's shoulder, and he squeezes me even harder than before. He's barely holding on, no matter how tight he hugs me. Hell, so am I.

The nurse finally turns to us and says, "I'm so sorry for your loss."

We both nod in recognition and say, "Thank you."

"I'll call and make all the arrangements. Do you want to wait in here, be with her, until they get here?"

I nod again, wiping my eyes, almost glad we have these decisions to make, to distract us a little bit from what just happened. "Y-yes, thank you. We'll wait with her."

In a soft voice, she says, "Okay, just let me know if you need anything," then she walks off into the living room.

Dad and I hover over Mom for a while. Both of us just stand there, in silence, holding each of her hands, until they show up to take her away.

* * *

LATER THAT EVENING, Dad and I sit at the kitchen table. I push a few noodles around in the takeout container of pasta we ordered from DoorDash. I didn't feel like driving and it's not like Dad can go anywhere with his ankle bracelet. I doubt he still has a driver's license anyway.

Once we're done eating, we both stand up to go throw the takeout containers away.

I'm about to walk back to the table when Dad stops me.

"We need to talk."

I'm not really sure what he wants to talk about right now, so I raise my eyebrows and say, "Okay? What's up?"

He looks down at the floor for a moment, then back up at me. "I'm sorry, Meadow."

"It's okay, Dad. She's not in pain anymore. That's the only thing getting me—"

He shakes his head. "No, not that. I'm sorry. About what happened with me, leaving you and your mother all alone."

My jaw sets a little. He wants to do *this, now*? "You already apologized."

"No, not like this, I didn't. I got to say what I needed to say to your mother, but not to you. Not the apology you deserved. Not just saying I'm sorry in the middle of an argument to try and end it prematurely. I *have* to look you in the eyes and tell you I'm sorry and mean every word of it." He takes a deep breath to compose himself. "I am so sorry. It was the biggest mistake of my life. I have regretted it every single day since, and I will always regret it. It haunts me—every damn day."

I stand there, thinking, processing. I know he's right; he did need to do it *this* way. He means what he just said, and I know I have to be truthful in this moment, no bullshit. "You know, Dad, I told you I forgave you. And I wanted it to be true. Please know that. I wanted to mean it. I'm sure you could read the situation, same as I could, same as Mom could. She knew we, well, *I* was pretending to get along for her. But I'll be brutally honest, giving you another chance scares the living fuck out of me. It's *so* hard for me. I told myself a million times there's no way I'd ever even look at you again. When you kept calling, and every time I heard that goddamn automated voice from the prison, I wanted to smash my phone across your face."

He pales a little, as if this might not be going exactly how he expected.

I start to say something else, and I just stop. My brain can handle a ton of bandwidth, but apparently my heart is not as good at handling emotional traffic. There is so much running through me right now, so many feelings.

Finally, I look down at the ground and mumble, "I heard you guys."

He leans back a second, regarding me skeptically. "Heard us?"

"You and Mom. After we got the news from the doctor. And we said our goodbyes, then I left the room, and you were alone with her."

His eyes widen as the recognition sets in. "You, umm, you heard that?"

I nod, and it's impossible to hide the slight grin at the way Mom handed him his ass. Before he can respond, I say, "And I'm glad I did, even if I wasn't supposed to. I didn't know that side of Mom existed. I never knew she felt that way, growing up, and I felt like such an asshole because I was always running to you. I always thought she was the mean one and you were the fun one. And that you got me, and I was nothing like her. I had no idea she was so jealous of you, and I was the reason for it."

He inhales a deep breath. "Well, she'd be mortified if she knew you heard that. She did more to protect you than I ever could. And she did resent me, a lot." He sighs, like he's reliving the past. "Yeah, because I was the fun one, and the way I would come home, and you would smile and sprint to me with your arms wide open. And your mother, Meadow, she was the most fun woman I ever knew. She was so much fun, full of vibrance and life. But she took being your parent seriously. Very seriously, more than I ever could, more than was humanly possible. We made a deal never to argue in front of you, which we kept our entire lives, well, almost, it seems. Your mother thought someone had to raise you to be a responsible adult, and that person most certainly would never be me, even if I *was* a professor with tenure, or a businessman, she knew the real me too. She pretty much sacrificed herself, her desires, when you were born, because I loved being a dad. And I don't want you to feel bad about that, because it's what she wanted, more than anything. She *wanted* the two of us to have fun. She *wanted* us to be close. And she only complained about it that one time, and she deserved to every day of the year. She never tried to make you feel guilty about it, because the only thing she wanted in life was for you to be happy. It was the single, most important goal in her life. It was her entire purpose for being on the earth. She believed that with all of her heart."

His words sock me right in the chest.

I start to say something, but he holds up a hand.

"That was the only thing. And she was right. And I know you think she went easy on me when I screwed up, ruined everything, and that she should've completely cut me off when I went away. I know all that went through your brain and you couldn't understand why she still had anything to do with me. But she made my life a living hell for it. Trust me. The only reason she kept in contact was to yell at me to fix the things that happened between us, because she couldn't bear that void I left in you. Yes, she forgave me, and we still loved each other. And yes, we remained in contact and she visited sometimes, but she kept her heel firmly dug into my back when it came to you."

He stops and looks at me for a long few seconds.

I don't even know what to say, because now my mom is like this entirely different person that I want to know even more, and I can't.

"I know you think you're just like me and nothing like her." He stops and shakes his head, looking like he might tear up again. "You're wrong, though. You're so wrong. You got the math and the finance and the computer brain from me, but that stubborn attitude, how you charge into a room like a bull and take control." He shakes his head. "That's *not* me. Not even close. You probably think the work you do with impact funds, and your heart for charity projects, and the recycling, and all the things you do to try to save the world, is some kind of response to what I did. Like you're trying to right the wrongs of the world to pay for my mistakes. But that's not it, Meadow. You got that stuff from her."

I raise an eyebrow.

"Your mother was a nature-loving hippie who would give anything to anyone who needed help. You just didn't see it much because we moved to the suburbs before you were old enough to remember anything. When we were at U of C and got married, I couldn't give her more than five dollars at a time when she went places, because she'd give all the damn money to any homeless person she saw."

I grin. "Really? Mom?"

He nods, smiling for the first time in days. "Hell yes. Didn't matter if it was five bucks or eighty bucks, she wasn't coming home with it. Drove me insane, because some months I worried if we could pay our rent or not."

This time I laugh.

"She was the leader of every damn student group possible for politics, the environment, standing up to fascism or whatever the hell the cause was that week. We were complete opposites, other than the fact I could make her laugh, and the first time I saw her I knew I was done for."

I lean back against the kitchen counter, relaxing a little. "I want more of *these* stories. So many more. Not all right now because I want to make them last."

"Deal," says Dad.

"One other thing."

"Yeah?"

"I've seen how you've been with Mom. I *do* notice things." I lock eyes with him. "I *noticed*, for ten years, when you still tried to call me, three times a week, on the dot, every damn week. I know those were probably some of the only phone calls you were allowed to make, and you spent them on me, knowing I wouldn't pick up. I still noticed, and those things still meant something, even if I hated you. You never quit. It's the only reason I can say what I'm about to and actually mean it this time." I take a deep breath and close my eyes, worrying if I'm about to fuck up again, but I can't hold this hate in my heart anymore. I just can't. When I open my eyes, my gaze meets his. "I forgive you, Dad."

He rushes over to me and wraps me up in his arms. "Thank

you, sweetie." He kisses the top of my head. "I will never quit. Ever." He squeezes me even tighter.

Honestly, I think this might be one of the only things that gets me through this time. Wells Covington is the other.

Wells Covington.

Shit. "Dad?"

"Yeah?" He lets go of me and backs up a step. "What's up?"

"I need to make a phone call."

"Sure, whatever you need to do. I mean, you're an adult now and all that, so yeah."

"I know this is going to be tough to hear too, but we're going to need to make the arrangements for Mom. Do you want me to handle that stuff?"

He shakes his head. "No, no, it's my responsibility, whether I want to do it or not."

I nod. "Okay. Mom had a will. And there are other things laid out in it, end-of-life plans. I made her sit down and do it like five years ago. Had all the tough talks in case something like this ever did happen. So, I mean. Yeah. She left everything, specific instructions in there about what she wanted. I think it'll make this a little easier, not having to make so many decisions."

He nods. "Yeah. Yeah. For sure, that's great. Thank you for making her do that."

I hold up my phone and gesture toward the other room. "Okay, I'm going to go make my call."

"Okay."

I turn to walk off.

"Meadow?"

"Yeah?"

"Thank you, again. I won't let you down."

WELLS COVINGTON

MEADOW'S on her way over right now.

I can't think of the last time I talked to a woman on the phone as much as I have. I've gone to see her, met up for coffee, just been there for her every time she's asked me to.

Her mom died yesterday, and my damn heart broke for her. I think it's hitting her extremely hard because it seems she put her mom on hold for a while, trying to save the world, work, do the things you do in your twenties to prepare for the future. She shouldn't fault herself for having ambitions, noble ones at that, which is much more than I can say for myself.

Hell, short of breaking the law, my twenties and beyond has been focused on winning at damn near any cost, proving everything I could to anyone who matters. I maintained some ethical lines I wouldn't cross, but as far as I was concerned, it was take or be taken from. I think that's another reason Meadow intrigues me so much. We're so alike, yet I find her challenging my core beliefs to be refreshing, interesting. She makes good points, whereas most people are afraid to criticize me, or just reinforce what I already believe because they want to kiss my ass, because they want something from me.

The sound of Orson's footsteps heading toward the door lands in my ears. She must be here.

I'll be damned if I don't still get that same rush, that same chemical spike every time I'm about to see her, regardless of the circumstances. I know this is going to be anything but fun, but I don't give a damn. I want this time with her. I want to comfort her, take care of her. It's what I was put here for, what I was born to do. I believe that in every fiber of my being. I just feel it, down to my bones, on an atomic level.

I reach for Orson's arm as he's about to open the door and shake my head at him. Then, I open the door and there she is, the most beautiful woman I've ever seen.

I step to the side and say, "Come in."

Then, she does it. She smiles, for just a brief second, despite everything that's happened. That smile is for me, and it makes me the happiest fucking man on the planet. I'm the only one who can get that smile from her.

My stomach tightens in the best kind of way when she's in my presence.

She takes a step past and says, "Opening your own door, huh?"

Before she gets three steps in, I have her wrapped up in a hug from behind and kiss the side of her neck. "Only for you. That's the absolute truth." I take her by the hand and lead her to my bedroom.

Once we're in there I sit down next to her, turn, and say, "I'm sorry. I'm so damn sorry."

All the air seems to leave her as she sighs. "She's in a better place."

It's interesting to me how Meadow can be such an exceptional human, IQ off the charts, and yet even the most intelligent of our species still resort to the same ways to comfort themselves in a time of grief. It's hard wired into us.

I could say a thousand different things, but I don't. It's not my job right now to have an intellectual discussion about grief, I'm just here to listen and support, something that would probably be impossible with any other person on the planet, but with Meadow, it's all I want to do.

"I'm sure it's still hard."

She nods and says, "Yeah."

I reach over and slowly guide her eyes to my face. "I'm here. I'll be whatever you need me to be, a shoulder, a punching bag, anything."

Her hands move to her lap, and she fidgets with her fingers. "Thank you. I mean it. You've been great through all of this. You made it easier on me, and I appreciate that."

I reach down for one of her hands and bring it up to my lips and kiss along her knuckles.

The second I do it, she starts to quiver, and I wonder if I've done something wrong. I just want to console her.

Tears stream down her cheeks, and I move her hand from my mouth. "Sorry. I didn't mean—"

She shakes her head, but the tears come even harder. "No, please, do it again."

My brows rise, but I do it again, just because she asked me to. Once I kiss her knuckles again, she lunges into me and kisses me. It takes me by surprise, but I kiss her back, and fuck it feels so good. My dick hardens against my pants, so much it's almost unbearable, impossible to not rip her clothes from her body. She makes me crazy, hungry for her.

I roll her over and pepper kisses down her neck, though the guilt of doing this while she's in so much turmoil gnaws at my stomach. I whisper in her ear, "Maybe we shouldn't—"

She shakes her head. "Please, don't stop." Her voice is almost pleading, more vulnerable than it's ever been. "Just make me forget for a while."

I trail more kisses down her.

She whispers, almost like she's somewhere else, "Just make me forget."

It feels all wrong, but I do what she asks. I work my way down, stripping her shirt from her, then her bra, and I take one of her nipples in my mouth. I don't know if I've ever had sex with a woman when it's so emotional and raw like this.

She gasps out a breath when I bite down on her nipple, and her chest arches her breasts up against my face. I glance up, and her eyes are closed, but the tears are gone. If she wants me to make her forget, if it relieves an ounce of her pain, that's what I'll do.

She wiggles her hips as I slide her pants down, and the second they're off my mouth is on her, tongue licking, swirling. Her hands work through my hair, her nails dragging against my scalp, and momentarily even I forget the brevity of the situation.

I'm a hundred percent focused on pleasing her, making her happy, giving her whatever she asks for.

She whispers my name over and over as I take two fingers deep inside her, curling them up to hit the spot deep inside her just right. Her hips grind her pussy against my mouth, the insides of her thighs pressing against my cheeks.

I work slow, lazy circles around her clit with the tip of my tongue, and slowly increase the tempo.

"Shit, that's so good."

I glance up, still stroking her clit over and over, just to see the reactions on her face. It feels amazing, knowing I can touch her, lick her, please her exactly how she wants, how she needs me to.

"I'm close. So close." The words come out on a needy whisper, like it takes everything she has just to say them.

My hard cock pushes against the mattress, straining to be inside her. I want to fuck her so bad my balls ache with need.

I speed up my tongue, stroking her hard and fast, fingers stretching her from the inside as she tightens around them. Her nails dig into my scalp again, then she tries to push me away, as if it's too much to take. I don't let up, not one bit.

"Oh my God, Wells." Her hips arch from the bed, and I don't think there's a better feeling in the world than hearing her say my name out loud when I get her off.

She shakes and trembles, her thighs tightening around my face so hard I have to keep them pried open with both hands. My mouth clamps down on her clit, tongue circling as fast as humanly possible.

She moans my name once more as the orgasm rolls through her in huge undulating waves. Then when it subsides, she gasps out a breath she'd been holding the entire time. Her chest rises and falls her lungs practically begging for oxygen.

I immediately sit up and strip my shirt off, then look down at her. Her eyes are hungry, unsatisfied, as if the previous orgasm was just an appetizer, and now she needs more.

I unbutton my pants and fling them down my legs, freeing my dick. I'm so fucking hard it hurts, and when my eyes land on her glistening pussy, my nostrils flare.

Annoyed, I start to get off the bed to reach for the drawer, but Meadow's hand flies out and stops me.

I know exactly what she's suggesting, her intent clear just by the look on her face, and fuck me if I don't want it too. I don't know how wise it is, though. I don't want to take advantage of this situation and end up doing something we both regret. The burden falls on me to be the voice of reason right now. I know this, whether she does or not.

"Meadow, I need to get protection."

She shakes her head at me again. "I want to feel you. Please."

It's so reckless and stupid. My brain knows this. I have a multi-billion-dollar business it puts at risk. If she gets pregnant, something happens, it's dangerous.

But the look in her eyes, the thought of coming inside her, finally marking her, letting the world know she's mine—it's unbearable.

Before I know what's happened, I'm between her legs, my dick lined up, my forehead pressed against hers, staring into her eyes.

"You're sure?" Goddamn, the thought that with one quick movement of my hips, I can slide deep inside Meadow's hot pussy—the animalistic urges are overwhelming.

She nods. "Yes. I'm sure."

My lips press into hers as I slowly thrust forward, and holy fucking shit. Sex with Meadow is already an out-of-this-world experience *with* a condom. Without one, it takes it to an entirely new level.

She's so hot and tight, the physical differences alone are

enough for me to never want to use a condom again. But the real difference is all mental, emotional, the connection I feel with her now, like we're one, joined together. It feels so fucking good and right, and I don't know if anything has ever compared to this before, or ever will after.

I continue to kiss her, our tongues exploring one another as I slide in and out of her, over and over. She gasps against my mouth with each deep thrust into her, then her teeth come down and bite my lower lip.

I kiss down her jaw and up to her neck. "You feel so fucking good. You don't know how happy you make me."

The second I say the words, she clenches around me. She squeezes me so hard, I damn near pass out from the euphoria. I don't know how much longer I can take this, having her bare, but I guess I have all night long to do whatever we want.

It's all so surreal. Just a few months ago, I don't think anyone could convince me I would ever actually care for a woman. I would've laughed. Now, with Meadow beneath me, writhing against my chest, I don't think there's anything in this world I wouldn't do to protect her, keep her safe. I never want her out of my sight, which is so fucking unreasonable it makes my head spin, but that's what I feel inside. This unbelievable urge. She drives me insane in the most intimate, important ways.

This whole experience is different because I realize I'm making love to her. She's the only woman where there's been an emotional connection during sex. I've fucked many women, but I've never cared about them.

I kiss down to Meadow's collar bone as I thrust into her, over and over, trying to go deeper each time, feel a new part of her I've never felt before. Both of us begin to sweat, and our bodies glide together, panting, gasping, fingers roaming.

It's finally too much, and my balls tighten.

I reach down between us and stroke her clit with my index finger, hoping I can get her off again before I explode. "Fuck, I'm close. Are you?" I ask.

Meadow nods against me, her whole face tight, like she's barely holding on too.

I stroke her clit faster and increase the tempo of my hips. The wet clapping sound of my thighs driving up against her ass echoes through my bedroom.

"Oh God." Her nails dig into my back, hard enough to leave marks up and down my skin, and she shudders, then clamps down on my dick.

As her orgasm crests and she comes with me inside her, it's too much to take.

I start to pull out, and her nails dig even harder into me, yanking me against her. "Come inside me." It's the sexiest fucking words ever whispered in history.

My heart redlines at the sound of it, and I shove into her as hard and as deep as I can. I try to hold it, but it's too much, and hot jets of come shoot into the depths of her as I groan and grunt.

It's so primal, humanity on its most basic level, doing what it was meant to do. Fuzzy stars dance in front of my eyes, and this euphoric rush, just a complete daze wafts over me as I come so hard inside her it streams out the sides of my cock and drips down her thighs onto the mattress.

I'm not even sure how best to describe the feeling, the symbolism of what just happened. Sure, it's sex, and a biological release and all that. But it's so much more than that too. It's like we're bound on a spiritual level, souls intertwined, quantum entangled together. It's something we'll always have, and that's between only us and no other person on the planet.

It's special, something I will *never* forget.

One thing I do know as I stare at Meadow, our eyes locked onto one another, is that there's a satisfied grin on her face, and there are no tears in her eyes.

She's happy.

For at least one brief moment, I actually did make her forget, eased all the pain in her heart, and gave her a momentary reprieve.

I kiss her once more, then roll over and collapse on the side of her, pulling her close to me. We stay wrapped up, just like that, and silence stretches between us for what seems an eternity as I spoon her in my arms.

All I do is kiss the back of her head, her neck, her shoulders, over and over. I want to worship her nonstop, prove to her she's the only thing in the world I give a fuck about. Show her how special she is to me, how I'll do anything for her, and that I'll always be here.

She needs to know I'm not some stepping stone along her path in life; I'm a permanent fixture, here to stay.

Eventually, she just says, "Thank you."

I roll her over, so she's facing me, and shake my head at her. "You never have to thank me. I'll do anything for you." I stroke the side of her cheek with my hand. "*Anything*."

She leans into my hand, and her eyes close. I glance around, and only one thought crosses my mind. This is where she belongs. Not this physical place, in my house, but with me. She belongs with *me*, always, for the rest of our lives. I'd give up everything I own for just one fucking day of this if I had to.

I want her—forever.

She curls up against me, nuzzling into my shoulder, like she just wants to be protected from the world. She's the toughest woman I've ever met, but it just proves that everyone craves comfort when things get tough. They want safety, and I will fight to the death to give it to her.

She tenses up a little in my arms and says, "Can I ask you to do one more thing?" The way she constricts in my arms tells me it's going to be a very serious request. "I feel so bad, like I keep trying to take and take from you."

"Don't. I told you I'll do anything. I mean it. I *want* to be there for you."

Her voice cracks a little when she tries to ask, but she takes a deep breath and says, "Will you go to the funeral with me? I don't know if I can make it through this without you."

I lift her chin with one finger, angling her gaze up to mine so she can see the conviction in my eyes, and tell her everything she needs to know just with my stare. "Of course I will. Anything you want, I will do it."

She nods a little, as if to tell me how grateful she is, then nuzzles back into me. After a long yawn, she whispers, "Thank you."

I nuzzle up against her to let her know I'm not going anywhere. It's only about six pm, but within a few minutes, she's asleep in my arms.

Guilt riddles my stomach. Not that I'm hiding anything or doing anything wrong. I just hate profiting from her pain like this. Because while she's probably never been sadder in her life, I've never been happier with her in my arms.

MEADOW CARLSON

I'M a wreck at the funeral home getting things ready. Honestly, the fact Dad is here helping me might be the only thing that has kept this from being a complete shit show. I know Mom wouldn't care one way or the other, as long as everyone she loved was there and getting along. Her bar would seriously be that low.

Somehow, something tells me if this isn't perfect, it will dishonor her in some way. Maybe it's all the guilt from neglecting the time we did have together.

The fact is, doing something like this, it's something I would've asked my mom to help me with. I feel lost without her here. That hits me all at once, and I just—the only thing comforting me is that Wells will be here soon. I told him he didn't have to come early and help with stuff, but he pretty much told me there was no way in hell that was happening.

I just hate forcing this kind of situation on him. Truth be told, though, I'm super impressed with how he's handled this whole thing. Mom didn't have a church or anything, and I certainly don't go to one, so Wells talked to some friends at The Hunter Group, and they put me in touch with Pastor Jeremiah.

I was a little skeptical about the religion aspect, but to be honest, the man is perfect. He hasn't mentioned God or Jesus once, in fact. He's so helpful and says all the right things. We just met up with him last night, and he's helped Dad and I get through all the preparations for the service, and I couldn't have asked for someone better.

Despite everything Wells has done, I still have this vision of him in my head, only caring about his own interests, only doing what's best for himself. It doesn't line up with reality at all. He's been there for me more than I could've ever imagined, and I'm falling for him so damn hard and fast.

Who am I kidding? I fell for him a long time ago. He's pretty much everything I have, the only person I can really trust.

Dad is great and all, and we're mending things, but Dad is still Dad. He's just—flaky. It's in his nature. There's still a lot of distrust there, feelings that need to be dealt with over a much longer timeline.

Dad comes around the corner, looks at me, then says, "Shit, the programs." He spins on a dime, and it's so cute, as cute as it can be, I guess, that it momentarily takes me out of the fact I'm trying to prepare this place for my mother's funeral.

Pastor Jeremiah comes up and goes over the itinerary once more with me.

"Thank you so much."

"Not a problem." He puts a hand on my arm and whispers, "This shit's hard. Trust me."

I actually laugh. I've never heard a pastor talk like this guy. I might've actually given church a go if I knew someone like him was the leader.

He gets a serious look about him and says, "I want to tell you something."

"Okay."

"You will experience emotions you've never felt before once we're in the middle of this thing. Please, be in the moment, and just honor your mother. Feel how you feel, and don't try to force yourself to be one way or another. I will be right there as backup, so you can express those emotions however you see fit, deal with them in any way you wish. Do not worry about a thing. You don't have to put on an Oscar-worthy performance. Nobody is grading you. Just be yourself, grieve, and celebrate your mother's life. I'll take care of the rest."

I nod. "Seriously. Thank you. You have no idea what that means to me."

It's incredible how he anticipates every single thing, but he's like eighty and has probably done thousands of these, so I guess you get pretty good at your job.

"I need to go do a few more things. Holler if you need anything."

"Will do." I check my watch, to see if it's time for Wells to get here yet. I need him more than I need anyone else.

Pastor Jeremiah walks off to another room of the funeral home.

It's still fifteen minutes prior to the time I asked Wells to come. It feels like it's going to be an eternity, and I'm getting more anxious by the minute, despite Pastor Jeremiah's little pep talk.

The more I think about Wells, the more I realize I haven't even told Dad I'm dating someone right now. I haven't even mentioned him to Dad because I'm a private person, and my father hasn't really earned the right to know that kind of information yet. Over time, I think the two of us can heal, but right now, I'm still guarded around him.

Plus, I didn't really know where things were going with Wells until the day he called that meeting at my office. The way he took charge, wanted to handle everything for me but not take things over. He wanted to make my life easier, so I could focus on the things I needed to focus on.

I think that's really what it's all about. Finding someone who complements you, wants to ease your burdens, and you want to do the same in return for them.

I'm aware I really don't know a ton about his past yet because we haven't had a chance to really dig into those things. Everything has been so unconventional, not a standard courtship, so to speak. But I don't even care. I just know with him I feel like we've pretty much already been battle-tested more than most couples who have been together for years.

In a matter of a few months, we've been through a lot.

I used to make fun of people I knew for falling head-over-heels, but now I kind of get it.

Just as I'm thinking about him, how special he's become to me, the man himself walks through the front of the funeral home, ten minutes earlier than I asked him to be. I know he has to feel a million different ways about this; unsure, worried about how I'll react. I know he has to have a ton of reservations, but you wouldn't know it by looking at him.

He's one hundred percent confident, and God, I feel even more guilty for even noticing, but he looks phenomenal in his suit. I can almost hear my mother from the grave, giving me an elbow nudge and saying, "Well done, Meadow. That is a fine looking man."

We would've died laughing together, drinking a glass of wine and talking all about him after he left the room. I wish she could have met him. She would've loved him. I can picture him trying to win her over, wooing her, just to make me happy. She would've let him and enjoyed every second of it.

My eyes never leave his, but I'm somewhere else, thinking about him meeting Mom. Yeah, he would've definitely turned on the charm for her like no other.

I must be grinning right now, because Wells looks so somber and serious, then he sees me and smiles.

"Hey." He walks over like he can't get next to me fast enough, with huge, long strides. He kisses me on the lips but takes care to make it not inappropriate. His hands immediately find both of my arms and he caresses the backs of them. "What do you need?"

I look up at him, and for some reason, I just can't stop thinking about how much Mom would've loved him. It's not fair. If I'd just met him a few months earlier. That's all it would've taken.

My thoughts go to Dad, and how he'll at least get a chance to know him. Until he goes back to prison anyway, after all this.

Shit.

I need to introduce them. How did I not think about this

beforehand? Introducing my boyfriend to my father at my mother's funeral. It was the furthest thing from my mind the past few days. I'm a fucking wreck, but it's too late to do anything about it now.

"I don't need anything, but I have someone I want you to meet."

Wells looks intrigued. "Think I can manage that. Easy enough."

"It's my father."

Covington's eyes get big. "Oh."

Too late for warnings, I might as well rip this damn band aid off. I yell, "Dad! Come here. I want you to meet someone."

Dad comes hustling around the corner with his head down at first, rifling through the stack of programs. When he finally looks up, he freezes dead in his tracks.

When I say freezes, I mean he freezes.

Looks like he didn't just see one ghost, but a damn horde of them. His whole face is pale, and his hands tremble so hard he drops the programs all over the floor.

No, what is this? What's happening here?

My stomach tightens so hard I almost think I might be nauseous. Something isn't right. Something about how Dad stares. It's not good. I can feel the dread pumping through my veins. I don't want to turn back and look, but I can't stop myself. It's a natural reaction.

And what I find absolutely breaks my heart almost instantly.

Wells Covington might be the most emotionally controlled man I've ever known, has more restraint than anyone. He can sit there and take just about any kind of abuse with nothing but a cocky smirk on his face, like he doesn't have a care in the world, because everything will always work out in his favor. But I've never seen him look like this before. I don't know if anyone has ever seen him look like this.

His face is bright red, nostrils flared, teeth clenched shut. My eyes dart down, and both of his hands are balled into tight fists. Fists so tight the whites of his knuckles show.

What the fuck just happened?

"What is this?" I fold my arms over my chest, despite the fact I don't know if I've ever been so scared in my life. "What's going on here? Wells?"

He lifts one of his hands slowly and points his index finger right at Dad. "That's your father?" His words come straight through his teeth, and the tone in his voice rips me apart from the inside. All I can think is this is so wrong. This should not be happening, no matter what's going on, or what history there is here. "Him?" He yells the last part, so loud it echoes through the funeral home, all the way into the sanctuary.

I figured he would know who my father is, but not like this. I thought it would just explain why I hide so much of my past, to sever the connection to his name, so I can still do business with people. I didn't think he'd want to murder him.

Despite the fear, my natural instincts take over. "You need to lower your voice. This is my mother's funeral."

"I'm sorry. I should—" Dad holds up both hands and starts to walk out of the room to ease the tension.

"You're not going anywhere, you motherfucker." Covington takes off for Dad, and I leap over to step in his way.

My eyes go wide, and I worry he might just barrel right through me at first.

Fortunately, he sees me do it and stops himself.

"Hey!" I yell right in his face.

He glances to me for a brief second, but his eyes go right back to Dad. I don't know if it's because he doesn't want Dad out of his sight, or because he doesn't want to look at me. I can hear him snorting, he's breathing so hard in and out of his nose.

Finally, his eyes drift down to mine, but it's new, a different look than all the ways he's looked at me before. Something just changed. There's hate there, pure, unadulterated hate, and it feels like some of that is directed at me.

Finally, still staring right at me, he shakes his head slow and deliberately, and says, "Fuck this, and fuck you." He points right at Dad. "I can't believe you came from that. Good luck." He turns around and never looks back as he stomps all the way out the door.

I stand there, and it feels like I'm outside of my body. I feel like my life just spanned an entire spectrum in a matter of seconds, and I'm just tired. Tired of the roller coaster, up and down, to every goddamn extreme there is. I just want to be fucking normal, average, moderate, for ten minutes. I just want a small break from the peaks and valleys, a moment of reprieve.

As everything starts to crash into me, the reality of the situation, anxiety takes over, and I can barely breathe. It feels like walls are closing in on me. In the last month I've cried more than I have for the past ten years.

I've lost almost everything I care about in the world in the span of a week.

Dad walks up behind me, and I feel his hand on my shoulder, and I don't even have the energy to knock it away. I'm so tired of men in my life disappointing me, fucking crushing me, turning me into this.

My heart starts to crack right there, because I realize the only thing I want right now. It sounds so childish to say it in my mind, but I want my mom. I just want my mom for two seconds. I know we weren't super close, like some mothers and daughters, but nobody comforted me through grief like her. She would always wrap me up in her arms, no matter how old I got, and smooth down the back of my hair, the same way, every single time. I would give anything to have that right now. Literally anything.

But it's time to grow up. Mom's gone. She's not coming back.

"What happened?" I say the words at Dad through my teeth, then turn around to look at him.

There's nothing but shame there. He takes a deep breath. "It's a long story. I'm sorry, Meadow. For now, I'll just say he has every right to be that angry at me, but I'm so sorry you were caught in the line of fire."

I grind my teeth, not sure whose ass I want to kick harder; Covington's or Dad's. Surprisingly, I think Covington just took the lead, but I'm sure it'll switch once Dad tells me the story behind that. "I wasn't caught anywhere. He took aim right at me." I want to lay into him, make him feel a little of what I just felt, but I can't. Because I'm just fucking exhausted. I don't think anything could surprise me anymore. I finally just sigh and say, "What happened?"

About the time he starts to explain, people arrive, walking through the front door. Thank God it's acceptable to look like you've been crying when you're in a funeral home. Because I have to greet everyone with puffy and swollen eyes, and do the things I need to do, for my mother. I just want to focus on Mom, why is that so hard to do?

I greet people and welcome them as they go in and have a seat, relatives, people I haven't seen in ten or twenty years, Mom's friends.

I'm supposed to give her eulogy.

It's going to take an act of God to get through it. I've never been crushed like this before. It's like pure torturous pain, bound to every strand of my DNA, just strangling me at the cellular level.

I don't even know how I'll be able to stand up there now. Wells was my plan. He was going to help get me through this, if I had a breakdown, if I got stuck. He promised me that he'd be there, every step of the way. Now, he's just gone.

He left me at my mother's funeral.

That fact plays through my head, like the stock ticker loop on CNBC at the bottom of the screen, over and over.

What the hell could have happened between him and Dad? Is this even real life?

One thing I do know, is this is not fair to my mother. I will *not* let this tarnish her memory. It was just her and me for over a decade, by ourselves. We didn't need men then, and we don't need them now.

I take a deep breath.

I have to get through this. I have to honor her.

Then, I may kill both of these motherfuckers, starting with Dad.

MEADOW CARLSON

I KEEP GLANCING down to Mom's face, and it's literally the only thing getting me through her eulogy. Dad's in tears in the front row, but every time I make eye contact with him, he can't even look at me. It's shame, regret, and I know he feels bad, but it doesn't make me not want to rip his head off.

I look down at Mom's empty shell of a body, pretending she's still in there, and I'm talking directly to her. Then I think about everything Pastor Jeremiah told me. His words are the only thing that gets me from one word to the next.

People aren't gasping or walking out, so I must be doing this right, but it feels like I'm just going through the motions. My heart is just a constant dull throb. An ache so deep it's crippling.

Finally, I make it through, walk around to Mom's body, kiss her on the forehead, and tell her I love her. The second I turn around, it's like a giant wave hits me. That's how it's been the past few days, like waves on a beach, over and over. I'll start to think maybe it's not so bad, maybe I can do this, move forward, and then another wave, and another. Then Wells showed up earlier and it was just a damn tsunami. Maybe that's how it works for everyone, sans the boyfriend showing up and yelling, "Fuck you," in your face. I pray that hasn't happened to anyone else, because I wouldn't wish it on anyone.

Pastor Jeremiah was right, too. There are emotions specifically related just to grieving for my mother that I've never felt before. She's the only person this close to me who has ever passed away.

You try to prepare yourself for things like this in your mind, always knowing when you're with people you care about, that one day they'll be gone, or you'll be gone. But no matter what kind of mental gymnastics I did, it never prepared me for this moment. Not even close.

I walk over and sit on a chair in the front row, next to my father, only to honor my mother and for no other reason. He reaches over for my forearm, and I glare at him. He immediately pulls his hand back.

I need to be better than this. I need to fake it, pretend everything is okay with him, at least until we're out of the building, but I can't.

Pastor Jeremiah takes over for me at the podium, says more nice things about Mom. He's so convincing you would've thought he knew her for her entire life. They play music we selected, and there's a slide show. I'm in about half the photos and it's Mom with friends in the others. There are some older photos with Dad in them, the three of us as a family. I can't stand the smile on my face in them. I wish I could go back and shake that girl, and say so many things to her, prepare her for everything that would come her way. Or maybe I just wish I could go back to being her, in a time when I was truly happy and thought I was the luckiest girl in the world.

I didn't think it could be possible when I woke up this morning, but now, everything hurts even worse. I had hope this morning, that maybe I could get back to being that little girl in the pictures, find her again. Dad came back. Wells and I seemed so perfect.

Now, the world feels pretty useless. What's the point of even being here?

I have zero hope for my future.

I look over at my mother's body once more. She was the only one who never hurt me. She was the only one who put me before herself, no matter what she was feeling, what she wanted.

Tears stream down my cheeks, and I just thank her, over and over in my mind. I hyper-focus on how much she loved me, and the sacrifices she made for me. I don't really know if I deserved the type of love she had for me, but it was unconditional. She's the *only* person I can say that about right now.

Finally, it's done, and they close the casket. I'm a blubbering mess, and so is Dad.

Everything hurts.

I just want to go home and disappear. I just want to sleep for days, and maybe eventually, I'll find the strength to come out and try to start over. Pick up all the pieces.

Feeling like a zombie, my feet drag me through the motions, the mingling, accepting condolences from people. I really don't mind. I love the stories some of Mom's friends tell, but by the end, if I hear one more person say, "She was so young," I might gouge my eyes out.

Once everyone makes their way to the front of the funeral home, we walk out and get in the car. I take a deep breath.

You're halfway through this. Just relax.

I didn't do a limousine for a family car because it's just me and Dad. It seemed unnecessary.

But I now realize Dad can't fucking drive of course, so I probably risk our lives trying to get us there in my current condition. I should've hired a car and a driver. Honestly, I figured Wells would drive us. So much for that. So much for assuming things and expecting things from people.

Won't be making that mistake again any time soon.

We weave our way through downtown Chicago, lightly drizzling bleak weather providing the perfect backdrop for the most somber day of my life. I just follow behind the two police officers on their motorcycles and the hearse, praying I don't pass out behind the wheel.

Dad hasn't said a word, and it's probably the smartest thing he's ever done in his life.

When we arrive, we have another smaller ceremony at the cemetery, and then they lower Mom's casket down into the ground, the skyline of Chicago filling the scenery behind us. For some reason, I just keep waiting for Wells' hand to slide into mine, for him to put his arm around me, hold me like he did in bed the other night.

The night when he fucking promised me he'd do anything for me, no matter what.

I know better than to count on someone else, to trust someone with my heart, but it still hurts so bad.

We finally leave the cemetery, and I manage to get us back to Mom's house. As soon as we're inside, I head for one of her guest rooms. Dad starts to say something, and I just hold a hand up at him and keep walking.

I don't want to hear any of what he has to say right now. I don't even care. I just want to be alone. I want to grieve for my mother without any asshole men opening their goddamn mouths, taking any more of this day away from me than they already have.

Honestly, I don't want to know what happened between the two of them. Not yet.

The second I get next to the bed, I collapse face first into it, and within seconds I'm out. I just completely pass out, because I don't know if I've ever had that much dumped on me in my entire life.

My heart can't take any more today.

WELLS COVINGTON

I PACE back and forth in my living room. I don't even know what I feel right now, all I know is it's coursing through my veins and I just want to purge it. I want it gone. It's like a sickness, a virus of emotion I've never had inside me, invading me from every angle.

I can't think straight, I can't even see straight. Colors, my whole world, it's all out of alignment. It's like bugs crawling all over my skin, but it's just rage, anger I've never felt before. It's boiling, just waiting to burst out of me.

"Everything all right, sir?" Orson walks in from the other room.

I turn, furiously, and yell through my teeth, "Fuck! Off!"

His face goes white as a sheet. He spins on a dime and walks out of the room as my chest heaves and more guilt floods into me. I want to run my head right through the wall for treating him like that, talking to him that way. It's like I'm not even in control of my body, what comes out of my mouth. I've never yelled at him like that. I never yell at anyone.

I'm better than this. I thought I'd mastered myself, trained myself not to feel these things.

I go to swipe through my phone, to check Bloomberg Chat, and accidentally answer a phone call from Penn Hargrove from The Hunter Group.

"Covington? Hello? You there?"

I take a deep breath because I don't want to fuck up business relationships as well.

"Yes?" The word barely comes out.

"You, umm, okay? Sound a little—"

"What do you need?" I say it way too harshly.

"Yeah, man, sorry, I have more capital partners on the line with me right now. That you asked me to round up. We were scheduled to talk about the investment property through the impact fund. The old Parker project."

Meadow's dream project. The one I've been running for her, neglecting all my investors and employees in the process. The fucking gift I gave her when she couldn't even tell me who her family was.

"Do you want to proceed? Is it a good time?"

Rage consumes me, and I grit my teeth. With Penn and all the other investors on the line, I say, "It's a loser. I wouldn't put a goddamn dime in it." I hang up the phone, then turn around when I hear a noise behind me.

It's Orson. He stands there, staring at me. I rake my eyes up his old wiry frame, but his face is different. I've never seen him look at me the way he is. It's not the way an employee looks at an employer.

He stares at me the way a father would to a son. The resolve on his face says he's not leaving, not until he's sure I'm okay.

I stand there, my legs barely holding me up, and my eyes start to burn, and I don't know how much longer I can do this. I collapse to my knees, and I don't know how Orson moves as fast as he does, but he catches me just as I go down. I can't even breathe. My whole life has been ripped away from me, everything I care about. I try to suck in breaths and it's like I can't get any oxygen, and I fight it even harder, because I don't know how to give in. I don't know how to not fight for what I want, even when it comes to getting air into my lungs.

"Relax, sir. Relax."

The fact he still has the dignity to call me "sir" after the way

I just treated him, makes me want to lash out at myself even harder.

"Easy, just calm down and breathe easy." He starts breathing in front of me, long deliberate breaths, trying to get me to do the same.

I try as hard as I can, but I just can't. Somehow, despite my limited supply of air, I manage to gasp, "L-l-left."

"Shh, sir. Don't try to talk."

"Left l-l-left her."

"Left who?"

"I left Meadow, at her mother's funeral."

Orson's fingers tighten around my arms, as if he's semi-pissed but still wants to comfort me and get more information. I know he thinks Meadow is probably the best thing that's ever happened to me, but he's wrong about that one.

"Ms. Carlson?"

I shake my head and slowly manage to start breathing again. The relief that temporarily comes over me is enormous, but it still feels like the sky is crashing down on me. "Not her real last name."

He eyes me curiously, as if I've gone insane; I'm sure it probably appears that way.

"Okay, well, easy, let's get you up."

Somehow, I find my legs under me, and he helps haul me onto the couch a few feet away.

Tears stream down my cheeks, and I can't believe I look this weak in front of him right now. I've never been like this before, let alone in front of someone else, even though I trust Orson with my life. He's always been there for me.

I collapse on the couch, and he takes a seat next to me.

I immediately lean forward and catch my head in my hands. I can't even look at him. "I left her at her mom's funeral. I got so fucking angry." My face starts to heat up again.

Orson stands, and with a hand on my shoulder, guides me over so I'm laying down on the couch.

"You need rest."

I try to get back up, resisting against him, but he shoves me down, his face inches from mine.

"It's okay. Just get some rest. Nothing good will come from you getting up right now. Some things just take a bit of time, then you'll be ready."

I can't even fight against him because I'm spent. I just want to close my eyes and forget this fucking day ever happened.

Finally, I just nod. "I'm sorry."

"None of that now, you hear?"

I shake my head. "No, I have to say it. You probably hate me now too."

He gets me laid down on the couch and says, "Remember that day, at the orphanage?"

I lean up for a second. How the hell could I ever forget that? "Of course I do. I got my ass kicked, bad. Might've gotten myself killed if you hadn't been there."

"Right. Right. It was a good job. It gave me purpose, and I squandered it. I got messed up in a lot of things. But I knew you were special. And I knew you had great things lying ahead of you, even if you didn't see it coming. You were hurting so bad and didn't feel like you had anyone, and do you remember what I told you?"

I nod. "Yeah, you told me you'd always be there for me. Whatever I needed. That I always had someone in my corner, no matter what."

"Meant every word of that. And I did my best to live up to it, even after everything that happened to you, when your life was in ruin. When I got all messed up on alcohol and lost my job there, I thought I was going to drink myself to death. Didn't think anyone would ever hire me for anything again. Didn't think I had any purpose left in life. Suddenly, this kid that I'd made a serious promise to, who I'd hidden all my problems from out of embarrassment, to try to be some kind of a role model for him, found out about all of it. I thought you'd come and spit at me like everyone else, treat me like I was subhuman for the bad things I'd done, but you didn't." He points a finger at me. "You didn't. You gave me a job at your house, so you could keep an eye on me and get me back on my feet. And I'll never forget that, son. Ever. You may think you're this billionaire stereotype everyone likes to denigrate on the news and scream about to make them feel better about their politics, but you are not that man. I know you think you are, but you're not. You can scream at me a thousand times, and I'm still gonna show up, every goddamn time. So get that through your bloody big skull of yours up there protecting all them brains, okay?"

I nod, staring into his eyes. "Okay. Thanks, Orson."

He gives me a singular nod back, as if everything is final. "All right, then. Get some rest, mate. We'll talk soon."

I nod. "Okay."

I close my eyes, and my body just shuts off. It can't take any more pain.

MEADOW CARLSON

I GET up and walk to the kitchen at Mom's house. It's been two days, and I haven't had it in me to drive to my condo. I've stayed here both nights. There's something comforting about it, and I think some of it is guilt too. Like I feel maybe my mom is watching me, and I have to prove how sad I am, do all of this to show her how much I miss her. It's irrational, devoid of logic. I know this.

She can't see me, can't hear me. I just want her to know how much I loved her and make up for all that time we never got.

I didn't want to say a word to Dad, but I had to. It's been meaningless small talk and niceties, because I'm just spent. He is too. But, there's this tension boiling under the surface.

I know we have to have *the* conversation. I want to fucking know everything that happened between him and Wells, but at the same time I'm scared to find out exactly what it is. I can't figure out if I haven't asked him yet because I don't want to get mad at my father all over again, or if it's so I won't feel any sympathy for Wells. What could possibly justify what he did though? Is there anything in this world that would justify that? I haven't been able to think of anything, but maybe I don't want to, and that's why.

To Dad's credit, he has given me as much space as possible. He knows me so damn well, and I hate that about him. He's patient, like an expert chess player setting up a move, even if he doesn't mean to be. It's how he is. It's how I am too.

He's at the table when I walk into the kitchen, and his eyes dart up to mine, then back to the cup of coffee in front of him. Slowly, I walk over, pour myself a cup, then head over and sit down across from him at the table. I give him the look that says, *okay, it's time to tell me everything.*

When his eyes come up, he just looks so—ashamed. To his credit, he doesn't break eye contact.

He says, "I had no idea you were dating Wells Covington. I can't believe he didn't even ask about your last name."

"I changed it, legally, from Mayes to Carlson."

He nods as if he immediately accepts it, but I know how much the family name means to him, and how it ends with him since he never had any siblings or a son. "Distance yourself from me. I understand. I tainted the family name."

"What happened, Dad?"

He lets out a sigh, like he doesn't want to say but knows he has to. "When I was in Champagne, still a professor, he was a student in my advanced capital markets class." Dad gets this look in his eye that's almost nostalgic. "He was—different, as I'm sure you're aware, if you've been dating him. Sometimes, you just know. And I knew he was a student that would come along once in a hundred years, if ever. Off-the-charts intelligence, he understood complex models most of the PhDs—hell, all of them—couldn't grasp. I mentored him. He became like a son to me."

It almost makes me want to puke the way Dad's talking about him. Right before he started the firm, a few years prior, I noticed he became a little more distant. It sounds like I was replaced with Wells and didn't even know it. My heart squeezes even more, knowing Dad probably hurt him as bad as he hurt me.

"Why didn't you ever talk about him? I never once heard you say his name."

He shakes his head. "It wasn't like that, Meadow."

"What was it like then? You never talked about your work.

You never told me what you really did, just that you were a teacher, until you started that damn firm in the name of providing us all financial security. You know Mom and I never bought that excuse, right?"

He nods a little. "Still, it's not what you think."

"If you know what I'm thinking, why don't you enlighten me."

"I didn't want you exposed to my work, okay? I didn't want you anywhere near it."

"Why the hell not? You were my father. I wanted to know what you did, what made you tick. You were my fucking hero, Dad. All I knew was you taught at a college."

"Your mother used to yell that same thing at me." He takes a breath, realizing he just raised his voice about her in her own home. He quickly relaxes. "I couldn't expose you to it because it would've consumed you. The way it did me. I wanted you to be a little girl. And then a normal teenager. I had to protect your innocence."

He's right. I didn't see that coming.

Before I can say anything else, he continues, "Our brains don't work like everyone else's. There are always problems and we can't rest until they're solved. I didn't want you reading financial textbooks and doing advanced calculus in the fifth grade, and I didn't want you going off to college when you were eleven. I wanted you to play with friends, and dolls, or whatever you wanted. You had your whole life to be an adult and be a genius and solve the world's problems, but you deserved to be a normal kid first, and I was going to protect your innocence with every last molecule in my body. And I *don't* regret that one bit. It was the best decision I ever made."

I want to choke him even more now, because I think he probably did the right thing, and I want him to be wrong so I can be pissed off at him. Because of him, I actually did have somewhat of a normal childhood.

"What happened with Covington?"

"Like I said, he was like a son to me in Champagne. We would work on problems into the night. I knew he was going to do great things, but he had no use for academia. He really didn't even need to go to college at all. He wanted to go out and conquer the world. I wanted to help him. So we started the firm. That's the real reason I did it."

My eyes widen. "You started that firm because of *him*?"

He looks away. "I didn't know it was going to turn out the way it did."

"Did he know you had a wife and a daughter?"

He nods. "Yes, but I wanted you two far away from the firm for legal reasons too. To protect both of you, and I just—I made a lot of mistakes, okay? I know that, and I'd give anything to do them all over." He sighs. "Covington had the brain, but he didn't have a name, yet. My name was respected, known throughout the world in finance and economics. My name attached to the firm gave it credibility he couldn't have gotten on his own. I was trying to expedite the process for him. Get him access to capital to manage."

"I still don't understand, Dad. Two of the brightest minds in the world, and you had to fucking cheat and go to prison? Couldn't beat the game the legal way?"

He shakes his head and looks away. "I can't tell you why I did what I did. All I can say is Covington didn't know, and when everything crashed down on the firm, and he barely escaped being in prison with me, well—that's how you end up with what you saw at the funeral home. It took him almost a decade to start over from scratch, get anyone to trust him, earn back the respect of his peers and the public. What he's done since is nothing short of remarkable." He has this look in his eye like he's still proud of Wells. A look I thought was only for me, but it turns out he hurt the man I loved the same way. What are the odds?

The man you loved?

Did you really just think that?

Yes, because it's true.

"Tell me why you really did it," I say through clenched teeth.

He shakes his head, pure panic on his face. "I can't."

"Tell. Me. Now. There's always a reason, especially with you, and you know damn well why you did what you did."

He looks like he might break any second. "Please, don't make me."

"*Now*, Dad."

His hand trembles at his side as he looks in my eyes and says, "I did it for you and your mother."

All the air leaves my lungs. "Wait? What?"

He nods. "It's true. I could feel the firm consuming me. I was addicted to that money, but more than that, the rush, the math, the problems. The feeling when we took profits on huge gains and beat every other firm in town. I craved it so much every day, and it was steering my life. So, I cheated on a big opportunity that presented itself, so I could get our portfolio to a level comfortable for me to leave and never look back. I was just going to let Covington take the reins, and I was going to retire and come home to the two of you."

I shake my head at him. "Bullshit. It took them a year to investigate the case, and you never came back home. You kept on going, working there. And knowing what I know now, they probably suspended your license, at the least. So you weren't even trading, or allowed in the room to discuss trades. The fuck were you doing while Mom and I were at home? Mopping the floors? Cleaning toilets? Can't believe Wells even let you stay there. Did you promise him you were innocent? No matter what? Cost the firm even more money to defend you, instead of taking a guilty plea? Drag everything out in the press when you could've minimized the damage to him and the firm?"

He drops his head in his hands. "Yes. To all of that. I know. I was weak and selfish, Meadow. And I didn't want to tell you because I didn't want you to feel an ounce of guilt from knowing you and your mother were the reason I did what I did. It was my fault. My decision."

"Goddamn right it was." Even as I say the words, I still know he's telling the truth. And I do feel guilty, like us being here made him do what he did. I shouldn't feel that way at all, I shouldn't hurt, thinking I was part of it. It's not rational, but human beings and feelings never are.

The same time all this is happening, I can't help but feel bad for Wells. Should I? That's the million-dollar question.

Maybe if he hadn't left me at my mother's funeral. What's even worse is I relate to him even more now, it's just another thing we have in common; being crushed by the man sitting across from me. It makes me nauseous, just sick to my stomach.

"I would've told you if I knew you were dating him. I swear on my life, Meadow."

I stare daggers at him, but still I can't bring myself to hate him. He's the dumbest fucking genius I've ever known, but the more I process it, the more I can see how he could do what he did. "I know, Dad."

His eyes widen a little. "You do?"

"I said I understand. Not that you're off the hook. Fuck, why do I feel like the parent here?" I let out a long sigh. "When do you go back again?" I know when he goes back, but I ask the question just to stall a little, for time to think—process what I just told him.

"Tomorrow. I have two years left, then my lawyer thinks parole will be an option."

"What about all the restitution and that stuff? Are the financial burdens satisfied?"

He nods. "Yeah, they gutted the assets of the firm back when it happened. All our profits took care of all that, and every investor of ours pulled their capital. It left you all with nothing. Left Covington with nothing."

This is all so ridiculous I want to laugh. Like this can't even be real, but it is.

"Meadow, I had a lot of time to think in prison. Think about everyone I've hurt. Think about my bad choices. I was weak. There are no excuses. The fact is, I just wasn't strong enough for you, and your mother, and for Wells. I never stopped loving the two of you, though. Never. You'll always be my little girl. I was supposed to protect you, and I failed. I'll never stop blaming myself for that, and I'm so glad that the one thing I did right, was pick the greatest woman of all time to marry and have a child with. Because she carried this family."

I look at him for a long time, then say, "I know, Dad. And I told you. Mom forgave you. And so did I. It doesn't mean I trust you. I don't know if that will ever be repaired. But I really do forgive you, and that was so hard for me to do. So hard. You can't comprehend how difficult it was for me."

He gets up and walks around.

I stand up as he approaches.

He wraps me in an embrace and kisses the top of my head. "Thank you."

"You're still my dad. You'll always be my dad."

He lets go and takes a step back.

I say, "So let's make the best of it until you have to go back, okay? And then we'll stay in touch after and work on trying to get you out in two years." I hold out a hand, like it's a business agreement. "Maybe we can make something positive out of this situation."

He looks down at my hand, then nods and shakes it. "Let's do it. Deal, kiddo."

"Okay, I need to check my email and see if work needs me."

He walks away as I pull out my laptop, and the first email I see is marked urgent, and it's from Martha and John Freeport. It doesn't look good, and I wonder if Covington sabotaged the damn thing out of anger. I'm almost positive he did.

I huff out a long sigh. This shelter is going to happen, whether Covington wants it to or not. I don't give a shit. I made a promise to Martha and John.

I'll have to take this thing one issue at a time, one day at a time.

WELLS COVINGTON

WHEN I WAKE UP, I have no idea how much time has passed. I have no idea if it's fucking morning or evening.

What I do know is Dexter Collins and Cole Miller are sitting a few feet away, smirking their asses off right at me.

All I can do is groan the word, "Fuckers."

"Doesn't really pack a punch like it usually does." Dex grins right at Cole.

Cole shakes his head. "Nope, that's the most defeated 'fuckers' ever uttered by the great Wells Covington."

My middle finger shoots up, and at the same time, I say, "What are you doing here?" I love how they can take the biggest catastrophe of my life and still maintain a sense of humor. Who could ask for better friends, right? "What happened?"

It feels like I'm waking up from a dream, and as the reality sets in, so does the dread. It's like when you get so drunk you don't remember what happened, but you have a vague recollection. Then you have to go to your friends and piece the night back together, memory by memory. This is even worse.

"Well, he's alive after all." The voice comes from across the room. Lipsy walks over. "Orson called me, gave me their numbers. Then we showed up and hovered around watching you, Danny-style."

My eyes dart over to Lipsy. "*Salem's Lot*?"

He nods.

"Fuck, that was a good one. Well played."

Dex laughs. "He's not lying… It was a little creepy."

I want to be angry with Orson for calling them, but I'm not. He went above and beyond, like he always has, and I know it's because he cares. He's always cared, and I've walked around like he was the fucking help instead of one of my best friends, and maybe the only real father figure I've ever had. I never gave a shit about the things he did to get himself fired. Everyone deserves redemption. I've treated him like he was no longer important to me, and it wasn't fair. He took the brunt of the punishment for years, after the only other person I've ever trusted in my life gutted my business, wiped me down to the foundation, took *everything* from me, and now, he still stepped up when I needed him to.

Now, after I'd moved past it all, built something special, that asshole came back for round two and ruined something even more important to me, like it's never enough with him. My blood starts to boil again, just thinking of his face.

"What the fuck happened, man?" Dex stands up.

I make my way up from a prone position and sit upright on the couch. I rub my temples with my fingers. Slowly, I unpack the whole story for them. Everything. From college on.

"Wait? Meadow Carlson is Meadow Mayes? Professor Mayes had a daughter?" says Dex.

My eyes widen, but I don't even have it in me to remain angry, so I deflect with humor. "It seems so, try to keep up."

Cole laughs. "Glad to know you're still in there." He gestures to me as if I'm some object that's broken and in need of repair.

Dex tries not to laugh, but he can't help himself.

"What the fuck is funny about this?" I glare right at him.

He shakes his head as if he's genuinely remorseful, but he's still smiling.

"What the hell?" Cole tries to glare at Dexter, but he's trying not to laugh too, because this whole situation is absurd.

My shoulders eventually start to bounce because he keeps smiling like an idiot. "Just fucking say it already."

Dex, who never met a situation where he didn't make a joke, about to lose it, manages to say, "Just wondering if you had her tied up, you know? Whipping her in leather and shit when her dad walked in."

"Jesus fucking Christ." Cole looks away so he doesn't laugh where I can see.

Lipsy doesn't bother to turn away and laugh.

Dex shrugs, barely keeping a straight face. "What? It's a legitimate situation. It could've happened like that."

"Is that what you've been wondering? This entire time?" I stare at him like *what the fuck is wrong with you?*

"I mean, of course. Don't have high expectations for me. I'll let you down every day of the week."

I shake my head at him. "It was at her mother's funeral."

Dex's grin disappears, and he stares at me for a long time. "Stop fucking with me. You're trying to make me feel bad."

"Oh, it's true." I look right back at him.

He basically deflates, his chest sinking in. "Well, shit."

Lipsy, out of nowhere, says, "So how the fuck are we going to *Ocean's Eleven* that cunt for sabotaging your first firm then sodomizing your love life? Pay some guards to abandon him at shower time, then fill the commissary accounts of the three biggest inmates to do unspeakable shit to him like Little Puppet in *American Me*?"

Everyone turns to Lipsy at once. He looks dead serious.

Dex looks away, trying not to laugh again, and says, "Fuck, man."

I stare right at Lipsy. "He's in club fed, not some max security death row prison with gangs and shit."

Lipsy glances around and shrugs. "I mean, it's just a rough draft. Spitballing. We can iron out details."

It sounds ridiculous, but I think this is maybe just what I needed. To have these guys around.

Friends.

Humor.

Something that lightens this load on my shoulders.

I think Orson might know me better than I know myself, knew exactly what I'd need when I came around.

"So what the fuck *are* you going to do?" says Dex. "Gotta do something. Idle doesn't suit you."

I shrug. "Hell, I don't know. Not much I can do really. Go back to work. Put all this in the rearview."

"Oh bullshit." Cole stands up, looking more determined than I've ever seen him. Also, more intimidating. It's like he just stepped back into the octagon.

My eyes widen a little at the sight of him.

He takes a step toward me. "You love her, right?"

I sit there, trying to convince myself I don't. That I could never love anyone, but I know the answer. Orson knew the answer a long time ago.

Our eyes lock, and I shake my head. "Doesn't matter. It's done."

This time, he takes another step, but his eyes plead with me. "But if you could save it, would you?"

My collar tightens around my neck. I don't want to think about this shit right now. I just want things to be normal again. I want my old life back, before I met Meadow, but I know it'll never be the same. "It's futile. The situation is unsalvageable. I left her at her mother's fucking funeral. Blew up on her and her father, with her dead mother one room away. She's not some random thirsty chick at a bar, she has a brain. A very big fucking brain. And I know her better than any of you. She doesn't forgive, and she will probably never trust anyone again, especially now that I know who her father is."

Cole seems hellbent on not giving up on this. "Seems like she forgave her father if he was there. He must've fucked them over too, the family. Went away. You don't even know that side of the story."

I stand up and pace the room, because I don't know what I'll do if they don't drop this. Maybe I need to be pressed about it, but not now. I need some time to fucking breathe.

"We're just trying to help," says Dex.

I wheel around on him. "Well don't—" I stare at all of them, trying to stop myself from laying into them. It's what got me into this shit. I've never had a temper in my life, but seeing his fucking face, it just brought it out of me. All the things I'd suppressed for so long.

Dex takes a step toward me, both hands up. "Look, man. We know you better than anyone."

Lipsy and Cole both nod as he says it.

"You don't quit. If there's one thing we all know about Wells Covington, it's that he never stops fighting. And you damn sure won't let her go, especially if you care about her the way we know you do. You don't take no for an answer, *ever*. So when you strip everything away, the periphery, and get to the heart of it, it all boils down to one question."

"What's that?" I know what it is before he says it, but I ask anyway, because I know being all dramatic like this is what he does. And I know I'm not thinking straight right now. I need these guys, whether I want to believe it or not. More than that, he's right. I need Meadow. I'm so goddamn empty without her, constantly in pain knowing how much suffering I caused. Knowing I left her when she needed me the most, and when I lash out at everyone, it's really just me attacking myself and my own insecurities. How can I ever live with myself after what I did? How can I look her in the eye and promise I'll be there no matter what, after I abandoned her? Even if he is her father. How could I get so mad I walked away from the best thing that's ever happened to me?

Dex stares at me for a long time before he says, "Can you forgive her father? After what he did to you, could you still *forgive* him, if it meant having her?"

I look down at the floor. Just hearing him say that out loud and everything that goes with it; I've never felt so ashamed in my life. All the shit that happened with Mayes, it was never really about the money, or the firm. It was about him abandoning me, betraying me, almost landing me in a prison cell next to him. I never understood how someone who seemed to care so much about me could do that. He was the only person outside of Orson

I'd ever really trusted in my life. Then, I met Meadow, and everything just clicked. I fell for her, so fucking hard, and he came back. Showed up again.

I know I'm more angry at myself than him. This time wasn't his fault. It was mine. I threw it all away when I walked out of there. I should've been there for her, fought for her.

Slowly, I bring my gaze up to Dex, because I know the answer a million times over. Everyone in this damn room knows the answer.

I nod at him. "Yeah, I'd do anything for her." My eyes roll over to Lipsy and Cole. "Any. Fucking. Thing."

A huge grin spreads across Dex's face. "Well, fortunately for you, I have certain services that can be rendered. You, my friend, need a big romantic gesture."

"Oh fuck," says Cole, rolling his eyes.

"What's happening here?" says Lipsy, looking clueless. "Tha fuck? What services?"

Dex points right at him but still looks at me. "This'll be right up your cinematic alley, Lipsy. It'll be glorious, better than the *Dirty Dancing* lift, the *Titanic* 'I'm flying', the *Notebook* slow dancing in the street, Luke and Lorelai's first kiss in the gazebo."

I have no doubt he could keep these references coming for hours with the kinds of movies he watches.

Lipsy stares right at him, wide-eyed, shaking his head in derision, and says through his teeth, "What kind of a fucking man, just, pussy flicks—" His words trail off like he can't process what he just heard, and he looks away at the ceiling, then glares back at Dexter. "Jesus Christ."

Dex, unfazed, turns to me, with a smile plastered across his face. "Here's what you're gonna do."

MEADOW CARLSON

IT'S BEEN one week to the day since the entire shit show that was my mother's funeral and everything that followed. It's been hard trying to focus on her, honoring her memory.

When Dad's parole officer finally came, and they took him away, it was even harder than I thought it'd be. The emptiness I felt inside as he drove away, watching me through the back window—I didn't know I would feel that again. I miss him, and he's all I have left, as far as family goes.

Now, I have to face this. I have to walk into my office and try to salvage the shelter project after I gave my word to Martha and John. I promised them I'd see this to the end, and I'm almost positive Covington is going to take all the investors he lined up and sabotage everything. He won't care how much money he loses; he'll do everything he can to destroy it. Why wouldn't he? That's how people in this business operate when you wrong them. He'll probably leak my identity, have me blacklisted.

I don't know how I'll pull any of this off, but I'll find a way. I don't break promises, unlike other people in my life.

My biggest fear is that he's going to be in the room when I get there. It's always theatrics. Billionaire hedge fund managers always drive home the point. He's still on the board of the project right now. I just know he's going to show up, look me in the eye, smile, then have all of them walk out, right in front of the Freeports, and crush their dream—our dream.

I walk through the front door, and I can see my small conference room and the suits sitting all around the table. My only hope is that he just decided to move on. It's a small hope, and I don't know why I hold onto it, because it'll probably make this even worse when it happens.

Please don't be here.

As I round the corner, I let out a sigh of relief, because he's not here, and all the other investors are. The second I walk in, every pair of eyes in the room lands on me. I can't read their expressions. I can't think, process, the way I usually do. I can't get a read on the room. It makes my skin crawl, not knowing. I can always see two steps ahead, and now, I'm flying blind. How the hell am I going to get through this?

I plaster on a fake smile, try to project confidence, but I know they see right through it. I'm about to bomb like a shitty comedian on open mic night. I can feel it.

I stop at the head of the table, take a huge breath, and turn to face all of them. "Hello, everyone. Thanks for coming. I know the last few weeks have been turbul—"

Footsteps.

Pounding on the floor, heading toward the conference room. They go off like bombs in my ears, every one of them, every last detail and sound frequency.

My heart squeezes in my chest. I know who it is before I even turn to look.

The second I lay eyes on him, I want to just crumble into a pile on the floor.

Please, no.

He's going to make an example of me. He'll exact some kind of revenge for what my father did to him, let everyone in this room know that if they ever do business with me again, they'll suffer the same consequences I'm about to receive. He'll chase any investment money away from anything that involves me, probably make calls to politician friends in DC to revoke their grants, bury me in paperwork. Anything I care about, he'll try to destroy.

I look up at his eyes, trying my best to remain calm and save face as much as I can. Maybe I can salvage something out of this if I keep it respectful. Covington doesn't look angry though, he just looks serious, determined.

His eyes are locked on mine as he makes his way straight toward me.

I need to do something, so as if nothing's wrong, I say, "Mr. Covington, we were just getting started. If you want to take a seat." I hold out a palm at an empty chair on the side of the table.

He doesn't flinch, doesn't slow, just walks straight at me, eyes locked on mine.

Fuck. Fuck. Fuck.

I pretend to be surprised, glance around a little like *did he hear me?*

My heartbeat pounds on my eardrums relentlessly. My palms start to clam up.

Once he's right in front of me, looking down at me like the rest of the room doesn't even exist, he stops and just stares for a long moment. He looks like he's curious, searching to see if I'm still in there somewhere, the Meadow he cared about. I can't look away from him. All I can do is stare into his eyes and see the pain in them. It reflects my own right back at me. He's hurting so badly, and despite all this, I have an urge to hug him, comfort him, and he looks back at me the same way. I don't see any malice there.

Before I can analyze his look any further, he drops to both knees, right in front of me, right in front of everyone.

There are a few gasps, eyes glancing back and forth around the room. They're probably wondering who the hell is this man and where the hell is Wells Covington?

I don't know if I've ever felt so much relief, and yet wanted to strangle someone at the same time. My blood heats up the more I look at him, especially now that he's in a vulnerable position, exposing himself to me. I thought for sure he would walk into the room and crush me like an ant under his boot.

He starts to say something, but his words catch.

Now, guilt floods my veins for thinking so little of him a few moments ago. For thinking he would really try to hurt me more, but it's still clouded with the anger from what he did a week ago. I've never been so—confused, pulled in opposite directions like I'm being emotionally drawn and quartered.

He closes his eyes, then opens them back up at me and they're glossy, welled up. I seriously can't believe he's doing this in front of the people in this room. Wall Street will have word of it within minutes after this, that's how fast news travels in financial circles. Once you're seen as weak, people come for you, come for your investors, like ravenous wolves.

"I-I'm sorry." He manages to croak out the words.

A giant wave of relief washes over me. For the first time in weeks, I feel like I can breathe again. It doesn't change how much I want to tear into him for what he did, but still, a weight has lifted from my shoulders.

I chance a look around the room and eyes are wide, watching the scene unfold in front of them.

I start to say something, lay into him, or tell him we need to step into the hallway to continue this, but he holds up a hand like *just wait.*

"What I did was wrong, it was childish, immature, hurt-ful." His eyes sear into mine, and a tear slides down his cheek. "Un—" He takes a second to compose himself. "Unacceptable. I, look, Meadow, I have no excuse for what I did. I was supposed to be there for you, like I promised, and I wasn't. I will have to carry that burden for the rest of my life, and it will eat at me every single day. I'm sure you thought, when I walked in here, that I was coming to destroy this project, bury you under the rubble. The man I once was would've done that to anyone who did to me what your father did, and I would've destroyed their family and everyone they loved right along with it. But I'm not that man anymore. I don't give a shit about any of this." He waves an arm around at the room. "I don't give a shit about anything—but *you.*" His eyes lock onto mine as he says it. He continues to struggle to get the words out. "You changed me. You make me want to be—better, decent. I'm on my knees, begging you for a second chance. I'll give all of it up, everything, because I can't l-live one more day without you. I've been in constant pain, agonizing pain, and it's not going away. My soul hurts without you. I miss talking to you, holding you, being with you. There's a hole in my heart, a giant void in my chest, and it can't be filled without you in my life. No amount of money or wealth can replace that. Please—" He pauses, and our eyes lock. "I'm *begging* you. Please don't write me off. Please, just give me a chance to prove myself."

I start to say something, but my throat is so damn dry I don't know if I can get any words out. My fingers tremble. My jaw clenches, and finally, very slowly, I say, "You *left* me at my mother's funeral, all alone. Do you know what that did to me, Wells?" I start to cover my mouth, then manage to stop myself, because I have to keep it together.

He looks like he might fall apart the second I say it, and he starts to look away, but then his eyes are right back on mine. His voice trembles, and he says, "I know, and I'm sorry."

I glare right at him because he's saying the right things, but how can I trust his actions? What about the reality of the situation? How can I possibly believe he could handle what would come if I gave him another chance? "What about my father? What about the animosity there? How could you possibly think that will ever go away? He's my dad. He's going to be a part of my life. It would never work, and you know it. What? Would I spend time with you, separately? Like a kid with divorced parents? I don't want to be with someone who can't be strong for me when I need them to be. I can't be with someone who can't stand my family. I have to be able to count on you one hundred percent of the time, not just when things are easy, but when they're the most difficult. That's when I needed you the most, and you weren't there." The tears start when I say my last sentence, and I thought I could keep it together, but I can't. My hand comes to my mouth, because I want to believe what he's saying so badly, but then I remember the look on his face in the funeral home. I'll never forget that look. It's burned into my memory forever.

He nods. "I fucked up. I know I did. And this is me taking ownership of that, putting myself in a position of weakness in front of people who only value strength. This is me not making excuses. What I did was wrong, and I accept full responsibility. That's what leaders do, right? In business and in their personal lives? They take ownership of their problems, and then proceed with a solution."

My lips mash into a thin line. "You think this is going to solve the problem?"

He shakes his head. "No, but this is the first step I'm taking. Because I will never let you down again." He glances over at the door to the conference room.

Every eye in the room follows him, including mine.

Covington hollers, "You can come in now."

My father walks through the door, and his gaze finds me at the head of the table. Now mouths are really on the floor around the table. My father is a notorious Wall Street felon, blacklisted in every circle there is. He's deemed toxic by the Street, and anyone who touches him is deemed toxic too.

Part of me wants to punch Covington in the face for exposing me like this, but at the sight of Dad, all the air leaves my lungs. I glance down to see there's no ankle monitor. "What? How?" I feel dizzy. This isn't possible.

"I called every single person I know who could help directly or indirectly. The governor, judges, law enforcement, politicians. I used every ounce of leverage in my arsenal, made promises you wouldn't believe, in order to have the man I've hated for over a decade, released from prison early."

"It's true, Meadow." Dad nods. "He's not lying. I'm a free man because of him. I don't deserve it, but it's true. And I guarantee you he didn't do that for me."

Covington's eyes roll up to mine, and his hands open and close, like he wants to reach out and grab me and it's taking everything he has to restrain himself. "All I want is for you to be happy and have everything you need. That's the only thing I want, whether it includes me or not. The thought of anything causing you more pain makes me sick to my stomach. I will *not* allow it." His eyes move around the room, a non-verbal warning to everyone witnessing this, and all of them scoot back in their seats a little when he does it. Finally, his eyes move back to mine. "Even if you never want to see me again. I put everything on the line, risked all my credibility. I'm responsible for the next two years of your father's life, the assets of my firm are collateral if he doesn't complete his parole obligations, and all the jobs that go along with managing that. I put it all at risk so he can be with you."

I want to believe him so badly.

So badly.

A few tears roll down my cheeks as I stare at him. "When we leave this room, nobody will ever do business with me again. I'm exposed."

People in the room whisper back and forth to each other. Despite Covington's warning, it will leak. It'll be on the front page of the *Wall Street Journal* tomorrow. Meadow Carlson is actually Meadow Mayes.

Covington stands up, and there's no more pain in his eyes, just pure determination, power, strength. "Take me back, Meadow. Fuck the people in this room. Fuck the Street. We'll join our firms together, and you'll be able to finish the shelter and take on any project you want. If any person in this room or anyone else fucks with us, we'll crush them, together. I'll make an example out of anyone who dares to utter a bad word about you."

The faces around the table pale, and they all know he means it. I know what he says is true. He's thought this through. But I don't even care about that, not really. I'm just scared to trust anyone again. That's what it all comes down to.

He reaches down for one of my hands, then looks at me. "Did you forgive your father?"

I nod, hesitantly.

His fingers wrap around my wrist, practically begging me to let him back in with just his touch. His voice softens to a pleading tone. "Then forgive me too. I love you. I love you more than anything. I don't care about my reputation or my job. I'll do anything for you, for the rest of my life. I just want—*you*. Please?"

I glance down at our hands, then back up at him. His eyes plead with me, begging me to give him another chance. Finally, I just nod a little. "Okay."

"Okay?" His eyes widen.

I nod again, then squeeze his hand back. "I love you too." It feels so good, like all the pain is transferred out of my body. In a split second, before I know what's happened, he yanks me into him, and his mouth is on mine.

He kisses me with that same Wells Covington power and strength and confidence that knocked me off my feet the first time, and still has the exact same effect. When we finally part, he's smiling so big and wipes at his eyes with the sleeve of his jacket.

I can't believe he just did all that, cried in front of all these people.

I expect to see people on their phones, but they're not. I glance around the room, and they're all smiling too. Wells and I grin like idiots at each other for a long moment, then all of a sudden, I remember.

"Dad!" I take off running over to him and wrap him up in a huge hug.

Wells walks over behind me, and I squeeze Dad tighter.

He hugs me back with equal intensity and says, "I love you, sweetie."

"I love you too.

"Thank you."

I lean back a little, curious as to why he's thanking me, but he's not. His eyes are locked on Covington behind me.

"I don't deserve it. I don't deserve this."

"It's water under the bridge. Let's start over, wipe the slate clean." Covington holds out his hand.

Dad shakes it. "I'm just—I have no words."

"I do," says Covington. He turns to everyone in the room.

"Apologies, everyone. Meeting rescheduled for tomorrow. I'll have food catered in and compensate you for your time."

People start to stand up and walk from the room. None of them look frustrated, but it's probably just an act.

"They're all going to talk," I say.

"Fuck 'em." Covington looks at me and smirks. "They won't do shit. The first one who makes a move gets a pile driver, Undertaker-style. The rest will fall in line."

"And, he's back." I smile at him.

"Back with you." He kisses me again before I can respond.

Someone clears their throat behind us, in a playful way.

I turn around to see Martha and John. They're about the only ones in the room who look concerned.

"So what does this all mean?" asks John.

Covington cuts me off when I start to say something. "I'm sorry for all this. It was my fault, but I'm telling you right now. You will have every resource possible at your disposal to mold this shelter exactly how you two and Meadow want it. I give you my word, even if I have to do it solely with my assets. Starting tomorrow, it *will* be back on track."

I don't blame them for looking skeptical. I feel awful that they've become political pawns, exposed to the harsh realities of venture capital situations. I feel awful that my personal life put their dreams at risk. I need to reassure them.

"He's telling the truth, I promise. It has all been ironed out. Just stick with us a few weeks and you'll see immediate progress and forward momentum."

They glance back and forth at the two of us, and Mr. Freeport says, "Okay."

Mrs. Freeport nods in agreement with him.

On their way past us, she stops and turns to Wells, gives him a thumbs up and says, "You nailed it, by the way. Well done."

He snickers and says, "Thanks."

They all leave, so that it's just Dad, me, and Wells. I don't even know where we go from here, but I know it makes me happy, having a path. Gives me hope. I never saw the past few months of my life going this way. I can't believe how much I've been through, the ups and downs.

But I do know I love the two men in the room with me, even if they are colossal idiots sometimes.

The best thing though…

I know my mother is smiling right now. She knows I won't be alone, and that I have a family again.

EPILOGUE

Meadow Carlson
Three Months Later

I GET ready to head out to the construction site for the new shelter. All the contracts are in place, and we're finally going to break ground on the renovation. The whole thing is equipped with a press release; media will be there, future tenants of the building, investors, politicians—it's going to be a big deal, a show for the public, and I'm a little nervous about it.

The past few months have been a whirlwind, but it's been amazing. We probated Mom's will and got everything transferred to Dad. Mom left almost everything to me, but I know she'd want it to be this way. Dad needs a place to live, and I have my apartment, so it just makes sense.

Covington rearranged office space so our firms are now in his building. We're working on merging everything together under one umbrella company to make things more efficient. Honestly, life has been great.

Covington walks into my living room, still half asleep and definitely not dressed.

"You need to get ready. The hell is wrong with you?"

He yawns like he doesn't have a care in the world. "Shouldn't have kept me up all night."

I turn around and try to scold him, but I can't get rid of the grin on my face. "Me? Kept *you* up all night?"

"Yep." He nods and walks toward me, and it's dangerous. He'll make us late if I allow him to, and I almost always give in.

"That's a bit of revisionist history."

"I write history however the fuck I want." He reaches out and pulls me into him, then kisses me full on the lips. It starts to get a little intense, and his hands slide down to my ass, and for a moment I contemplate letting him make us tardy.

There's a knock at the door, and he sighs against my lips. "Saved by Orson." He gives me a little play spank.

I faux glare at him. "You need to get your life together."

He grins and walks over, opens the door, and Orson looks away from his naked body and hands him a suit bag.

I walk over there, putting an earring in on the way. "Thank you, Orson."

"My pleasure, Ms. Mayes. Do you require anything else?"

"Privacy," says Covington. He waggles his eyebrows at me as he says it.

"We're fine. Ignore him."

"Oh, I'm very practiced at that discipline." Orson cracks a smile right at me.

I lean up and give the old man a kiss on the cheek. "Thanks for keeping him in line."

"It's my pleasure. I'll be down in the car."

"We'll be down in five," I say to Orson.

"Fifteen." Wells tries to override my order.

I whisper, "Five," and hold up one hand showing all five fingers to Orson.

He nods as if we just made a secret pact, then walks off down the hall.

When I close the door and turn around, Covington's hand comes out of nowhere and has me lightly by the throat, but it catches me off guard.

He still manages to surprise me every day and it's so hot. I want to give in, badly, but he doesn't even give me a chance to respond.

His mouth is right next to my ear, and it drives me insane when he does this. "I won't make us *late*, today." His hand slides down, straight between my legs over my midi-length skirt. "But you'll be late next month. That's a fucking promise, Meadow." He kisses me on the cheek and walks off with his suit to get ready, leaving me panting and breathless.

Holy. Shit.

I'll be damned if he doesn't emerge from the room in four minutes, looking like he could be on the cover of GQ magazine.

"I fucking hate you." I glare right at him.

He smirks. "Haters gonna hate."

I shake my head at him as he walks past acting as if I'm the one who's going to make us late now.

Yep, this man makes me happy. So damn happy.

* * *

WE GET to the front of the building, the same building where I first ran into Covington. The place where this craziness began. I cannot believe I wanted to stick it to him so badly I orchestrated the vandalizing of a twenty-five-million-dollar wall and then got caught on purpose. It doesn't even seem real now, feels like it was ten years ago with all we've been through.

Crazy how life can change.

I glance around, and everything is set up. There are media vans from all the major Chicago stations and surrounding areas, and even a few national outlets. This is a very big deal.

Dad meets us up front with a smile. He told us he didn't want to come, in case it invited scrutiny, but we assured him he should be there. He has strict parole rules for another year and a half, and all his licenses to trade securities were revoked for life. He's not allowed to consult with anyone, nor have anyone invest on his behalf. Basically, he can't touch anything stock market related, or consult anyone on investments.

He nervously came to me the other day, asking if I could

help him. The same familiar pang of anxiety hit me, like he was going to ask for a self-serving favor of some kind, but what he asked surprised me. He wants to see if he can petition the courts to allow him to teach personal finance to former inmates and low-income people, to help them learn how to build wealth. He wouldn't have even come to me, except with the impact fund, he thought I might have some connections.

We'll see what happens. I have my reservations, given the nature of his personality and how he throws himself into things. Maybe if it's heavily supervised, but he needs something to do. He's going to drive me insane.

Wells smirked at me, cocky as ever, when I told him, and said he has the solution to all our problems. Then proceeded to tell me Dad just needs some grandchildren.

The three of us walk up and meet the other investors on the stage. There's a giant multimedia screen, loudspeakers, a podium with a mic, and the cliché golden shovel every company and project in history uses for a photo op during ground-breaking ceremonies.

Penn Hargrove, from The Hunter Group, walks over to us. "Everything look okay? All set up?"

Covington nods. "You did good."

Penn shakes his head. "Not me, Decker. He's the PR expert. Even got some national news here."

Wells' face tightens a little. "Tell that asshole I said thanks."

"Tell me yourself, bitch."

We turn around, and all the Collins brothers are grinning, along with their significant others. Dominic and Mary are also present. Lipsy walks up with some of the PMs from the fund too. Honestly, I think of most of these people as family now. I've spent so much time with them. Especially Lipsy, Dexter, and Cole.

Wells looks like he's in a tough spot. He and Decker have a past.

"Thanks." Wells shakes his hand.

He's told me everything about what Decker has done. From having the firm look into companies owned by the hedge fund, how he almost exposed him while he was working with the FBI, and his visits to BDSM establishments. God, the press goes even more crazy about that now, because Wells and I continue to go in there, and we've even tried out a few things. I really do think it is helping make an impact, that public perception is shifting on the issue.

Wells keeps glancing over to Dex, Cole, and Lipsy, and they keep sharing those boyish grins, like when ornery school kids are up to something. The problem is, they're all billionaire men with far more than enough resources to employ their immature pranks.

"What's that all about?"

Wells straightens up, as do the other three. "Nothing. What?"

"Mmhmm, something is happening."

"Pshh." Wells looks away. "You're nuts."

I narrow my eyes on all four of them. "Better not embarrass me."

Their faces all go white.

Harlow Collins gives me a fist bump. "I still like her." She turns to Covington. "A lot."

I turn to face her. "Thank you." Truth be told, Harlow might be the scariest woman I've ever met. Beautiful, but intimidating as hell with jet-black hair, icy-blue eyes, and sleeves of tattoos on both arms.

Penn walks over to Wells and pulls him aside for a minute, to go over something. It's curious. I know I trust Wells, but there's still tiny bits of doubt that linger every once in a while. I don't know if it will ever go away, but it's manageable.

I don't know what those two are up to, but the fact he didn't call me over to discuss it with them gives me pause.

I don't say anything though. Truth be told, Penn has been an incredible asset from The Hunter Group. He does incredible work for charities, especially on the administrative side, and he's a brilliant, albeit extremely cocky, man. I'd love to have him come work for the impact fund, but he's unshakably loyal to Donavan Collins. They're best friends from Columbia Law

School. You have to admire that in someone, that kind of mutual devotion.

Penn nods to Wells, then breaks free and walks up to the podium to begin the ceremony. He talks about the project some, a forty-thousand-foot view of the mission, what we'll do, then introduces Martha and John. They're amazing, and I know they'll sell this story to the public better than we ever could. They play a professional video we had produced up on the big screen for everyone in attendance to watch. We gave the media access to the video feed and the audio, so they can all broadcast it through their stations.

I stand there, pretty emotional, just by what all of this represents. Everything we all went through, bringing it to fruition. It's incredible. Martha and John nail the delivery, like I knew they would, because this is their baby. There's no way Wells or I could convey the passion they have for this, to the city, and the rest of the world.

When they're finished, Wells and I, joined by the mayor and the governor, say a few words and conclude everything. The broadcasts all start to shut down, but suddenly, the screen comes back on behind us.

All I hear over the speakers is, "Meadow, turn around."

I turn around, and Wells is up on the screen in what looks like some kind of home video or a Zoom call that's being broadcast. There's a time stamp at the bottom, and I'll never forget that date. It was the craziest day of my life. He starts talking to me from the screen.

"Meadow, this is the day I showed up in your office with your father." Dad peeks his head in and waves at the camera, then disappears. "I haven't come after you yet, but I'm about to. If you're watching, it means I was successful. I just wanted to record this and tell you, I'm going to marry you. Soon. I already bought the ring." He holds up the box. "But asking you one time to marry me is not enough. I'm going to ask you every single day until the day comes when you say yes. I love you, Meadow Mayes. I will always love you, every single day. I will fight for you when we're in the same room and when we're apart. I will always be there. No matter what. I hope you enjoy this moment right now, because you deserve it. Love, Wells from the past."

The screen cuts and there's a date time stamped on it, one day later. Wells is with Dexter, Cole, and Lipsy. They're drinking at The Gage.

"You're so annoying, always Meadow this, Meadow that. It's been one day." Dex turns to the camera. "Please say yes, so he'll shut up about this. We love you and all, but it's getting old already." He grins the whole time he says it.

Lipsy nods. "Yeah, Meadow. You gotta say yes after this shit. Dude went full *Officer and a Gentleman* on you."

I laugh.

Cole says, "Just give in to the dark side, Meadow."

Wells appears on the screen like he yanked the phone away from them, glares in their direction, then smiles into the camera. "I don't have much time, you're in the bathroom right now. But, Meadow Mayes, will you marry me?"

The screen cuts to the next day. Wells is outside in the back-yard of his giant mansion. He's smoking a cigar with Dad. "Sorry about the smoke, it's the only way your father and I could get away so I could ask you something. You probably don't know what it is, so you'll just have to wait."

Dad appears on the camera. "Meadow, I never thought the day would come when a man would ask me for permission to propose to you. I definitely never thought I would have the opportunity or had earned the right to accept. But Wells wanted to honor the tradition before he even knew if you'd take him back, and I have to say, while whatever happens beyond this is one hundred percent your choice, I can't think of a better man for a son-in-law. So, I told him he has my blessing."

Wells appears. "Meadow Mayes, will you marry me?"

It keeps going on and on, sometimes Wells is alone, hiding in the house at night, whispering into the camera. Once he's in the middle of handing Dominic and Mary keys to one of his yachts. He's with friends. One is in the middle of Manhattan for a busi-ness trip he had to take to Wall Street. All our closest friends, family, clients, they all urge me to accept. Some are sweet, some are hilarious. And every time, at the end of the clip, he always says, "Meadow Mayes, will you marry me?"

As the dates get closer to today's, my stomach knots up, but I can't look away. I don't want to miss a single detail, and I'll probably watch this video a thousand times throughout the rest of my life, but this is the only occasion where I will watch it for the first time. I can't believe this is real life right now, and once again, he's reduced me to tears, but the best kind. I feel like I could float into the sky, but my eyes stay locked on the screen. Finally, today's date appears on the screen, and Wells is on one knee in the camera, holding up the box with the ring on display, and he looks right at me and says, "Turn around."

When I turn around, he's right in front of me, the same way he was on the camera. It was a live shot of him. My eyes dart over to where Dex has a video camera trained on us so we're broadcast over the media system.

I start to tremble all over, while all our friends and family and colleagues surround us, watching intently. Women clutching their chests. Wall Street investors, some of them who don't seem to be capable of having a soul, crack smiles.

My eyes lock with Wells, and I've never seen him look more determined in his life.

And just like that, he says, "Meadow Mayes, will you marry me?"

I nod emphatically, smiling and crying, and say, "Yes. Yes."

He takes the ring—a gorgeous round-cut diamond solitaire in a platinum setting—and slides it onto my left ring finger. His hands shake so much he almost can't get it on, but once he does, he jumps up and his lips are pressed to mine. His fingers dig into my waist like he'll never let go of me as long as he lives.

I don't know how he does it still, but like always—I feel invincible when he's near, like nothing can hurt me, like I can do anything.

"I love you." He says the words against my mouth.

"I love you too. So much."

We both look at each other and giggle, like we're just a

couple of innocent children, and the world around us doesn't even exist.

"Did I do okay?"

I nod. "Yeah, you did good."

"Great." He turns to Dex. "Kicked your ass." He then turns to the other Collins brothers, Dominic, and Cole Miller and says to each of them, "Kicked your ass. And your ass."

I give him a playful smack to the chest while he does it, and his eyes are back on mine.

"You know it's true."

I shake my head at him, all of them really, but out the side of my mouth where only he can hear, I say, "Totally did. Yours was the best of all time."

Wells nods at me with a satisfied smirk. "That's right."

We turn to face the crowd, and everyone cheers and goes nuts. People walk up and congratulate us, everyone. Wells looks impatient as we have to say thank you to everyone over and over, and finally, he just scoops me up over his shoulder like he did the first time at my apartment, and carries me right through the middle of them. It appears he's had enough waiting.

"Sorry, everyone." His eyes land on mine and heat me up from head to toe. The look of determination, hunger in them is so intense I get butterflies in my stomach. "I made a promise to her before we left."

Holy. Shit.

His words are front and center in my memory.

"But you'll be late next month. That's a fucking promise, Meadow."

I have a feeling he's going to put a baby inside me before the week is over. And that's okay. Because there's nothing I want more than to start a family with this man. I've never been more excited.

I glance up at the clouds and smile. I smile so big, because I know my mother is ecstatic, looking down on us.

* * *

SLOANE AND ALEX thank you so much for reading Wealthy Playboy. As always they have a special bonus epilogue for you, grab it HERE.

If you're new to us or maybe you missed an earlier book in the series, you can one-click one of our boxset HERE.

To pre-order book eight, Pretty Playboy, one-click HERE.